WALK
in the
AFTERLIGHT

J Merrill Forrest

This edition published by The Moon Tiger 2020

'Walk in the Afterlight' is a revised version of
'The Waiting Gate' published 2017 by Hashtag Press

Text copyright © J Merrill Forrest 2020
Cover design copyright © Lawston Design

A CIP catalogue for this book is available from the British
Library.

ISBN: 9780956795441

The Moon Tiger

www.jmerrillforrest.com

'Afterlight'

The light visible in the sky after sunset;
twilight afterglow; a view of past events;
retrospect

2009

Chapter 1
Flora

Keeping to the shadows at the back of the last house of the terrace, Flora stood on watch while her mother worked at prising away the board nailed to the window frame. The whole street was due for demolition and there hadn't been any sign of a security patrol, but still they had to be careful.

Rachel swore as she struggled with the boarding, and then there was a tearing sound as one side came away. The rest of it was much easier and soon she'd pulled it off and dropped it to the ground, saying a soft and relieved "Hallelujah!" because there were no panes of glass in the window. Flora was hoisted up onto the rotting sill and she climbed through onto the draining board of a small kitchen. Dust puffed up around her feet as she jumped nimbly to the floor, and her nose wrinkled against the musty smell.

She swung around her precious pink torch to get her bearings. It wasn't a nice place. Thick cobwebs covered the pipes below the window where the sink would have been and the doors of the mismatched kitchen units hung crookedly from their hinges. Mouse droppings and dead insects littered every surface.

Flora stood back as the black plastic dustbin bags holding their possessions were pushed through the window, then Rachel heaved herself in and landed lightly in front of her.

The torch beam flickered and Flora shook it, relieved when the beam brightened again.

Rachel bent down and lightly tapped the tip of Flora's nose. "Come on, Munchkin, we need to get settled as quickly as we can."

Gathering up their bin bags they moved into the hallway. Beneath a fine layer of dust the black and white floor tiles were cracked and stained, and green and brown blotches marked the walls. It was creepy and Flora wrinkled her nose at the horrible smell, not wanting to think what could be making it.

The first door Rachel tried jammed against something behind it and no matter how hard she pushed she couldn't get enough clearance even for Flora's tiny body to slip through. She tried the door on the other side, heaving a sigh of relief when it swung open unimpeded, but the room was pitch-dark because of its boarded-up window.

"Give me the torch."

Flora handed it over and Rachel tried to shine it through the narrow gap.

"I can't see a thing," she said, peering into the room. "Never mind, let's try upstairs."

She closed the door and Flora saw that her mum was making a funny face at her in the gloom, trying to cheer her up. "I know you're scared, sweetheart. Remind me to get some candles and matches tomorrow, they'll always come in handy. Now come on, we're both tired, so let's find ourselves somewhere to sleep. It's been quite a day and we need to rest, and I'll sort everything out in the morning. Let's go."

She led the way up the stairs, testing each step carefully before putting her full weight on it. Flora followed slowly, wishing with all her heart that they could just go back and she could sleep in her own bed, with her nightlight keeping her safe through the night.

The uncarpeted stairs creaked beneath their feet, but at least the last of the daylight still filtered through the planks haphazardly nailed on the inside of the window at the top of the staircase, so they could make sense of their surroundings.

There were two bedrooms upstairs, one tiny and filled almost floor to ceiling with broken furniture, the other a good size and empty except for a dead pigeon lying in a ragged pile of its own feathers on a stained mattress.

"Hey, look at that!" said Rachel. "Something to sleep on, what luck!" She dumped the bags just inside the door and beckoned Flora to do the same. "It may not be cosy but at least it's dry. Here, help me tip this up and I'll brush it off. It'll be fine if we lay our clothes on top of it." She paused, seeing the doubt on Flora's face. "I know this is horrid, but it's getting dark, it's raining, so we'll just have to make the best of it. We'll have all day tomorrow to find somewhere better. Come on, give me a hand with this."

Wordlessly, Flora helped to sweep the mattress of dust, dirt and mouse droppings, and Rachel emptied one of the bags of clothes onto it and spread them out. Flora rolled up two sweaters for them to use as pillows. She was so tired she would have lain in the dust on the floor if she'd had to, but she was grateful for the softness of the mattress, if not for the nasty smell that came from it. Why did everything in this place smell so bad?

They ate some chocolate biscuits and an apple each, then, exhausted by the bewildering day she'd just had, Flora curled herself into the warmth of her mother's back and closed her eyes. She expected to fall instantly into a deep sleep, as Rachel did, but was dismayed to find herself wide awake and staring into the blackness. She snuggled closer, wondering how they had ended up here, forced to spend a night in such a horrid place. How had they ended up breaking into an abandoned house for shelter? When she was very small they'd lived in a flat high up in a tower block with lifts that rarely worked. It may have been tiny and basic with noisy neighbours on both sides and above, but Flora had been well-fed with quite a few pretty clothes in her wardrobe. Then, as far as she'd understood it, her mum had lost her job, been unable to pay the rent, and had been thrown out by the horrible landlord.

It might also have had something to do with her mother's boyfriend, who came and went and smoked something that made him behave a bit odd. He'd stolen money from Rachel's purse, Flora had seen him do it.

Anyway, following the eviction the boyfriend was never seen again and they'd stayed with friends for a little while, both of them sleeping on the big sofa in the front room. Flora had liked the friends, and really loved their fluffy, purring grey cat that liked to curl up in her lap, but they'd all too soon moved on from there because, her mum explained, they mustn't ever impose on friends for longer than a week. Flora hadn't understood that, for if they were friends, surely they wouldn't mind how long she and Rachel stayed? They were scrupulously tidy, and Flora was careful not to make any noise or get in anyone's way.

From there they had moved to a tiny basement room of a three-storey house that seemed to Flora to be home to about two dozen people. She hadn't liked it at all, and was glad when, in the dead of night, Rachel had ordered her to help pack up their few possessions and they had crept away once Rachel had gone round like a burglar searching in drawers, pockets and under sofa cushions for any cash.

Flora had been frightened in case they'd been caught, but Rachel had said, "They're all stoned, don't worry about it." Flora worried that her mother had hit them all with a stone.

For a time after that it seemed to Flora that they never spent more than a night or two on a sofa or blow-up mattress on the floor, Rachel telling her to wait in another room and not make a sound while men came to chat to her in private. She always seemed unhappy after the men had been, but they must have enjoyed talking to her because they gave her money. Some of the men offered a lot more money to talk with Flora, if they spotted her before she'd crept away and hidden herself, but this had made Rachel shout a lot and quickly shove them out, barricading the door and quickly moving the two of them on again.

4

For this Flora was grateful, for sometimes she heard things that frightened her and she didn't like the way some of the men looked at her.

One day, a day Flora hated to think about but often couldn't help herself, Rachel had muttered something about Flora being too pretty for her own good. She had gone out and come back with a pair of dark trousers, a couple of baggy sweatshirts and a pair of scuffed grey trainers. They had both cried when Rachel had cut Flora's long, wavy hair with a large pair of scissors, cropping it close so she looked like a boy.

But some men still gave her that strange look. She didn't understand what it meant, that look, but it gave her the creeps.

Time went on and her mother could not get work and they never seemed to have any money. Every few days Rachel would shrug on her one good coat, by then several sizes too big for her, ordering Flora not to move from the room. She would disappear for hours and when she returned would look really plump until she'd emptied the pockets of food and shrugged off the coat to reveal layer after layer of clothes. She'd remove the price labels of the clothes by biting through the plastic tags with her teeth.

Then, about a month ago, they had moved into the spacious flat of a man called Hemp, a huge, red-faced man with a short temper and a lot of men friends that came and went at all hours of the day and night. He was often away, but when he came back he was generous with his money, peeling off twenty pounds notes and handing them to Rachel. Despite this, Flora didn't like him or his friends. What she did like, though, was her own room with a soft, clean bed and a bathroom with hot running water across the hall.

Best of all, she was allowed to look like a girl again, letting her hair grow and wearing pink jeans and sparkly trainers.

Rachel had started to look better too, the hollows in her face filling out, her hair becoming glossy and smelling of apples. Her smile flashed more often, too, so Flora dared to hope that their fortunes had turned around and this would be their permanent home. Maybe her mum would marry Hemp, and he'd be her dad!

When she turned seven two months ago, just a few days before Rachel's twenty-second birthday, Rachel had said they should celebrate while Hemp was away on one of his mysterious trips. They'd gone into a supermarket and Rachel told her to choose a birthday cake from the many on display on the shelves. She'd chosen a small one, vanilla sponge with strawberry jam in the middle, covered in pink frosting, with a simple 'Happy Birthday' written in white curly script across the top. They'd eaten the whole lot between them in one go, washed down with lemonade, laughing as their mouths smeared with cream and jam. Then Hemp had come home in a foul mood and the birthday was ruined.

Things changed when Hemp had begun looking closely at her, his narrowed eyes following her every move with that expression that had made her nervous when other men had done the same. He touched her too, touched her in a way that really scared her, and then he'd told Rachel that they could make a lot of money if they put Flora on the game.

Flora hadn't known what kind of game, but it was clearly not a nice one, because Rachel had flown at Hemp and raked his face with her fingernails. There'd been a terrible fight, ending when Rachel smashed Hemp over the head with a lamp. He'd slumped to the floor and Rachel had dashed madly round the flat, stuffing money into her pockets and ordering Flora to pack whatever she could into some bin bags. She'd done her best, but she was so scared and crying so hard she'd left behind some of their best clothes, and they'd run from the flat before she had time to think.

They'd walked a long time, then Rachel had put them onto a bus, paying for tickets that would take them to the bus station. From there they had walked and walked, lugging the full bin liners, until they'd arrived in this street that was lined on both sides by boarded-up terraced houses. Graffiti covered every wall, even scrawled across all the 'keep out' signs nailed to the doors, but Rachel had picked this house, its two bay windows solidly boarded-up so their only option was to go round the back and get in through the kitchen window.

And now here they were, holed up in a derelict house on a mattress that was home to who knew what kinds of creepy-crawlies.

Rachel turned in her sleep and Flora looked at her face, barely able to see it in the gloom.

Her mother was pretty, with thick, reddish-blond hair, the same texture and colour as her own, that flowed in shining waves all the way down her back. Her eyes were huge, blue or deep green depending on what she was wearing or what mood she was in, and long-lashed. There was a smattering of freckles across her neat nose, and she had small, even, white teeth. When she smiled her whole face lit up.

But leading up to this latest escape, Rachel had rarely smiled, and she'd rapidly lost weight.

Flora must have drifted off to sleep at last, for suddenly she was being shaken awake. She sat up, teeth chattering because of a chilly and damp draught. Heavy rain drummed against the window. Rachel handed her a chocolate biscuit and what was left of their bottle of water, whispering that she was going out to find them something to eat.

"There's no point in us both getting soaked so you stay here. You need to be really quiet and you mustn't go *anywhere*, understand me? I'm not sure how far it is to the nearest shop, but I promise I'll be as quick as I can. I'll get as much food as I can carry, we'll have ourselves a little feast, and then we'll move on as soon as the rain stops and find somewhere better to stay tonight. Okay, Munchkin?"

"Okay, Mum. And don't forget candles and matches."

Rachel pinched Flora's chin and kissed the tip of her nose, then quietly left the room.

Flora listened to her footsteps on the stairs until they faded, then snuggled back down under the pile of clothes and, despite the chill of the room and the gnawing hunger in her tummy, was soon asleep again.

When she next woke up it was because it was raining even harder and she badly needed to pee. Was she not meant to leave this room at all, which would mean going to the toilet over in the corner, or would it be all right if she went to the bathroom? Where was the bathroom? She didn't remember seeing one. Some of the places they'd stayed in had bathrooms downstairs at the back, but she was sure there'd been no other doors leading from the kitchen besides the one to the hallway.

She decided to count up from one and keep going all the way to a squillion, and hope that Rachel came back as she wasn't sure she knew how to count so high. She sat in that damp space, mice droppings all around, trying to count and trying to keep her mind from thinking how desperately she needed to go. She wasn't helped by the sound of the incessant rain, and in the end her bladder was too painful to ignore. Shivering with cold and fear, wincing as she unfolded herself from the mattress because her limbs had become painfully stiff, she quickly pulled on another sweater and her anorak and crept out of the room.

There was a door next to the smaller bedroom so she peeked inside and was relieved to see a toilet. The room was hardly wider than her outstretched arms, the toilet had no seat and the water in it was a dark, murky brown with an oily film on top. On the floor was a roll of toilet paper, wet and flecked with grey and black mould. Thick cobwebs swayed above her head, but she didn't care, her need was too great now to bother about spiders, so great in fact that she almost didn't get her pink jeans unzipped and pulled down in time.

Once relieved, she looked for the flush handle, but the cistern was very high up on the wall and the pull chain out of reach, even if she stood on tiptoe. She contemplated standing on the toilet bowl, but shuddered at the thought of slipping and her feet going into that horrid brown water that she'd just added to.

She scurried back to the bedroom to wait for her mum. After a while, when too much time seemed to pass, she crept to the window and peered out, careful not to show too much of herself. Her lip curled as she noticed how close her foot was to the dead, decomposing pigeon beneath the window sill, its scaly clawed feet pointing to the ceiling.

The room was at the front of the house, so the window looked out onto the deserted street and the blank faces of the boarded-up houses opposite. There were no cars, no people, in fact no movement at all that she could see. Not having a watch she had no idea what time it was, but it felt as if Rachel had been gone a very, very long time. Maybe the shops were miles away? She'd be soaked through and they'd not brought any towels from Hemp's place.

More time passed. She ate the last two biscuits in the packet, now slightly stale, and folded up the clothes they'd used as their blankets, placing them carefully in the bin bags. Still her mother didn't come and Flora was getting scared. Really scared.

There was a noise downstairs, a scraping sound like something being dragged across the floor. Her spirits rose in anticipation of Rachel's return and something good to eat, but there was no bright voice calling her. Unable to wait any longer, Flora crept out of the bedroom and peered down into the narrow, gloomy hall. She listened hard but her ears caught no more sounds. Maybe Rachel had gone into the kitchen, though she couldn't think why as she'd seen nothing useful in there yesterday.

The banister rail wobbled as she touched it, so she went down each step carefully, keeping herself close to the wall. From the hallway she could only see a glimpse of the kitchen, but the living room door was wide open, and unlike the blackness of the day before, there was light within. Footprints in the dust, too. Feeling confident that her mum was in there, having bought candles and other supplies, and making everything as nice as it could be before she called Flora down to join her, she skipped down the last few stairs, clearing the bottom two steps with one jump.

Rachel was not there, but Flora didn't worry about it, just looked with delight at the things in front of her, glad of the lantern on the hearth that lit the room with a soft glow. There was a sleeping bag rolled up and secured with string on the hearth of the fireplace, a large canvas satchel leaning against it. In front of the hearth was a cooker ring connected to a small, round, bright blue gas bottle, a carton of milk and pizza box. Why hadn't she come up straight away to check on Flora, and to bring her down to show her what she'd brought?

Flora darted forward to lift the lid on the box, disappointed to find that there was only a quarter slice of pizza left in it. Had Rachel eaten the rest of it and left just that little bit for her? Her stomach grumbled, a mixture of real hunger, annoyance and nagging fear; where had her mummy gone?

"Mum?" she called, her voice wavering. She cleared her throat and tried again. "Where are you? I'm scared!"

Flora waited, hardly daring to breathe. She could only think that Rachel was fetching in more things and she'd just have to wait.

She spotted the pile of yellowing newspapers and a little stack of wood to the right of the fireplace; how lovely it would be to have a fire to drive away the dampness of this room. She gazed hungrily at the pizza, then snatched up the slice and ate it quickly, stuffing it all in her mouth at once so it filled both her cheeks and she could hardly chew. It was cold and soggy and didn't taste very nice, but she used her fingers to wipe the congealed remnants of sauce and a few strands of hard cheese from the box. She tore open the carton of milk and drank deep; it was deliciously cold and refreshing.

Now she decided to investigate the dark green canvas bag, wondering where her mum had got it from and hoping there would be batteries for her torch inside. When she had undone the two buckled straps, she pulled out its contents and set them on the floor: a battered tin cup; box of matches; pouch of strong-smelling tobacco; flat packet of cigarette papers, of the kind she had seen often in the various places they'd stayed; multi-bladed penknife with a scratched, red handle that had a white cross on it; plastic disposable razor with black whiskers caught between the twin blades; a small, locked, square tin that was heavy and rattled when she shook it; a metal ring with lots of small keys on it; a bottle half full of purple liquid.

At the bottom of the bag she found several items of men's clothing, all filthy and greasy to the touch. Eyeing these things left her in no doubt that her mum had stolen the bag from someone. She swallowed hard.

There was that scraping noise again, and she could tell someone was in the kitchen. She froze at the sound of heavy footsteps tramping along the hall, for she knew they couldn't belong to her cat-footed mother. They stopped outside the half-closed door and Flora felt her mouth go dry.

What should she do? Announce herself straight away and apologise that she had touched his things, or hide until she could see what type of person he was? Where, oh where was her mum? What if she had stolen these things and the owner had followed her here to get them back, or Hemp had managed to trace them and had hurt her before coming for Flora?

Frantically, she checked round the room, a perfect square except for the bay window, no nooks or crannies, no cupboards. No way could she climb into the fireplace and crawl up inside the chimney. No way could she push her way out of the boarded-up window. There really was nowhere for her to hide, no way out but past whoever was standing in the hall, someone she could hear breathing heavily on the other side of the door.

Deciding her only hope was to make a run for it, she crept forward, keeping her head down, ready to whip the door open and barge past whoever was waiting out there, scared witless that even if she got past that obstacle, she might be caught before she made it to the kitchen and out of the window.

Gulping back her tears she made her move and yanked open the door, ready to run as fast as she could. But her escape path was blocked and she careered full pelt into the bulk of a man that seemed like a giant to her, his foul body odour making her gag. Her head ramming into his stomach forced the breath from his lungs with a whooshing, hissing sound, but he stood his ground and shoved her violently away from him.

As she staggered back, unable to keep her balance, Flora registered that it wasn't Hemp. This man with the rough, dirty clothes and long black hair stringy with grease, was a stranger. And he looked as terrified as she felt.

PRESENT DAY

Chapter 2
Alex

A long, flatbed truck blocked the entrance to his engineering works when Alex drove up, so he parked round the side of the building and walked back to watch it being unloaded. It was a delivery of steel and other metals for a number of jobs they had on the go, and Alex enjoyed the shouts and banter of the men as they unloaded and organised where the heavy, unwieldy material was to go.

When the fun was over and the lorry had backed out and driven away with a trailing cloud of black smoke from its exhaust, he strolled through to the office to be greeted by Trish. She had not long joined the firm as a part-time administrator, hired by Alex's manager to run the office and deal with all the paperwork.

"Good news is we're getting busier, boss," Bill had said to Alex. "But as a consequence we're getting behind with the invoicing. Dave says his wife has relevant experience and is looking for a part-time job, so I think we should call her in. Now you're so busy with other matters we really do need someone dedicated to the paperwork, keeping track and making sure the invoices are paid on time. It'll be worth it, Alex, trust me."

Alex had inwardly smiled at Bill's 'other matters' knowing he was quite bemused about what it was that kept Alex away from his own factory so much these days, but had agreed to Trish being hired.

He went to make himself a mug of tea before tracking Bill down and having a general walkabout with him so he could be updated on the latest orders.

The little kitchen was still a shock to the eyes and nose, not because of the state it was in but because of the state it *wasn't* in. He always expected to see unwashed mugs and used teaspoons piled up untidily in the sink and on the draining board, spilled coffee powder, grains of sugar and puddles of milk on the worktops and on the floor. On top of that, the whiff of an old, much-used dishcloth left wet and balled up for too long. He'd suggested they go to plastic cups and spoons but the outcry had soon put paid to that one, so the large, thick mugs and metal spoons had stayed, along with the mess.

But there was no mess on the days Trish came in. On finding out that she was regularly washing-up and cleaning the kitchen, even taking it upon herself to bring in clean tea towels and take the used ones home to launder, Alex had gathered Bill and the five other men who worked in the factory and told them that he did not want her doing this.

"Wash-up your own things," he'd said. "And use the paper towels provided to dry your mugs. Trish is here to do the invoicing and make sure you get your wages paid on time, she is not here to clean up after you."

No-one had taken any notice, and Alex knew that they still left it for her to do, and she did it without complaint. He sighed as he chucked a teabag in a mug, a mug that didn't even have brown stains in the bottom of it any longer, and filled it with hot water from the dispenser. He was stirring in a splash of milk when Trish appeared in the doorway.

She hesitated, as if not sure whether to come all the way in. From the beginning Alex had sensed she held herself back, as if she was a little nervous of him, and he could think of a few reasons that might be. For one thing, he was the boss. But, the real reason for her slight agitation in his presence was the same as Bill's and all the other members of staff: it was

14

the fact that he was very publicly a psychic medium. That made a lot of people nervous.

He smiled at her. "You still clean up in here, don't you?"

She gave a rueful, slightly apologetic grin. "I really don't mind. The guys are busy, and of course their hands are always dirty because of the jobs they do. I know they appreciate it," she laughed. "And I really can't *stand* an untidy kitchen! Please don't worry about it."

Alex laughed, knowing she was right, and who tidied up the kitchen was a battle he shouldn't even try to win.

"Well, thank you. I certainly appreciate it, it's nice being able to make a drink without worrying if I'm going to get salmonella or something equally nasty. I hear you're doing a great job for us, I hope you're enjoying it?"

She nodded, saying that she had a lot of fun because all the men were so friendly and funny. They looked after her really well, she said.

"Bill told me that you volunteer at Rainstones House?" Alex said. "I go there sometimes. The staff there are very open minded and invite me along at the request of patients who want the kind of reassurance they feel I can give. What do you do there?"

"I help out in the Day Patient Unit once a week. It's basically meeting and greeting guests, making refreshments, helping out with whatever entertainment has been laid on. Such a wonderful place, I really enjoy it."

Alex, his senses on alert, felt her hesitation and knew there was more. She dropped her gaze and said, "A great-aunt died in the hospice some years ago and my father's in the dementia wing."

He had a vague sense of someone with her, and heard in his mind *pat-a-cake*, spoken in the merest whisper. He tried to focus on whoever it was, thinking it could maybe be the great-aunt wanting to remind Trish of a childhood game.

Unable to make a connection though, he simply said to Trish, "Oh, I'm so sorry. That must be very hard for you."

"It is. He was diagnosed with Alzheimer's in his eighties and he's a hundred and one next month." She laughed at the look on Alex's face. "I'm a product of his third marriage and he was sixty when I came along. Shall I tell Bill you're here?"

"I already know!" Bill's booming voice rang out just before his rotund frame filled the door widthways, trapping Trish in the kitchen. "Hey there, boss, how are you? Everything set for the wedding of the year? Remember, we'll all want to see pics of you in the monkey suit!"

Seeing Trish's puzzled expression Bill said, "Alex's brother-in-law is getting married. He's a very successful agent in the entertainment business, so it'll be a grand do and there'll be quite a few famous faces amongst the guests." He winked at Alex. "Including our Alex, eh boss?"

Trish smiled uncertainly, and muttered that she had to get back to work. She sidled past Bill, who had stepped back to give her room, and Alex watched her go to her tidy and dust-free desk, grabbing the phone almost before it started to ring.

Bill said, "She's an absolute bloody treasure, Alex, you've no idea. The invoices are up to date, she chases late orders and payments like a terrier, taking no shit from anybody. And she keeps this bloody room clean and disinfected, as you can see!"

"And she keeps the swearing down, I hope."

Bill laughed, his jowls and big beer belly wobbling. "Yes, there is less of the bad language when she's around, I must admit. Now then, let me bring you up to date. And the first thing I have to tell you is, Clive is leaving us."

"What? Why?"

"He and his missus have decided to retire and move closer to family. He's our longest serving member of staff so we'll need to give him a merry old send off. But don't worry, Trish is on the case and she's going to put an ad in the paper and help us find a replacement. It'll be a month or two before Clive moves, and I'm certain we can keep on top of the orders even without him in the short term."

Pleased that his factory was in the capable hands of Bill, Alex followed him round while he gave a running commentary on the jobs being worked on, reflecting for the thousandth time as he listened to Bill how much he missed being here on a day to day basis. It was his business after all, he'd started it and was the sole owner, and he loved it. But the TV show where he demonstrated mediumship had brought recognition beyond his wildest dreams and taken him to a point where he was constantly in demand and just couldn't be here full-time any more. That's why he'd promoted Bill to factory manager, knowing he'd do a great job of keeping the place running efficiently and ensuring that the reputation of Kelburn Engineering and the goods they produced remained of the highest quality.

He inhaled the familiar smells of hot metals and oils while casting his eyes around the bays where projects ranging from utilitarian sheet metal work to ornate spiral staircases and everything in between were being made by his highly-skilled team. The high-ceilinged factory rang with the ringing, buzzing, hissing sounds of hammers on steel, heavy duty bandsaws, grinders and drills and welding equipment, making Alex long to grab some gear and get his hands dirty doing something. Anything. But with Bill managing the factory, a great team making the goods, and Trish so efficiently running the administration side of things, he really wasn't needed here.

Tour over and satisfied that all was well, in fact very well indeed, Alex decided to go home to Beth. She would be back from work by the time he reached the house, and he thought he could get some paperwork cleared and then the two of them could go out for dinner.

The drive home took him through the village and past the road where he'd lived during his and Beth's painful separation.

He recalled with a shudder the incredible shock felt by everyone when his next-door neighbour, Scott, had died after being hit by an out of control van. That accident that had almost taken Alex's life, too.

Yes, there were a lot of painful memories packed into this part of town, and he was glad to leave them behind to go home. He searched out Beth as soon as he arrived for a hug and a kiss. She was in the kitchen, standing in front of the open fridge door.

"Hot flush?" he quipped.

"Oh, ha-ha, but I'll have you know I've got many years to go before you should risk making a remark like that! How come you're back from the factory so early?"

"Well now, the sad fact is I'm not needed at my own business these days, so I thought I'd come home where my qualities are still appreciated by my beautiful wife."

Beth turned her attention back to the contents of the fridge, saying, "Hmm, well I'll certainly appreciate you if you come up with something we can make for supper."

"I thought we'd go out?"

"Ooh, lovely! Have you booked somewhere?"

He shook his head. "I'll do it now. Anywhere you particularly fancy?"

Beth said she didn't mind where they went, then had second thoughts and named a place a colleague at work had recently mentioned to her as a good place to eat. It was a little Italian bistro, tucked away up a side street in the town, with checked tablecloths, candles stuck into wax-covered Chianti bottles, cheerful service and good, wholesome food.

"Sounds perfect. I'll find the number and book us a table. It's a lovely evening, so as soon as I'm done with some paperwork let's go into town, have a walk along the canal and a drink in the Old Bear before dinner."

He ambled into the little downstairs room he used as an office, where a quick online search took him to the website of the restaurant. He dialled their number and booked a table for two for seven thirty.

As he was making the reservation his attention was drawn to the pad beside the phone, a small notepad which had printed across the top of each page 'Kelburn Engineering' and below that the address and phone number in a plain, dark blue font. He'd never bothered with a website because they were listed on all the online local business pages, but Bill had said a couple of times lately that they should have one to showcase what they made. After the update today Alex could see that Bill, yet again, was right, so made a mental note to look into it soon. In fact, maybe a little rethink about their letterhead, business cards and the general company image would give Alex something creative to do that was concerned with his own business.

Right now, though, he had something else to attend to. From his in-tray he took a pile of papers in different colours and sizes, letters that arrived daily from people who watched the show and were desperately hoping to see Alex for a personal reading. He wished he could help all these people, but there were so many it would simply be impossible, and to pick out just a few would be unfair on the rest. So he always read every one of them and made notes on each so a member of Paul's staff could send gentle refusals and suggestions how they could find other, equally reputable mediums to help them.

He was struggling to decipher the small, spidery handwriting of a woman who wanted to make contact with her late twin brother when his mobile rang, startling him because he was so deep in concentration. He saw that it was Paul's office and grinned to himself at the thought that Paul, his agent, brother-in-law and best friend, was getting married soon. No-one thought he'd ever settle down, but Adele had won his heart and Alex couldn't be more delighted.

"Hello, Alex, it's Marcia."

Ah, Paul's very attractive, extremely efficient and rather frightening PA, until you got to know her and learned she had a wicked sense of humour.

"Hi, Marcia. How are you? I hope you're not calling with a message from my brother-in-law, because he swore to everyone that he would give one hundred per cent attention to his wedding arrangements and we wouldn't hear from him until after the honeymoon."

"Oh, he tries calling several times a day but I just ignore him! The reason I'm ringing you is to tell you that Eselmont Productions want to commission another series. Congratulations."

"Thank you! I know Paul never doubted it, but it's a relief to have it confirmed. Did they say when they want filming to start?"

"They're going to get back to us with the details. They did say, though, that they want to change the format a little. They'd like for you to have an occasional guest, for instance, either to give a mediumship demonstration as you do, or something a little different. If you have any names we could put forward could you pop them in an email and I'll pass them on? Eselmont will then check them out and see if they'll fit in with what they have in mind."

Alex didn't have to think very hard about it, for one person that sprang immediately to mind was his good friend Linda Chase, a medium and healer. Linda had helped him so much after his baby daughter had died, she deserved a shot at appearing on television, and Alex knew she'd be brilliant on camera.

Two other people were also worth considering, Lars and Rosemary Magnusson, he was a medium, his wife an amazing psychic artist. They always worked together, Lars delivering messages and Rosemary quickly and accurately sketching in pencil or pastels those the messages were coming from.

"No problem there, Marcia, I can think of a few people straight away. Anything else?"

"Yes, a couple of other things are being considered, but they'll talk to you directly about them when they have the first production meeting. One idea which seems firm, though, is one which Paul is aware of from earlier negotiations, and it's the introduction of one-to-one readings in people's own homes, so there are discussions that need to take place about the how and the who. Paul thought you should be paid more now the series is such a success, so I was told to accept the commission should it come in while he was away, but to tell them that the renewal contract is to be negotiated on his return."

Alex thanked her again, and after asking and being told that there was nothing he needed to be doing with regard to Eselmont other than email her some names and contact details, he rang off.

The popularity of the TV series had surprised him, and it still astonished him to be recognised when he was out and about. How on earth had he leapt from working in small venues like Spiritualist churches and village halls to being a media personality with thousands clamouring to see him?

There was his autobiography too, *A Different Kind of Life*, that was, to use Paul's words, still walking off the shelves. It had humbled Alex when the book had come out and he'd travelled around doing book signings that there were so many people willing to queue for his autograph on their purchased copies.

There was more money in the bank than there'd ever been, allowing Beth to reduce her hours as an administrator at the college while she trained to become a bereavement counsellor to parents who'd lost children. It wouldn't be long, Alex thought, before she was able to work as a full-time counsellor, a job she would love and be exceptionally good at because she had personal experience of such loss.

Like Beth, he loved helping people. He'd been fortunate to have been born with a special gift, one he could use to bring comfort and reassurance to as many grieving people as possible.

Television had brought him this unexpected fame, something he was a little uncomfortable with if he was honest, but at the same time television, sensitively done, was the best way to serve large numbers rather than just a few. Yes, he'd be happy if he still had the time to run his engineering business himself rather than be an absent boss, but he believed that he was doing what he had been placed on this good Earth to do, and was grateful for all the hard work Paul had done on his behalf with Eselmont.

Thinking of his brother-in-law brought up memories of the sequence of events that had run up to the forthcoming wedding of the year. If Amber hadn't died, Beth wouldn't have insisted on a separation and Alex would not have rented the house in Saxon Road next door to Lily and Scott Miller. If he hadn't become friends with them he would never have met Lily's sister, Adele, and neither would Paul.

But he could recall in clear detail Adele and Paul's first meeting, the day he and Beth, a short while after they'd reconciled, were moving out of the rented house and into their new home on the other side of town. Paul had unexpectedly turned up with champagne (and cut glass flutes, of course), invited himself to the farewell party at Lily's house, and Adele had been unable to take her eyes off him from the moment he'd strolled into the room as if he owned it. No-one had been surprised when the engagement had been announced just six months later.

But those happy memories brought back with a painful jolt the tragic deaths of his little girl, Amber, and of his friend Scott Miller. He needed to see Amber right now. He opened his mind and called to his father, who was also Alex's guide and gatekeeper to the spirit world, working with him every time he did a demonstration of mediumship, whether it was taking place in a village hall or the television studio.

"Dad, are you there?"

"Yes, I'm here. Great news about your show, I look forward to it! I know you want to see Amber, here she is."

Alex opened his mind still further so he could see his little girl. When she'd passed from a brain aneurism she'd not even had her first birthday. Now she was a toddler, a cute and giggly toddler. It did his heart good to see her and he knew he was fortunate to have the gift that enabled him to do so, but he still wished he could physically hold her.

Beth called out that she was ready, so Alex said his goodbyes to his dad and his little girl and set aside the letters that still needed to be read. Now he was ready to enjoy a nice meal and a bottle of good red wine with the most amazing woman in the world. The evening would end, he hoped, with a long, loving session in the metal-framed bed that he had made with his own hands as his wedding gift to her.

It had taken a while to regain the intimacy they'd enjoyed up until Amber died, but they had sensibly allowed themselves time to find their way back to each other after their reconciliation. Nowadays, Beth didn't immediately dissolve into tears after lovemaking, apologising over and over again that there could be no more children. He was sad about that too, of course he was, but Beth meant the whole world to him and he was prepared to reassure her of it until his last breath. As long as he had her by his side he could cope with anything.

He grabbed his keys and joined Beth, giving thanks to the Universe for his great good fortune that such a wonderful, beautiful woman loved him as much as he loved her.

Chapter 3
Kallie

Yawning until her jaw hurt, Kallie wondered what had been the cause of last night's nightmare that had her waking in a sweat in the early hours, fighting the duvet that was wrapped tightly round her legs. It had stayed with her while she showered and dressed, only beginning to dissipate as she and her grandmother had eaten breakfast.

Now in the car on their way to Rainstones House, she cast a quick glance at her grandmother sitting so serenely in the passenger seat, humming quietly to the music. It wasn't her choice, she was so tired she'd prefer something modern, loud and lively that she could sing along to, but classical music calmed Verity so she always had a couple of CDs in the car for when she was a passenger.

Verity was very frail these days, and Kallie worried for her as her grandfather's death now seemed imminent. How would she cope when her soulmate was gone? Kallie shuddered at what was to come and her stomach fluttered with butterflies. Since she'd been little, she coloured her imaginary butterflies in different shades: red for excitement, yellow for nervous tension, muddy brown for sadness, bright blue for joy. Today's butterflies were dark grey and black. Or maybe they weren't butterflies, but moths or miniature bats. She shuddered at the unwelcome image of bats with their huge ears and leathery wings and forced herself to concentrate on the country roads they were travelling along.

At last they arrived at their destination and she swung the car between the ivy-covered stone gateposts of Rainstones House and headed for the car park. It appeared to be full already, but just as Verity was starting to fret, as she fretted about every little thing these days, that they might not find anywhere to park, someone waved for Kallie to stop and wind her window down.

"If you go all the way past the dementia wing to the end you'll find a space at the far end. I've just this minute parked next to that space and you're the first car I've seen come in."

"Okay, thank you very much," said Kallie, and carried on as directed.

It turned out to be a tricky space between a white minivan and a low stone wall, but Kallie manoeuvred her small car into it with ease. Careful not to clip the wall as she opened the door she squeezed out and walked round to help her grandmother get out. She gave her the walking stick, then took her other arm, and they walked slowly back to the hospice wing of the complex, Kallie apologising to Verity for not thinking to drop her off at Reception before parking.

"I'm fine, Kallie, it's really not far and the walk is good for me."

Once inside the building, Verity insisted she was all right to go on ahead on her own and Kallie, taking that to mean that her gran wanted some time alone with Walter, took her time writing their names and the car registration into the visitors' book before following her.

By the time she entered the corridor Verity was out of sight, so she must have marched along at a surprisingly fast pace, wanting only to get to her husband's bedside as quickly as possible. Kallie slowed her own pace right down, intending to give her grandparents five minutes alone together. It was so sad that he was here, but it was a beautiful place, and it was where he wanted to be for his final days.

When he'd first been diagnosed Verity and Kallie had been able to look after him, but as his illness had progressed to the point he was almost bedridden, Walter had grabbed at the chance offered by his doctor to arrange nursing and palliative care at home.

"I don't want my Verity nursing me through the worst of it," he'd growled to Kallie when Verity had been out of the room, his eyebrows low over his fierce gaze. "And I certainly don't want you nursing me either, washing and changing my nappies, though I know you'd do it with good heart and without a murmur of complaint. Get onto Rainstones House and arrange help, and when the time comes, I want to die in the hospice."

When Verity had overheard that last bit she'd cried and told him she wanted him at home, but he'd replied, "I'm not dying in our bed, woman!" He'd softened his words with a loving gaze and a stroke of her hand, but continued, "I want you to be able to go on sleeping in this bed and remember me fondly when I'm gone. Besides, have you given any consideration to how they'd get a stretcher up and down our stairs?" He'd snorted at the thought. "I shall die peacefully and with dignity in the hospice, I know it and you know it, so there are to be no arguments when the time comes."

And now the time had come, and there had been no arguments, for Verity, tearful and worn out despite all the extra help that had been arranged, had capitulated with her usual quiet grace when the doctor had said he would make arrangements for Walter's immediate admission.

When the Rainstones House ambulance had come they'd known he wouldn't return to the tiny old cottage the three of them had shared since Kallie's birth, with its bathroom downstairs beyond the kitchen and steep and narrow stairs up to the bedroom.

Walking slowly along the corridor now, her mind running over these heart-breaking times, Kallie spotted the sign above the door that informed her it led into the Day Patient Unit. From the beginning of his illness until he'd been too unwell to go, Walter had spent a day each week there to give Verity a break, a day which had her worrying rather than relaxing, but he had enjoyed it very much, calling it 'the jolly old DPU'.

Kallie hadn't seen it because she was always working, but Walter had told her how he enjoyed spending time there because everyone was just lovely.

Kallie's throat tightened as she wondered how much longer her precious grandfather had. The last two days he'd only been conscious for short periods of time. It had been agonising watching Verity grasp his hands, kiss his face, all the while telling him it was okay for him to go, that she would miss him and mourn him; he knew that Kallie would look after her.

But he was still here, still fighting to have a little more time with his beloved wife and granddaughter.

Still dragging her feet, Kallie paused halfway along the passageway, where another corridor led off to the right, leading to the therapy rooms and the chapel. She could smell the sweet perfumes of aromatherapy oils, so familiar to her, and longed to see inside the rooms and meet the therapists. She knew that anyone in the hospice could ask for treatments both practical, such as manicure and pedicure, and holistic, including aromatherapy, reflexology and acupuncture. Maybe she could offer her services? How wonderful that would be. She thought she could work it so she had two half days a week here, even one full day, and still keep all her clients happy at the salon, where she worked with another beautician and two hairstylists.

The sweet smells disappeared immediately as she pushed open the door into the Inpatient Unit, which always smelled different to anywhere else in the hospice wing. It wasn't unpleasant, just a mixture of odours that marked the place as a medical area.

The beautifully decorated single rooms were on one side of the modern, purpose-built wing that had been added to the old stone building about a decade before. Each had a hospital bed, wall-mounted television, radio and DVD player, small en suite bathroom, and sliding glass doors that opened out onto a private patio. Here, if the weather was warm and dry, patients and their visitors could sit and have their meals, read books of their own or borrowed from the many donated to the library, or simply gaze at the spectacular, beautifully landscaped grounds against their backdrop of rolling Wiltshire hills.

The door to her grandfather's room opened as she approached and a young nurse came out, carrying a shallow metal bowl covered with a cloth.

"Hello, Kallie," she whispered. "Your grandad's asleep at the moment, but he might wake up soon. He had a peaceful night."

Kallie could only nod as her throat was so tight now she was unable to force any words out. Showing complete understanding, the nurse gave her a sympathetic smile and told Kallie to come and find her if anything was needed during her visit.

She crept into the room and kissed Walter before carrying on outside so Verity could be alone with him but call her back in if she needed to. Turning a patio chair so she could see into the room as well as into the garden she sat with her elbow on the little metal table and gazed towards the water sculpture that had become the symbol of Rainstones House Hospice & Dementia Care since its installation in the early 1980s.

It was a slender tower of unusually shaped quartz stones hung with small copper bells. The stones glistened and sparkled in the water that flowed over them from the top. The falling water caused the bells to knock against the quartz, making the most beautiful sound. She knew from the literature Verity had been given when they'd first investigated the place that the name Rainstones was a bit of a mystery, but it had provided the inspiration for the sculpture that had been commissioned and donated by the grateful relative of a patient. She thought she might stroll over there before leaving today, just to see it up close and hear its music more clearly than she could from where she was sitting.

Being the first room nearest the entrance to the unit, her grandfather's terrace was sheltered by the golden stone wall of the older part of the building that housed the therapy rooms and other areas of the hospice, and it was exceptionally warm today. She tipped her face up to the sun, closing her eyes tight until the colour behind her eyelids flared and glowed deep orange and vibrant red.

She was glad she'd been able to clear her diary to have these few days off, because she didn't think she'd be able to work competently knowing her grandmother was sitting alone in vigil by Walter's bedside, hour after hour, until Kallie could get back here again.

Someone coughed from the patio next door, screened from Kallie by a low wall and trellis that dripped with clematis. Kallie opened her eyes and observed a group of gardeners arriving to start work on the large ornamental flower beds. They were all volunteers, she knew, and thought what a wonderful job that would be.

Hearing the bedroom door open she swung her head to see who had arrived. It was Bronwyn, the lovely senior nurse who'd been looking after them all from the day Walter had been referred for hospice care. Kallie had quickly come to admire her steady manner and straightforward approach to her job. Bronwyn said a few words to Verity and then came outside.

"I'm just about to finish my shift, but I like to check on all my patients before I leave. How are you, Kallie?"

If that question were asked anywhere else and by anyone else she would reply with the usual, 'Fine, thanks. How are you?' But here they genuinely wanted to know, and Bronwyn's open gaze and soft Welsh lilt made you want to open up to her with honesty, so her reply was, "Shit-scared."

It sounded shocking spoken within earshot of Verity, who did not approve of even the mildest bad language no matter what the circumstance. Bronwyn hugged her, a deeply personal gesture Kallie would never have expected from her,

29

and she had to bite her lip hard to keep the ever-present tears at bay.

"Your grandfather is where he wants to be, and it's the best possible place. You know that, don't you? He's in no pain and we'll take very good care of him in the time he has left." Bronwyn glanced back at Verity. "Your grandmother is an amazing lady, isn't she?"

Kallie nodded and swallowed hard so she could speak.

"She really is. She's worn out with worry, but, you know, she always wants to look beautiful for him. She chooses her outfit the night before we come, making sure it's pressed and her shoes are polished, and she sits at her dressing table to do her hair and make-up while I dash about like a headless chicken. I'm worried that she's become so frail, but she's far more stoic than I am, yet her loss will be far greater. I hear her telling him it's okay for him to go, that she'll be fine because she knows it won't be long before she joins him, and it breaks my heart." A sob caught in Kallie's throat on the last word.

Bronwyn patted her arm and smiled. "It's her way of reassuring him. I've seen it all since I've worked here. Some, like Verity, can let go of their loved ones calmly and with dignity, others just need to rant and rave at their going. We're all different, and of course it depends on age; far harder to let go of someone young. But if you're worried about your gran's health we can check her over." She glanced at her watch. "I really must go, or my daughter will be very cross with me. I'm on call, though, and I'll come straight back if I'm needed. Stay strong, Kallie. It's all you can do."

Kallie managed a small smile, but by telling her she was on call, Bronwyn was letting her know that she expected Walter to die very, very soon. The thought made her stomach churn anew.

Verity was coping admirably now, at least outwardly, but Kallie couldn't imagine how she was really feeling. She and Walter had been together since Verity was sixteen, Walter a couple of years older, but now the time they had left was ticking away hour by hour, minute by minute, to a matter of—what? A couple more days? Maybe only a handful of hours? The bats in her stomach chittered and stirred their leathery wings at her troubled thoughts that it could be that very day.

Moments after Bronwyn had gone, leaving the room after a quick check on Walter and a quiet word to Verity, Kallie crept back into the room and leaned back against the wall, taking in the scene of the still figure lying on the bed, the beautiful lady sitting so serenely beside it.

Her grandfather had lost so much weight he barely made a mound under the sheet and thin blanket that covered him. But then, so had Verity. Kallie saw for the first time how her clothes hung off her shoulders, even her shoes seemed a size too big. She saw movement in the bed as Walter flexed his legs, then his eyelids flickered and opened, his gaze searching for and locking on to Verity.

"Hello, my love," he whispered, and Kallie had to swallow hard at how much she was moved by all the love contained in those simple words.

Her grandmother's face was luminous as she smiled at Walter, and Kallie could only wish that one day she would find a love like theirs.

"I've been having the most wonderful dreams," Walter whispered. "A garden, oh the most beautiful garden you've ever seen. It's full of people, ordinary people just like me, and I see my mum and dad, my brother. But there are also these …" He stopped and shrugged his thin shoulders. "Oh, I don't know what they are or how to describe them. Maybe they're angels!"

He grinned at Verity and Kallie, his face boyish for a moment.

"There's a bright light waiting for me, just like you read about, and I'm not at all afraid. Truly, I'm not afraid, my love. But they're not taking me yet."

He noticed Kallie then, and beckoned her over.

Kallie, marvelling both at the length of her grandfather's speech and at what he was saying, crept up to the bed and bent down to kiss the whiskery, paper-dry cheek. She noticed that his lips were dry and cracked, so she moistened a cotton pad in water, always kept handy on the bedside table, and tenderly dabbed the mouth of the elderly man she loved so, so much.

"Shall I massage your feet for you, Grandad? I've brought some mint-scented lotion just for you, I know you'll love the smell."

"Maybe in a little while, darling." His voice was weak and raspy. "Right now there's something else I'd like very much."

Kallie smiled down at him, wondering what it could be.

"I'd love a cup of tea!"

Her grandmother reached for her stick and started to rise, saying she would go and find someone to make it so Kallie could sit and have a chat with her grandad, but Walter stopped her with a surprisingly strong gesture.

"Kallie will make it, won't you, pet? Make a proper pot, my darling, no dunking teabags in mugs!"

"Of course, Grandad!" She couldn't keep the happy surprise out of her voice.

All he'd wanted these past couple of days was a little lemonade mixed with tepid water. Perhaps this was a good sign. Hadn't he just said that he wasn't going yet?

"I'll see to it straightaway." Kallie headed for the door, but was called back by that thin, reedy voice.

"I love you, Kallie, you're a special girl."

She blew him a kiss. "I love you too, with all my heart. I'll be back in two minutes."

Kallie hurried to the small kitchen provided for visitors and deciding to make a bit of an occasion of it as her grandad clearly wanted, she located a small milk jug, three cups with matching saucers, a stainless-steel strainer, and a china teapot that she warmed through before making the tea with leaves, not bags. She found a freshly laundered white cloth with which to cover the tray, and a small box of shortbread. Taking just three biscuits, she lifted the tray and headed back.

She entered the room backwards, pushing the door open with her hip, swinging away from the bed as she came in so she could place the laden tray down on top of the chest of drawers. Quickly, she set the cups on saucers, added milk and poured tea through the strainer, wondering if her grandfather would be able to manage to keep the delicate cup in his grip.

"Tea for three, just as you ordered!" she sang. "It's Assam. Shortbread biscuits too. Shame we can't all sit out on the patio, it's such a lovely day and the garden looks beautiful, but we'll have our own little tea party right here."

She turned back to the bed, a cup and saucer in each hand. It took her a full two seconds to realise that her gran was crying, crying so quietly Kallie hadn't heard her while her back was turned, and another second to comprehend that her grandfather had gone. Really gone.

Forcing herself to place the cups back on the tray rather than just let them tumble from her numbed hands and smash on the floor, she understood that he had sent her away so he could be alone with his Verity as he'd taken his last breath.

Chapter 4
Sylvia

"Well done, Paul! A beautiful ceremony and a wonderful reception, and everyone enjoyed your speech. I was doubtful you'd ever settle down, you know."

He laughed, his face lighting up in a way Sylvia loved to see.

"Nor me, Gran. Any woman has a lot to live up to thanks to my having such gorgeous and amazing ladies like you and Mum in the family, but I've found myself a beauty, haven't I?"

He certainly had. Adele was a delightful young woman, and Sylvia suspected, the first to really steal her grandson's heart. Even the lovely girl he'd been engaged to a few years back had not been able to bring such tangible joy to Paul's life. Adele had calmed him a little and managed to pull him gently away from being a total workaholic who lived, breathed and ate celebrity business deals, and he was all the happier for it, not to mention nicer to be around.

Sylvia smiled at the way Paul's face softened as he switched his gaze from her to his new bride, who was across the room talking to her parents. Adele had chosen a simple, fitted, very elegant cream gown for her wedding dress, and wore no jewellery other than a scattering of tiny diamond pins in her short, dark hair to complement those in her bouquet of cream and pale apricot roses and her beautiful diamond engagement ring. Would they have children and make her and Simon great-grandparents again? Sylvia asked herself. If they did, how would Beth and Alex cope with that? Especially Beth?

No, no, Sylvia, she admonished herself. Don't go down that road.

She hugged Paul and told him how devastatingly handsome he looked before moving away in search of the other members of her family. She spotted Beth and Alex talking to Adele's sister, Lily, but where was Simon?

She scanned the room, looking for the long, rangy form of her husband, knowing when she found him that he would be running his finger inside his collar or pulling irritably at his cravat.

Paul had insisted on the men being kitted out in top hat and tails with wing-collared shirts and fancy waistcoats, and Simon's loud and sometimes furious objections, unusual for someone usually so mild-mannered, had been firmly overridden by everyone. When she'd finally seen him in the full get-up she'd thought he looked wonderful. Well, except for the hat. When he'd plonked that on his head the tops of his ears had folded downward beneath the brim and she'd had to stifle a giggle or risk setting him off on another rant.

She located Simon with a knot of people she didn't recognise standing in front of a beautiful arched window. He and all the other men had ditched the top hats at the first opportunity, but sure enough he was tugging at his clothes. If he wasn't adjusting the collar or fiddling with the cravat, just as she'd imagined, he was tugging the embroidered waistcoat down at the front.

As she neared him she could see how he gazed straight over the head of the much shorter man he was in conversation with, a blank expression on his face. Was he merely bored by his companion, or was it something else, that something she had begun lately to worry about?

Feeling her heart skip a beat, Sylvia moved swiftly to rescue the situation.

"Hello, darling. I'm in need of a drink, would you mind going to find me one please? A glass of champagne would be lovely."

He barely seemed to acknowledge her but moved off to do as she asked. Sylvia fastened her brightest smile onto her face and introduced herself to the man as 'Sylvia-grandmother-of-the-groom.'

She took in at a glance the artfully spiked hair, the air of supreme confidence, and gosh, was that make-up on his face and neck, mascara on his lashes? His lips were suspiciously glossy too. From the make-up and the rather dazzling sheen of his hair, face and clothes, Sylvia could be sure that he was a showbiz type, so very likely he was a client of Paul's. Very likely, too, that he was famous, but she was sure she hadn't seen him in anything

There were a lot of celebrities here, quite a few recognisable TV and film personalities. For that reason just one reporter and one photographer, professionals Paul knew and trusted, had been invited to cover the event. To protect the famous, and even the not-so-famous, other guests had been asked not to take photographs on this occasion, with the promise of free copies of the professional ones in due course. Sylvia suspected that any photos featuring the showbiz stars were destined for a society magazine for some great fee.

She made small talk, not at all surprised to find that the man was indeed rather boring, definitely self-centred and rather miffed that she clearly did not recognise him, until it dawned on her that Simon was not coming back with her drink.

"My husband's been waylaid, I think. I'd better go and find him, I really do want that drink. Lovely to talk to you. Enjoy the rest of the reception."

The man stiffly bowed his head to her, probably as relieved as she was to bring an end to their stilted conversation, and strolled away from her as she tried to guess where Simon might have got to.

For weeks and weeks she had worried about this day, how Simon would behave. Was she right to suspect that

36

something was wrong with him, or was he just going through something short term and she was making mountains out of molehills? Sure, he had moments of forgetfulness, but didn't everyone have that from time to time? Especially as one got older. It hadn't worried her unduly at first, just caused a little irritation now and again, but he was constantly forgetting appointments, names and phone numbers. His moods were erratic, and the displays of temper certainly unusual. And then he'd worry and obsess over silly little things, like did he have his wallet in his pocket, or was she sure she had locked all the doors before coming to bed? There were moments, just a second or two, when he seemed completely blank, as if he didn't know where he was or, even more alarming, who *she* was.

But he *was* eighty-four, six years older than her. Was it just old age? He had always been energetic, with a terrific mind that absorbed like a sponge and remembered with accuracy the knowledge contained in all the non-fiction books he read. He had several hobbies that required planning and manual dexterity, just like the experts recommended to keep elderly brains ticking over. She'd tried to convince herself that the changes in him were caused by having too much to think about. After all, they had a lot going on and were almost as busy even this far into his retirement as they had been when he'd been working.

And, she had to admit, though the sudden death of their little great-granddaughter had stunned them all, Simon had found it extremely hard accepting that Beth, in deep mourning for the loss of her beautiful baby, had separated from Alex and moved back in with her parents. Sylvia and Simon had had such a row over that, she still smarted to think about it.

It had started with Simon shouting, "What is *our* daughter thinking in letting *her* daughter walk out on her marriage? What about poor Alex? He's grieving over Amber too, isn't he? A wife's place is beside her husband no matter what the circumstance, so Beth should be at home with Alex."

Sylvia had countered by saying she felt they ought to support Beth, a grieving mother, until she could think straight again.

"Who knows what goes on inside a marriage, Simon, except the two who are in it? I understand what you're saying, but I don't want you saying anything to her other than you love her and want what's best for her."

From there it had escalated, with Sylvia only slowly comprehending that Simon's anger at Beth was his way of venting his own grief at the loss of dear little Amber, but when she'd said this he'd stormed off to his workshop. She was relieved at his going, though, as it meant he would take out his frustration on some inanimate object rather than her.

But she'd wondered herself why Beth had walked out on Alex. Of course, as she had said to Simon, they had no knowledge of other factors within their marriage which might have contributed to the break up, and she would not pry. She just thanked the heavens that they were back together and seemed very happy, both for their sake and for the wider family, for they were close-knit and she wanted it to stay that way.

Though the whole family deeply mourned baby Amber, who hadn't even lived to see her first birthday, they got on with their lives, for what choice did they have? Sylvia had been relieved to get settled back into their routine, and then Paul's announcement last year that he was getting married had been a delightful surprise that had lifted everyone's spirits.

Well, everyone except Simon, once he'd been told it was to be a wedding with all the bells and whistles, not only the morning suits for the men, but also big hats and fancy dresses for the ladies, a five-star venue for the ceremony and reception, a seven-course wedding banquet, and so on and so on.

Sylvia had been thrilled at the idea of such a grand event, knowing that with Adele's innate good taste, Paul's PR skills and business contacts, and the likelihood of Adele's wealthy father footing some if not all of the expense, it would be a beautiful and memorable wedding.

She, Anna and Beth had spent a few happy days hunting down their outfits and she'd looked forward to showing what she'd chosen to Simon. Unfortunately, he had marred things slightly for her by going into an almighty strop because of the amount she had spent and the reminder that he was required to hire his morning suit from a very expensive gentlemen's outfitter. Yes, Sylvia acknowledged, she knew he preferred to always be dressed in casual, comfy clothes, but surely one day in a tailcoat wouldn't kill him! Paul had offered to foot the bill, so surely her splashing out on a special dress with matching coat, shoes, handbag and hat wasn't something that Simon should be worrying about!

He'd accepted grudgingly that her new clothes were gorgeous but had gone on and on about the morning suit for days, until Sylvia had finally lost her temper and told him in no uncertain terms that he *would* wear the coat, the striped trousers, the fancy waistcoat, the shiny shoes, hat, starched shirt and even red silk underpants if their grandson required it, and she would not hear another word about it. And she hadn't. He'd simply closed his mouth with an audible snap, compressed his lips into a bloodless straight line, and not uttered a single word of protest about it since.

All through the fittings at the very fancy hire place and even getting dressed this morning he'd not complained, but she'd almost prefer it if he had muttered his quiet obscenities, because for quite a while it had been as if he'd shut himself away from her and become unreachable. And all over a suit!

Sylvia was brought back to the present by Beth's arrival at her side. She smiled with loving warmth at her granddaughter, who looked gorgeous in a cherry red dress, topped with a beautiful cream hat adorned with cream silk flowers that wound round the crown and spilled onto the brim. There were fine lines around her eyes now, but at least her smile reached her eyes these days. She was still far too thin in Sylvia's opinion, though Beth promised everyone she ate healthy food and plenty of it.

"Having fun, darling? I'm looking for your grandad."

"Pops is outside talking to Mum and Dad, and Alex has just gone over to join them. The men all look so handsome in their get-up, don't they? When I saw Alex it took my breath away!" She laughed as she said, "Until he put the hat on. I bet Pops hates it? Dad and Alex certainly do, and I know the minute we get home Alex will pull on his tattiest jeans and most raggedy rugby shirt."

"Yes, and Simon will change into his usual comfy trousers and checked shirt. Do you know, I've hardly ever seen him in anything else since he retired? He always wore suits and ties when he was working, so handsome! But now it's casual every single day, no matter what we're doing. Open his wardrobe and that's all you see, dark trousers and checked shirts. And all his belts and shoes are brown."

"Well, I suppose it makes getting dressed easier! Shall we go and join them?"

Sylvia took Beth's proffered arm and they strolled out onto the grand terrace that ran the full width of the magnificent hotel. Stone steps, curved and sweeping, perfect for the official wedding photographs, led down onto manicured gardens of stunning flower beds and emerald green lawns mown and rolled into stripes. There were about a dozen pretty, beribboned awnings dotted about, sheltering white-clothed tables from the sun, laid out with canapés, exotic sweets, party favours, cocktails and drinks of all kinds.

Anna, Felix, Simon and Alex were in front of the bar housed in a grand marquee, Simon holding a half-full pint glass of beer and a full flute of champagne, so Sylvia was happy to think he had at least had the intention of returning to her with the drink she'd asked for.

She curled her arm round his waist, mindful of the wide, feathered brim of her hat bumping against his arm.

"There you are! Is that for me?" She took the glass and sipped. "Mmm, heaven. Isn't it just the perfect day?"

Simon had clutched the glass for a little too long so the bubbly drink was no longer ice-cold as she preferred it, but no matter. She wouldn't ask him to change it for a fresh one.

She beamed round at her beloved family, but she hadn't missed the look of puzzlement on Alex's face before he'd seen her approach and gathered himself to smile at her. What had Simon been saying to him? Or what had Alex *seen* in Simon? Her grandson-in-law spooked Sylvia a bit, because of what he did. She didn't quite understand it, she wasn't even sure she believed in it. She'd watched his TV show with a mixture of disbelief and awe and she'd read his autobiography, but whether it was due to his having psychic powers or not, she knew with certainty that he was unusually sharp and perceptive about people. His seventh sense, he called it.

Now, however, with Anna and Beth in earshot, was not the time to ask him, and she hoped Alex wouldn't say anything to Beth later if he had any concerns about Simon. Beth would be sure to tell Anna, as she shared everything with her mum, and at all costs Sylvia wanted to protect her daughter and granddaughter, especially her granddaughter, for as long as she could if it turned out that Simon had the illness she was more and more suspecting he had.

Beth was a strong woman in many ways, incredibly so, but Sylvia knew there was also a fragility in her that had always been there and could easily rise to the surface again under pressure.

During the months Beth had lived with her parents, Anna and Felix, after Amber had died and she'd separated from Alex, Sylvia had seen and despaired of her vulnerable state and the depression she descended into. Yes, Beth was grieving for her baby, and everyone knew that would take forever and a day, but she had somehow got it into her head that she was not worthy of Alex, which added to her sense of profound grief and loss.

When Alex had at last confronted her and finally sorted it all out, Sylvia had been so relieved. But still, you never got over a bereavement of that nature. No parent should have to bury a child, any generation having to bury one of a younger generation that wasn't the right order of things.

Beth and Alex truly loved each other, she could see that, but there were times she found herself wondering if they'd managed to repair their relationship so it was unbreakable in the face of any further trouble or tragedy, fervently hoping that it was as secure as it seemed to be. These worries about her family were always bubbling under the surface in her mind, and that, she knew, was the burden carried the moment one became a parent.

Come on, Sylvia, she warned herself. Stop it now or you'll be crying.

A loud handbell started clanging. People stopped their conversations mid-sentence and turned as one towards the source of the sound, wondering what it might mean. A man, a town crier no less, in full livery of long red coat with gold braiding, white shirt with elaborately frilled cuffs, buckled shoes polished to a mirror shine, and black tricorn hat with a large white ostrich feather on it, strode among them, ringing his bell and exhorting everyone to go inside as the newlyweds were preparing to leave.

Careful of their slender high heels sinking into the grass, Sylvia, Anna and Beth linked arms and walked ahead of their husbands to join the others gathering beneath the chandeliers of the room where the reception had been.

All the tables and chairs and been cleared away and Paul and Adele were standing hand in hand on a low platform at the far end, dressed now to go straight to Heathrow airport for their flight to a one-month safari honeymoon in Kenya.

To get Paul away from his business for so long was yet another sign that Adele was a very special woman.

Sylvia found herself next to Adele's widowed sister, Lily, clutching the hand of her adorable little girl still wearing her delightful bridesmaid's dress and spangled shoes, and Adele and Lily's mother, an elegant but rather glacial woman.

Once the newlyweds had left in a dark grey limousine trailing tin cans tied to the back bumper with white ribbons, Sylvia said to Simon it was time they went home. The party would continue until late with a disco and a live band taking turns to entertain, with some of the guests—those that could afford the five-star prices—staying overnight in the hotel, breakfasting in style the next morning before returning to real life.

She and Simon had been given the choice to stay the night, but as the grand country hotel was less than an hour from their own home, they'd decided they'd prefer to wake up in their own bed the next morning.

It took a long time to extract themselves as there were so many people they needed to say goodbye to, so it was a relief to finally climb into the back of the chauffeur-driven silver Mercedes that Paul had arranged as their transport for the day.

Sylvia kicked off her shoes, flexed her toes, and leaned her head back with a tired but contented sigh. Taking Simon's hand, she said, "I bet you can't wait to get that suit off, darling, and return it and that ridiculous hat to the hire shop."

He slowly swung his head towards her and she felt alarm grip her insides at the glazed look in his eyes. "What are you talking about? What hat?"

Sylvia realised then that he'd left the hat at the hotel and she'd have to call as soon as they got home to make sure someone retrieved it. But more concerning than that, far more worrying, was the blank expression on Simon's face.

She felt her heart flutter a little and her stomach turn sour, as it had started to do every time Simon had one of his 'episodes'. Suddenly overwhelmed with tiredness and anxiety, she leaned her head against the window and wondered, for the thousandth time, what on earth she should do.

Chapter 5
Alex

Alex was only half-listening as the production team discussed a new backdrop to the stage for his television show. Various designs were scrolling across the large screens that dominated the far wall, and each one was being assessed as if it would be the end of the world if the wrong one was chosen.

He'd been quite happy with the one used before, just a plain, slightly shimmery silver wall that showed him up to good effect in the dark suits he favoured when working on the programme. He could say so, he supposed, but who would listen? He'd learned pretty early on that they didn't like getting suggestions from outsiders, even if one of the outsiders happened to be the star of the show.

He tuned out while the discussion went on, hardly believing that something so trivial merited so much serious attention.

Virginia, a fairly new researcher on the team, brought him back into the meeting with a question.

"What do you think, Alex? Do you like this one best too?"

For a moment he couldn't think what it was he was meant to like, then he saw that the images were no long scrolling and they were all looking at a picture of his studio stage with the backdrop coloured sky blue and his stylised signature in navy blue blown up large and placed diagonally across the centre. Wanting to laugh at the absurdity of it, he agreed that it was most impressive, avoiding catching Paul's eye because he would know Alex really didn't care about the small detail either, and then the producer asked him how he felt about having some one-to-one sessions filmed for inclusion in the programme.

"We're still figuring out the best way to do this, Alex. We could select members of the audience that you haven't been able to talk to and invite them to meet you on another date. Or we could invite applications for one-to-ones, though Paul says his office is already inundated with letters from people trying to get to see you. Whichever way they are chosen, we feel they should be done in a small room at your hotel, more intimate that way."

After giving it some consideration Alex replied he liked the idea of selecting audience members who hadn't received a message during the initial recording, but he really didn't mind where the meetings subsequently took place.

"Could you do a couple immediately following the taping of the show, do you think?"

Alex shook his head. "I'd prefer not to, though I appreciate it makes it easier all round. It's very tiring working in front of an audience for several hours, so I wouldn't be able to give it my best."

"In that case we'll concentrate on getting the shows taped, then set up sessions on future dates so you can do however many one-to-ones in a day that you're comfortable with. We'll edit them into the rest of the show."

Alex gave his agreement and then there was a pause, the only sound was the producer tapping his pen on the pile of notes before him on the table. Alex's psychic faculties came on alert as he sensed another new suggestion was forthcoming, one that the producer was wondering how to phrase.

Eventually he cleared his throat. "One of the team put forward this next suggestion, Alex, and Virginia has already looked into the possibilities it may offer. This article in the local paper gave him the idea." He handed over a photocopy of a newspaper cutting.

Alex scanned it quickly. It was a short article about the discovery of human bones wrapped in a sleeping bag six weeks ago during the building of a swimming pool in the garden of a house in Manchester. When a digger had uncovered the skeletal remains all work had had to be stopped while police investigated.

Forensic testing and pathology had proved that the bones had been there for around ten years or so, back when the area had been Victorian terraces. The state of the skull indicated some blunt force trauma, so any further construction of the pool was halted while an investigation into a possible murder took place. Thus far, the police had no idea of the identity of the person who had been buried, they had no missing person reports that matched the height and build of the remains so couldn't check dental records, and no-one had come forward with any information.

The only clue they had was fragments of an anorak, some pale green wool which might have been a sweater, pink denim that had once been jeans, a pair of small, scuffed pink trainers, and a rusted pink torch, making it more than likely the victim had been a little girl.

Frowning, he looked up from the piece of paper in his hand at the producer. "And the idea is what exactly?"

Paul spoke up for the first time since the meeting had started, and Alex caught the excitement in his voice as he said, "The idea is for you to identify the body and find out what happened! Just think, Alex, if you could communicate with whoever this is…"

Alex, aware of the high excitement and expectation in the room, was unsure about it all. It was just a child, for heaven's sake. He asked some questions, made some observations, and said he needed a little time to think about it.

"Okay, Alex," said the producer. "Could you let me know by the end of the week so we can make arrangements? Great. Let's call it a wrap, folks, good meeting."

When the Eselmont people had gathered up their papers and files and hurried back to their desks, Alex and Paul left together to return to their cars.

"I hope you're not going to say no, Alex," said Paul, his eyes on his phone checking all the messages that had come in during the meeting. He glanced up when there was no reply and Alex shrugged.

"I'm not sure. It could uncover something very unpleasant, and then what?"

"You won't like this, I know, but the more unpleasant it turns out to be, the better the PR we'll get out of it. Why don't you go there, let them film it, and just see what happens?"

They reached Paul's car first and Alex asked if he was going back to the office.

With a rueful grin and a light in his eyes, Paul replied, "Actually no, I promised Adele I'd be home early tonight."

Laughing as he walked towards his own car, Alex replied, "I don't know what you did to deserve it, but she's the best thing that's ever happened to you. Don't screw it up!"

***

Back home, while Beth was sitting at the dining table revising for some upcoming exams that would see her on her way to becoming a bereavement counsellor, Alex poured himself a beer and sat in the antique-red chesterfield armchair that had been his father's. He loved the smell of the deep-buttoned leather, the comfort of the chair that was both physical and spiritual. Here, he could rest his head and rub the scrolled and padded arms with his hands, knowing that his dad had done the same thing so many years ago.

He opened his mind, rousing his psychic senses. Immediately, there was a change in the room and Alex relaxed, expecting it to be his dad. But the power of this presence was far stronger, so powerful it set his ears ringing.

It could only be Grace.

Feeling like he'd been punched in the gut, sucking in air and blinking hard, Alex waited as the outline of a figure shimmered in front of him, growing brighter and brighter until he had to shield his eyes. He waited for her to rein in her energy so he could comfortably look at her and hear her deep, musical voice.

"Hello, Alex. Do you know why I have come?"

Alex regarded her with the usual curiosity and admiration. He did not truly understand who or what she was, or why she'd chosen to stay close to him since their meeting during Alex's near-death experience, but he felt it was a privilege. An impressive being, her form was tall and slender, her beautiful, impassive face was dominated by huge eyes that were obsidian-dark, eyes that flashed as if reflecting stars.

"I can only imagine it's about what I've been asked to do, to try and identify those bones?"

Grace bowed her head. *"It is indeed. There are lessons to be learned by you. You will do it."*

Chapter 6
Flora

There was a vibration, a sensation on her skin so slight she wondered if she'd really felt it. In all the time she'd been there, Flora had never felt anything like it. It was an odd sensation, something she imagined a spider might feel when a fly landed on its web.

She stood still, straining her ears and eyes for any other changes, but for a while there was nothing. Thinking she had been mistaken, she started to walk towards the oak tree, the tree where Grace, the tall lady with the strange eyes, could always be found.

The sensation hit her again.

And again.

Someone was thinking or talking about her!

And it wasn't her mum. She was always aware when Rachel thought about her, which was almost all the time, but this was different. Mum's thoughts never felt like this.

She started to run, sure that Grace would know what was happening. She felt the nerves flutter as she ran, because she was a little afraid of the tall figure that had led her away from that horrible house, and brought her here, to this lovely place.

When Flora had asked who she was and why she was there, Grace had replied, "I am Grace. I am one and I am many. I am here and I am everywhere. I am here to help you."

Now, as the special oak tree came into view, Flora slowed to a walk and stopped as Grace appeared, for it seemed as if she'd just stepped out from inside the tree. Flora stopped running and waited, biting her lip as the tall lady strode towards her.

"Flora. Walk with me. Tell me what is on your mind."

Grace towered over Flora, but she measured her steps so Flora could keep up, her robes flowing over the meadow flowers without touching them. It was things like this that made Flora both love and fear her. She was unlike anyone she had ever known in her young life, and she was pretty sure that nobody else could do the things Grace could do.

She swallowed and said, "Someone is talking about me, but I don't know who it is, or what they are saying."

Grace looked down at her, silver flashes sparking in her extraordinary eyes, and then she smiled. It was so beautiful and so unexpected that Flora felt her breath catch in her throat and she had to blink tears from her eyes.

"Indeed," Grace said. "Someone special *is* talking about you, Flora. He doesn't know you yet, or what happened to you, but he will come to see you soon. Be ready, sweet child, and trust him, for he will help you do what you so long to do. You will then help someone else. And once it is done, you will be able to leave here and grow up as you should."

Flora knew what Grace meant about what she longed to do, for she wanted more than anything to talk to her mother, but she didn't understand why she would be able to grow up afterwards. What could that mean? Although it seemed a long time ago, she remembered her ninth birthday as if it were yesterday, and she still felt the same age. If she grew up, how would her mother recognise her?

Chapter 7
Sylvia

Sylvia peered into the cupboard under the stairs but couldn't see what she was looking for. She reached round for the pull cord to turn on the light and then saw that what she wanted was right at the back, just visible behind the vacuum cleaner, ironing board, laundry basket and sewing machine. Tutting at the thought of hauling everything out, she heard Simon's cheerful whistling as he came in from the garden.

"Could you get the kitchen clock down for me please so I can change the battery? I can't get to the little folding steps without emptying the cupboard."

He reached up and took it off its hook. "I'll see to it."

"Okay, I'll get a new battery and…"

But she was talking to herself, because he'd turned away from her, loudly whistling a different tune, and was heading for his workshop with the clock tucked under his arm.

Deciding to leave him to it, though it meant the clock probably wouldn't be put back on the wall for several hours because he always got distracted by something else he was working on, Sylvia went outside to deadhead some roses.

As she ambled amongst the flower beds, she couldn't stop the thoughts about the increasingly worrying symptoms Simon was showing. His anxiety over whether he had his wallet and that the doors were locked every time they went out, or up to bed, didn't cause her too much alarm, but the tantrum over the wedding outfit had been shocking. Then he'd left the hat behind at the reception and seemed to have entirely forgotten that the suit was on hire and needed to be returned.

His changeable moods were making things increasingly difficult, with Sylvia constantly having to soothe and placate him, not knowing half the time what had upset him.

The old Simon would apologise and immediately try to make amends, but this Simon sometimes looked at her with pure dislike, and that was like a knife being thrust into her heart. Would he go to the doctor if she asked him?

She paused at the sight of a particularly beautiful rose with perfect petals, creamy yellow with a golden centre, and bent to smell its soft perfume, asking herself why she was hesitating to talk to him about this. They talked about everything, every little thing, it was the basis of the enduring strength of their long marriage, but she was so worried about what the episodes of forgetfulness and bad temper might mean she couldn't bring herself to voice her concerns out loud.

She wasn't even sure if Simon was aware of his changed behaviour. How would she even raise the subject of dementia? Even thinking the word made her shudder, she couldn't possibly suggest to Simon that he might have it.

But what if it were the other way round? She sat back on her heels and looked up at the sky. What if it was *her* manner that was changing in a worrying way, if it was *her* forgetting things and fretting over inconsequential stuff all the time, wouldn't she want Simon to tell her? She was sure she would, and she was also sure that she would make an appointment with her doctor straight away and deal with it.

"Tonight," she told herself. "I'll tackle it tonight."

An hour later she went inside to make tea and sandwiches for lunch. There was still no clock on the wall and no sign of Simon, so she fetched a battery from the drawer in case there were none in the workshop, and went to his workshop to call him in. On the workbench, lined up neatly in a row, were the clock components of back plate, clear plastic front, black metal hands, movement mechanism, screws and battery casing. The dead battery had been placed in a chipped glass ashtray that Simon kept despite giving up smoking decades ago.

Simon had his back to her, rummaging through a drawer. When he turned around he was holding a tiny screwdriver and a magnifying glass.

With a teasing note in her voice, she pointed and asked, "Did you take it apart deliberately or did you accidentally drop it?"

"What do you mean? Of course I didn't drop it."

Wary of his tone, Sylvia gently said, "But why is it in pieces? It only nee—"

Glaring, he interrupted her and spoke with exasperation, "You know why! It stopped working. You asked me to fix it and I'm fixing it!"

Feeling that horrible prickle as she looked at this man she hardly recognised, knowing he wasn't joking but nevertheless wishing passionately that he was, she could only try to explain and hope he calmed down.

"It stopped working because it needs a new battery, love, that's all."

Simon's mouth worked as he looked from Sylvia to all the bits on the bench, and she willed him to laugh, to tell her that he just wanted to see how it worked and have the challenge of putting the clock back together again. But he said nothing and, if anything, looked as if he was fighting back tears.

Placing the new battery beside the pieces of the clock, Sylvia suggested he come in for lunch, and turned to lead the way out. But, two steps away from the workshop, she heard Simon curse and turned in time to witness him sweep everything off the bench with his arm. Bits of plastic and metal hit the wooden floor and bounced and rolled, the smallest screws falling straight through a hole, but Simon didn't stop to pick them up. He marched out, pushing roughly past Sylvia, and stalked away across the garden and into the street.

Shocked into silence, Sylvia watched him go, deciding not to chase after him. She wouldn't talk to him about her worries when he came back either. He'd need time to calm down, she needed time to work out exactly what to say and how to say it.

I can't do it today, she thought. I'll wait a bit longer, until I know it's the right time.

When an hour had passed with no sign of Simon returning, Sylvia drank two cups of tea and ate her lunch and left a covered plate of ham salad sandwiches for when he came back. Maybe he'd gone to the pub and had a bite to eat there, or maybe he was just walking off his temper.

As time ticked on with no sign of his return she found herself changing her mind yet again, concluding that she simply must initiate a discussion with him when he got back. For too long she'd been flip-flopping like this over whether to talk to him or not, but the manner of his disappearance today combined with the realisation that there would never be a 'right' time finally brought matters to a head. She had no choice now but to tackle him head on so they could do something about it.

He was brought home three hours later by their next-door neighbour, Len Keene, who looked very worried. He had Simon by the elbow on one side and his well-behaved, cream-coloured poodle on the other. The dog sat patiently outside as Len led Simon into the house.

"I was walking past the pub and I saw him sitting at one of the tables outside, just staring into space. I spoke to him, asked him if he wanted to come inside and have a pint with me, but... well, it was as if he didn't know me. Didn't seem to know where he was, either, so I brought him back. Is everything all right, love? He hasn't had a knock on the head or anything, has he?"

Hiding how frantic she had become during the long wait and swallowing down the tears of anger and relief that threatened now he was safely returned, Sylvia managed a bright smile and told Len an outright lie. "He's on a new medication for high blood pressure and it seems not to be agreeing with him. You know, sleepless nights, a bit of confusion, that kind of thing. It needs to be changed again, obviously. Thank you so much, Len, for bringing him home."

Len seemed happy to accept her explanation. Sylvia, out of politeness, offered tea and was relieved when Len refused, saying that it was the dog's dinner time. He left to go next door and no doubt tell his wife all about Simon's strange episode.

She sat Simon down in the living room and pulled the foot stool over so she could sit directly in front of him. Their knees touching, she took both his hands in hers and shook them gently.

"Simon? Can you hear me?"

Apparently, he could not, or if he could, he was ignoring her or was incapable of responding. Pushing away a flutter of fear, Sylvia rose and went to the phone, scrolling quickly to the number of their doctor's surgery. She explained to the receptionist what had happened, and was told to bring Simon in an hour, if she could. Their own doctor was not available to see them, but they had an emergency appointment available with someone else if she was happy to see her instead.

Twenty minutes after their appointed time they were sitting in front of Dr Safeer, a very beautiful woman dressed in a sapphire blue sari edged with gold.

Simon was becoming more responsive but was still a bit dazed. Sylvia quickly explained everything that had been happening, and what had happened that morning. Dr Safeer asked lots of questions about Simon's age and if he had been in an accident where he'd hit his head, if he'd complained of headaches, and if there were any medical issues Sylvia thought could be relevant.

Thinking of how she'd lied to Len Keene, she shook her head, saying that her husband didn't even have any of the usual things associated with age, such as high blood pressure, high cholesterol, blood sugar issues, hearing loss. Not even arthritis in any joints. She spoke the dreaded words, the first time she'd said them out loud: "I'm worried that it's Alzheimer's."

Looking sympathetic, Dr Safeer told her not to jump to conclusions. "We need to do some tests, including a brain scan, so I'll make the appointments," she said. "Diagnosis takes time, though, and isn't always definitive when it comes to dementia, so I can't offer any treatment until we know what it is we're dealing with. In the meantime, I can only suggest you keep a close eye on him and make sure he comes to no harm. Have you family nearby? Close friends?"

When she said yes to both, Dr Safeer continued, "Then I suggest you let them know what's happening so they can help you. I appreciate you may want to keep things to yourself until you know for sure what's going on, but it wouldn't be wise to try and cope with it on your own."

She talked some more about the possibilities of what might be ailing Simon, including minor stroke or brain tumour, and advised her to pick up some leaflets from reception on her way out so she and her family could read about the symptoms to look out for.

As the doctor finished speaking, Simon suddenly snapped out of his trance and demanded to know where he was. When Sylvia told him, worried that he would get angry again, Simon simply said, "Oh" and meekly allowed Dr Safeer to ask him some questions, check his blood pressure, examine his eyes and ears and take a blood test.

They left the doctor's office with the promise that they would be contacted soon about an appointment for the brain scan and other tests, and Sylvia decided not to pick up any leaflets yet as she didn't want Simon seeing them. There was no point scaring themselves unnecessarily. Wait until they knew.

In the car, Simon hesitated as he pulled the seat belt round himself and asked who needed a brain scan and why. Trying not to cry Sylvia said they should wait until they were home so they could talk face to face, and she was relieved when Simon didn't demand to have the conversation there and then. She drove home with her mind trying to make sense of everything.

It was obvious to her that something was very wrong with Simon, whether it be a stroke, tumour, neither of which she'd considered until the doctor mentioned it, or Alzheimer's. Which would be preferable, she wondered: a tumour that could possibly be operated on, or dementia, which had no cure? She knew she needed to tell Anna, Paul and Beth about what was happening, but not today. She'd been indecisive for too long about Simon and didn't want to make the same mistake again, but she couldn't take any more today.

She would wait until they had a firm diagnosis and tell the family immediately. Right now, all she wanted to do was get home with Simon and lock all the doors to keep him safe.

Chapter 8
Kallie

Feeling as if she were in some kind of hideous time loop, Kallie once again moved amongst the same mourners who had come to Walter's funeral just three months before. The cottage being far too small for so many people she had hired the parish hall for both funerals, made the same buffet refreshments, gone through the same motions the whole day through, and now her beloved grandparents were resting side by side in the graveyard just over the wall that divided the church and its grounds from the cottage garden.

Three months, that's all it had taken for Verity to follow her beloved husband, leaving Kallie alone. With the benefit of hindsight, Kallie believed that her gran, already frail, had held on just to see that Walter's funeral was conducted the way she wanted, with utmost dignity, and then it seemed to Kallie that she had simply forced her body by sheer willpower to get sick and shut down.

"Kallie," Verity had said, taking Kallie's hands in hers with surprising strength. "I am old. I want to be with my Walter. I've kept it from you for some time, but there is something wrong with me. I'm not in pain, I assure you, so I ask you, *beg* you, not to let the doctor anywhere near me. Just let me go quietly, my dear. You have your whole life ahead of you and one day soon you'll meet your own soulmate and if I'm still here you'll be torn between setting up home with him, as you should, and looking after me. I don't want that for you, my darling girl, I want for you and me both to be free."

Kallie had insisted she be allowed to organise for the same carers who had looked after Walter to come back and look after Verity while Kallie was at work, but those arrangements hadn't come into effect before Verity had died.

Each morning, Kallie had helped Verity dress and get downstairs and had left her a little snack before she went to work. She'd organised her appointments so she could always be home for lunch, and she made sure she was always home as early as possible in the evenings.

For a while it had seemed as if Verity was perking up, for she talked about Walter as if he was with her all the time. Maybe he was, Kallie thought, but even if he was just a figment of the imagination it made Gran happy, so she would laugh and ask what Walter had to say for himself.

The morning Verity died, they'd had breakfast together as usual, Verity seeming contented but eating very little. Kallie had settled her in the living room with a blanket over her legs, a flask of tea, a plate of biscuits, and the television remote control close to hand, though Verity preferred to listen to the radio. She had made two rounds of sandwiches and put them on a plate, covered, with two pots of fruit yogurt on the kitchen table, ready for her and Verity to have for their lunch. She'd be able to get home for no more than half an hour, she'd said as she was leaving.

She'd come home at half past twelve to find Verity asleep in the chair, looking as if she hadn't moved from the moment Kallie had helped her sit there. But she wasn't asleep, she was dead. Kallie had been gone just a few hours, her gran could have drawn her last breath at any time in those hours.

"People are leaving now, Kallie."

Blinking, Kallie came out of her abstraction to notice that the crowd of black-clad mourners were gathering their things and preparing to go home. She moved quickly to the door to stand by her mother to say thank you and goodbye, wanting now for them all to be gone so she could tidy up and go back to the cottage.

Once the hall was empty of people, she went round the tables scraping the remnants of sandwiches, quiches and cakes, into the middle of the paper tablecloths, then balled the cloths up and stuffed them into bin bags ready to place in the large wheelie bin out the back. Her friends and a couple of neighbours offered to help, but Kallie thanked them and ordered them away, saying she and her mother would get it all done between them in no time.

She wanted to ask her mother to start stacking the dishwasher in the hall kitchen, but there was no sign of her, so she'd have to do it herself. She put in as much as would fit and set the superfast dishwasher running. It wasn't until she had emptied and reloaded twice more that her mother appeared, her face tear-stained and blotchy, her nose bright pink, making her look plainer than ever. Kallie had no idea where she'd been, and was further irritated when Celia simply leaned against the door frame with her arms crossed watching her put the clean and still hot plates and cups back in the cupboards.

She didn't speak until Kallie picked up a couple of wine glasses, and then she said, "I trust you're going to wash those by hand. The dishwasher will ruin them."

Kallie's brewing temper blew then, and she berated Celia for not contributing anything to the day, as she hadn't for Walter's funeral, her tirade ending in tears as she thought of how horrified Verity would be if she'd been there to witness this anger and frustration.

Not moving from the doorway, Celia said, "I don't think you know how hard it was for me to learn that Dad had died before I'd had a chance to say goodbye, and then to lose Mum so soon afterwards, with no warning. I should have been informed much sooner how ill he was. I should have been around more."

"Yes, you should have been! Gran called you the day Grandad went into the hospice, but you didn't come straight away, did you? And then you say you were overcome with grief when I called to tell you Gran had died, but you hadn't been to visit her for weeks to see how she was coping. *She*

61

was grieving, *I* was grieving, so how come this is all about you? I came home from work to find her dead, have you thought what *that* was like for me? I left her alone for just a couple of hours. When I found her it was as if she hadn't moved from her chair from the time I left for work in the morning and came back to give her some lunch. I've had to deal with everything, Mum, with no help from you! I had to make all the arrangements twice over, and now you're here crying that you weren't around much! Well that choice was yours, wasn't it? It was always yours."

She stood rigid in front of Celia, her hands in fists at her sides. Both of them were shocked by her outburst, Kallie herself having no idea how or why their mutual grief had degenerated into such a flare up. But wasn't it always the way with them? They were just toxic to each other.

Without a word her mother marched away, leaving Kallie to get on with washing the glasses in hot, soapy water. When Celia came back she was wearing her coat and carrying her car keys, and Kallie realised she must have gone back to the cottage to fetch her things.

"Well, Kallie, I don't think I should stay the night with you in the cottage and it's too late for me to drive all the way to Cambridge now, so I will go to a hotel. I'm sorry we had to argue like this on today of all days, but it seems it's how we're destined to be. I will call you in a week or two.

Utterly exhausted and wrung out with emotion, Kallie didn't try to stop her and when she heard her mother's car roar away from the hall she realised that the main emotion she felt was relief.

As soon as she got back home, she poured herself a large glass of wine and curled up on the settee, glad to be alone after such a harrowing day. Her eyelids felt heavy and she hoped she would sleep later, for she knew she needed to rest. She took a sip then raised her glass in a toast.

"I hope you didn't hear all that arguing between me and Mum, but you know what we're like! Here's to you, Gran and

Grandad, the most wonderful grandparents a girl could ever have wished for. I love you and I'm happy that you're together. I'll be okay, I promise."

Chapter 9
Simon

"Simon, I don't feel well."

Simon looked up from his newspaper, peering over his reading glasses to where Sylvia was sitting across from him, and was alarmed to see how white her face was.

"What do you mean, love?"

"It's hard to explain, but I didn't sleep well and I haven't felt right since I woke up, to be honest. I thought it was indigestion, but I've never had it like this. Whatever it is, it's getting worse by the minute."

He crossed the room to her, brushing her fringe back to feel her forehead. She wasn't hot, but her skin felt clammy. "A cold coming on, d'you think?"

Sylvia frowned as she rubbed her jaw. "More like flu. We should have had those jabs. You'd better go and get one as soon as possible, love, we can't risk both of us being ill!"

In all the years since reaching eligibility for the annual flu vaccination, they had joined the long queues at the local health centre. But this time, after long discussions about the benefits versus the side effects and the possibility that the media reports were correct that they hadn't got the formula right, Sylvia had made a convincing argument for not going ahead. The letter informing them of the date of this year's vaccination at their local surgery had gone straight into the bin and he'd thought no more about it. But, as she said, they ought to have the vaccination if it was still possible to do so.

"Okay, I'll sort it out. But what can I do for you now? Would you like a cup of tea? Aspirin?"

Sylvia shook her head, still rubbing her jaw. "I'm sorry, Simon, but I feel a bit sick. Could you get me a bowl from the kitchen? I don't know if I'm going to be, but I know I wouldn't be able to make it to the bathroom in time."

Worried, for Sylvia had never been like this in all the years they'd been married, he hurried off and opened and closed cupboard doors in frustration, staring like an idiot at the immaculately ordered shelves, not seeing anything but cups, mugs and small glass dessert dishes. Then he caught sight of the washing-up bowl in the sink, glad that it was empty and clean, and grabbed that. By the time he got back to Sylvia, her face had changed from white to ash grey and she was hugging herself, arms across her chest, hands gripping her shoulders so her knuckles were white. She rocked herself backwards and forwards.

"Sylvia? Hey, sweetheart, you're scaring me now. Tell me how you feel. Where exactly does it hurt?"

Sweat beaded on her upper lip as through clenched teeth she managed to say, "Everywhere. Call the doctor," before she burst into tears.

"I'm calling an ambulance!"

Keeping his eyes fixed on Sylvia as he dialled 999 and talked to the emergency services operator, he gave their address, her name, her age, stumbling over a couple of the details. He described her symptoms, trying to keep the wobble out of his voice as he looked at his beloved wife across the room from him, suffering and in pain.

He was assured that an ambulance was already on its way and he should stay on the line until the paramedics arrived.

"Hurry up!" Simon shouted and he hardly heard the soothing voice of the operator telling him to keep calm, asking questions about Sylvia that he couldn't answer because his brain felt like it was melting inside his skull.

Everything then went simultaneously super-fast and super-slow in a confusion of action and noise. When Sylvia slumped from the settee onto the floor he hardly heard the despatcher telling him to open the front door for the medics to get in as soon as they arrived because he dropped the handset and rushed over to her.

He could hear the siren getting louder as it neared the house. Telling Sylvia that help had arrived, he tried to hold her up but she fought him, wanting to stay lying down. Then there was the ringing of the doorbell and a pounding of the knocker, and he forced himself to leave her and let them in.

The room abruptly seemed full of people, though there were only two medics; a young woman and a man in his fifties, Simon guessed, and so broad-shouldered and muscular it was a wonder they found a uniform to fit him. The woman went straight to Sylvia, introducing herself as Alison and talking in a low, soft voice that seemed to reassure Sylvia. The man, saying his name was Bruce, kept his attention on Simon.

He indicated the handset on the floor by the table. "May I tell the despatcher that we're here, sir?"

"Oh, yes, yes, of course. I'm sorry. I…"

Bruce put a reassuring hand on Simon's arm. "Don't you worry about it, sir."

He spoke into the phone and replaced it on its cradle before joining his colleague, the pair of them talking in low voices to Sylvia and conferring between themselves.

Simon knew that he had to let them get on with it but it was hard to just stand there doing nothing while they helped Sylvia to lay out flat on the carpet and took her pulse and blood pressure. Simon became aware of a portable ECG machine on the floor by Sylvia's side, a display of lines dancing across the small screen in time to Sylvia's heart rhythms. He was aware too of Sylvia being asked questions, and questions being asked of him. He knew he should answer them, but he couldn't find his voice. He was frozen, just wishing the whole terrifying scene wasn't happening.

But if it had to happen, why not to him? Why should it be his Sylvia who suffered this way? Could it be, as she suspected, a severe case of flu?

Flu killed people, he knew that, especially older people, and he cursed himself for acquiescing to Sylvia's decision not to have the vaccinations. And they were old, he realised with a jolt. Okay, he knew he had memory lapses, but that was normal at his time of life. He and Sylvia ensured that they both kept active, mentally and physically, and they had a wonderful social life, hobbies that they did individually or together, lots of trips around the country and abroad. They were planning a cruise to see the Northern Lights.

Bruce was talking to him again, and although Simon understood what he was being told, the man's voice sounded as if it came from a long way away. The ECG readings showed that Sylvia was having a problem, the medic explained, and the mask over her face was to give her a little extra oxygen.

They lifted her onto a wheeled stretcher that Simon had no recollection of being brought in. They were going to take her to hospital. They were asking did he want to go in the ambulance with them or follow in his own car. Of course, he wanted to go with them. He wasn't going to let her out of his sight.

As he followed them outside, having the presence of mind to grab a jacket and pick up his keys, wallet and mobile phone from the hall table, it started to feel as if he were wading through treacle. And their voices, the medics' voices, he could no longer make out their words.

Their next-door neighbours were at the gate, a kind couple they'd known for years yet he simply could not recall their names. He could see the woman's mouth moving, but it was as if his ears were stuffed with cotton wool and he could not understand her. He registered the concern on her face, though, even managed a weak smile to acknowledge it, as he climbed into the back of the ambulance like a robot and sat where he was told to.

"I have to go back, I've forgotten my wallet."

"I'm sorry, sir, but we really can't delay."

About to object, Simon searched his pockets, relieved to feel the wallet and keys there. He steadied himself as the ambulance set off, lights flashing and siren wailing.

After that it was as if he'd passed into another dimension, one where he had no control, no part to play, no say in anything that was happening.

Within moments of arriving at the hospital Sylvia's stretcher disappeared and he had been politely but firmly held back by a male nurse, forced to answer yet more questions. But he had to, for her sake. Again, as with the emergency services operator, he recited her full name and her age. He gave her date of birth. Told the nurse making the notes she'd always been healthy, seldom got a cold, never complained of headaches. She was lactose intolerant and suffered from hay fever every May.

When a doctor came out and informed him Sylvia was having a heart attack and that she needed emergency bypass surgery he didn't believe it and started to shout at him. The doctor remained calm, compassion in his eyes, until Simon ran out of rant and stood there, wild-eyed, panting and terrified.

"Is there anyone you'd like us to call, Mr Savarese? A family member perhaps who could come and wait with you?"

It was then, finally, he realised how serious the situation was and he would have to contact Anna with this awful news.

"It's okay, thank you. I'll call my daughter." He pulled the mobile phone from his pocket.

With a shaking hand, he started to search for Anna's number, but the names on the tiny screen were blurred and he pressed the wrong one. He hung up and tried again, but his mind went blank and he couldn't think of the name he was searching for. He stared in panic as he scrolled through the list, his mouth going dry, because now he had no idea where he was and who he was meant to be calling.

Frantic, his eyes darted round the room, seeing people on rows of chairs, some sitting motionless and blank-eyed, others sipping coffee, or idly chatting. Staff members dressed in trousers and tunics in different shades of green, burgundy and blue, some with stethoscopes round their necks or poking out of large pockets, some with upside-down watches pinned on the tunics, were coming and going. He took in all this detail, yet couldn't remember what he was doing there.

Then, just as the receptionist called out to him, a concerned expression on her face, that moment of feeling utterly lost passed as quickly as it had come, and he dashed outside, found his daughter's phone number, which was, of course, at the top of the list, and called it before he could forget again.

She answered with such a cheerful hello that he choked up and could barely get the words out to tell her what had happened. Before he finished speaking Anna was crying, but she told him she was on her way, and the phone went dead.

Simon paced the floor, not knowing how long he waited, but at last Anna was there, rushing into the A&E, searching him out. Close behind her came Beth and Alex, and Simon thanked them for bringing her, remembering that his son-in-law, Felix, was away on a business trip.

Alex shook Simon's outstretched hand and asked what was happening. Simon could only swing his head from side to side and tell them that Sylvia had had a heart attack and been rushed into surgery.

"I'll go and see if I can find out anything more," Alex said, and hurried over to the reception desk.

Simon hugged his daughter close, then drew Beth to him as well, fighting back tears as he offered his handkerchief to Anna. Eventually, she sniffed and pulled away so she could look at him.

"A heart attack, Dad? I can't believe it."

"Nor me, Anna, my love. Nor me."

Beth asked what had happened, but before he could answer Alex came back over to them. "They can't, or won't, tell me anything more than you already know, Simon. Sylvia's

69

going to be in surgery for a couple of hours, though, maybe more, so they suggest we either go home or go to the cafeteria and have a hot drink, try to eat something, because it'll be a long while before you can see her."

Anna, highly distressed, said that they should stay where they were, but Alex, pointing out that there did not seem to be enough seats for them to sit together, convinced her that they should do as suggested and go to the café.

"They won't bring her back here anyway, she'll go straight to Intensive Care. Let's get a hot drink and then we'll find out where we need to go and wait for news there."

Simon, too, resisted at first, but with a little gentle persuasion from Alex and Beth agreed that it would be better to move, to do something, rather than just sit on those hard, plastic chairs with other people just as anxiously waiting for news of their loved ones or treatment for their own cuts and broken bones.

He allowed Alex to lead the way, and soon he, Anna and Beth were sitting opposite each other at a table by the window, clean but still damp from a recent wiping. Alex went to get drinks and some snacks.

Simon gazed at Anna and Beth, marvelling afresh at how much his granddaughter resembled Sylvia when she'd been that age. Beth's huge hazel eyes were teary and bloodshot, her make-up was smeared, her hair coming loose from the band of her ponytail, but to Simon she was beautiful.

For the first time, he registered that it was dark outside. It was eight o'clock in the evening so five hours had passed since Sylvia had first informed him that she felt unwell. It seemed like five years.

They talked about what had happened, Simon telling them in as much detail as he could remember.

"I'm glad Alex was able to bring you here," he said to Anna. "I'd forgotten until you arrived that Felix is away. It's a good job Alex was home, I wouldn't have wanted you driving while you were upset and worried."

"If he hadn't been," said Beth, "I would've taken a taxi and picked Mum up. I wouldn't have let her drive, Pops, nor risk driving myself in the state I'm in."

Anna put out her hands and Simon took one, Beth the other, and they tried to reassure each other that all would be well, because Sylvia was a strong woman who'd hardly had a day's illness in her life. She would fight her way back to them.

Alex returned with a tray laden with four steaming mugs, sachets of sugar and a selection of plastic-wrapped sandwiches and packets of crisps and biscuits. They each took a drink, milky tea for Simon and Anna, strong coffee for Alex and Beth, and Alex opened all the packets and spread the contents out so they could help themselves. Simon's stomach rumbled but he didn't think he'd be able to take a bite, let alone swallow any food.

Alex wanted to know exactly what had happened, and Simon recounted again what he'd already told Anna and Beth just minutes before, but he knew Alex needed to hear it too. It was all such a shock, he felt even as he went over the events of the last hours that he was talking about someone else.

Sylvia had shown no outward signs of illness whatsoever in the days prior to this one, so how could she be having a heart attack? And her symptoms had not given him an inkling of how serious it was until she'd started clutching herself and rocking forward and back, forward and back. She had told him that her jaw and shoulders ached, and by the time the paramedics arrived she had clearly been in a great deal of pain and distress.

Then, in the ambulance on the way to the hospital, she'd admitted with a whisper that she'd been having palpitations for a few days and this morning she'd been woken up by what she thought had been indigestion. Simon had felt terror grip his own heart then, and he felt it now.

By the time the hot drinks had been drunk, or half-drunk in Simon's case, and he, Anna and Beth had shared a couple of cheese sandwiches, Simon was impatient to find out if there was any news.

As they walked back along the harshly-lit corridors, Simon felt something snap like a twig in his brain. He kept walking but couldn't think where he was, or why he was there.

A woman was walking beside him on his right, there was a younger woman and a tall, dark-haired man who seemed familiar three paces ahead of him, but no names came to mind. The younger woman held hands with the man, whose shoes squeaked on the linoleum floor, and she turned to say something to Simon. She was looking straight at him, her mouth moving. He was struck by how much she looked like his Sylvia.

Or was it Sylvia he was looking at?

His wife, soulmate, best friend.

Confused, he was about to ask who they were and what they were doing in this place when there was another snap and the confusion disappeared as full memory slammed back into his brain: the man was Alex; the woman on his arm was Simon's granddaughter, Beth; the other woman was his daughter, Anna, and they were in the city hospital, because Sylvia was very ill.

Heart attack.

Emergency surgery.

He must be suffering from a panic attack. How else could he have forgotten, even for a split second, what was happening to his wife in an operating theatre somewhere in this huge, imposing building?

Chapter 10
Sylvia

It was a dream, yet not a dream. Sylvia, for the first time in her life, was lying on an operating table in a hospital. She could hear the monitors, the quiet requests of the surgeon asking for what he needed, the clinks and chinks of metal as a nurse sorted through the instruments and lined them up on a large tray, handing over forceps, scissors, clamps and keeping other surgical tools lined up ready. She wondered how she could hear it all and worried that the anaesthetic was wearing off. You heard about such things happening, where patients felt everything yet could do nothing to alert the surgeons that they were awake.

Terror gripped her as she braced herself for intense pain, but instead she came effortlessly out of her body and was looking down on the scene.

She had a bird's-eye view of the surgical team working on her, could see her physical self completely draped in green cloths. Only her head and chest area were exposed, her eyelids held closed by narrow strips of white tape, her rib cage cut through and spread open with something that looked like a medieval torture instrument. She could see her beating heart in the dark, gaping cavity. One gowned and masked figure asked for suction and another pushed a rubber tube into her open chest and there was a soft, gurgling noise.

She was a witness to all of this and yet felt nothing for the physical part of her that was laid out on that table, for somehow, she recognised it as the most unimportant part of who she was. It was merely a shell, the vessel that had held Sylvia Winston, Mrs Sylvia Savarese as she had been these past fifty-eight years. She was released from it now, yet it still felt like she was seeing with physical eyes, hearing with physical ears.

There was music playing; a light, soothing jazz. She searched for the source. Was it in the operating theatre or coming from somewhere else?

Her thoughts turned to Simon, who would for sure be able to identify both the music and the composer, and wondered where he was and how he was coping. He was due to have his brain scan; would he remember it? She had no idea how much time had passed, maybe he had already had the scan? Oh, she wished she'd told Anna what was going on instead of waiting for the tests to be done and a diagnosis given. Why did she have to so catastrophically collapse before she'd had the chance to sort things out?

Without knowing how, she found herself moving outside and away from the theatre, gliding along a wide corridor with cold strip lighting and a shiny, dark blue, linoleum floor.

A thin, stooped man was walking away from her, pushing a clattering cleaning cart with a wide broom and drooping grey mop sticking up above his shoulder. She cried out when she saw that Alex and Beth were walking towards her, Anna and Simon following behind, but it seemed none of them heard her and it was clear that they couldn't see her.

Anna and Beth looked almost childlike, she thought, they were both so much shorter than the two men. For a wild moment she wondered if Alex could be aware of her, but surely not. She wasn't dead. Or was she? No, it was obvious that he did not see her, nor did anyone else walking up the corridor in the same direction acknowledge her presence. She floated right up beside Simon, managing to keep pace with him as she peered into his face. There was a glazed expression in his eyes, a tightness to his mouth, a look she had come to dread.

Oh God, what if she didn't pull through when he needed her so badly, when they all needed her? Would Anna be able to manage things? And what of her poor darling granddaughter; how would Beth cope with another tragedy after the grief she had so recently come through of losing her little girl?

And Paul so recently married, he and Adele wanting to start a family as soon as possible.

Why did Sylvia's heart have to cause all this trouble now, when there was so much she needed to do?

For the sake of her family she had to fight this terrible thing that was happening to her.

She had to get back to her body and back to health so she could take care of her precious family.

Chapter 11
Kallie

Kallie made the usual social chit-chat with the two volunteers working behind the reception desk. She'd come to know them well in the time her grandfather had been a patient, and now here she was about to start working there as a part-time therapist. She clipped the security pass that was handed to her onto the waistband of her skirt and pushed through the double swing doors that led into the hospice wing of the huge building.

Avoiding dwelling on the entrance up ahead to the inpatients unit where her grandfather had spent his last few days, she turned right into the adjoining corridor and hesitated outside the first of the three therapy rooms. A list of available treatments was pinned on the door and she smiled to herself at the thought that this time next week she'd be administering those therapies.

Suddenly the door opened and a sandy-haired man beamed down at her. He was dressed in a black short-sleeved tunic, black trousers and electric blue trainers. Kallie noticed he wore a copper bangle on one wrist and had an intricate Celtic band tattooed on the other.

"I had a feeling someone was out here! Not lost are you?"

"No, I'm not lost," Kallie replied, wondering how he could possibly have known she was outside the door. "I'm a holistic therapist and beautician and I'll be working here on Thursdays from next week. I'm on my way to help out in the DPU, to experience what goes on there."

The beam got wider. "Oh, it's fantastic, you'll really enjoy it. I do Thursdays here as well so I guess we'll practically be roommates. I'm Kevin." He stuck out his hand and she shook it, giving her name in return. "You'll love it here, Kallie. I've been doing this for eight years and it's my favourite day of the week. We get a few coming over from the dementia wing, but it's mostly DPU guests who come to us, and if we're not too busy then any members of staff and volunteers are welcome to come and see us."

Kallie said, "I'm a little nervous about it but really looking forward to it. I'd better get a move on or I'll be late."

"Oh, that would never do!" he said with a wink. "Well, bye for now, Kallie. I look forward to seeing you around. There's no need to be nervous, you're in for a wonderful day. If you can survive the notorious induction training you can survive anything!"

Kallie laughed out loud as she waggled her fingers in farewell and walked away, thinking about that training. She had been warned that it was intense and likely to bring up all sorts of emotions, and this had turned out to be very true.

"Don't worry about crying," one of the two women giving the course had told her and the seven other new volunteers sitting in the seminar room. "Most people do get upset and it's entirely expected, so everyone's sympathetic. What happens in this room stays in this room. And we always have tissues."

This last bit made everyone break into nervous laughter as they cast sidelong glances at each other. It was a fair bet that they each had a tale of bereavement and loss to tell, and it would probably all come out over the next few sessions as they got to know each other and bonded as a group.

Kallie had found it difficult talking about the deaths of her grandparents, but she managed to get through it without too many tears. One would-be volunteer, though, had pulled out of the course after the second evening session.

They'd been shown videos of terminally-ill people talking about the different ways they were facing up to their imminent deaths. One had featured a forty-five-year-old woman who had a cardboard coffin in her living room that her three children and various other members of her family were busy painting in psychedelic colours and writing messages of love to place inside. She wished to be laid to rest in a woodland burial ground, and she had chosen the spot, written the service and made all the arrangements so her grieving family wouldn't have to. For some reason this had really upset this particular would-be volunteer and she had withdrawn. None of it had bothered Kallie as much as she'd expected, because for the most part she found everything she learned fascinating and, to her surprise, not at all depressing. In fact, it was uplifting!

This was a place where death and everything surrounding it was dealt with compassionately and without drama. They encouraged open honesty and discouraged the use of false hopes and euphemisms, telling the volunteers that it was preferable to always use straightforward language.

"We need to tell it as it is. We die. It's a fact that none of us can escape from, so let's not be embarrassed about it or skirt around the issue. Patients and their loved ones begin grieving as soon as the diagnosis is given, and this is to be expected. It's far better to be upfront and honest, and the patients you come into contact with will be grateful for it, believe me."

She had completed the training last Saturday, which had meant losing a day's earnings from the salon, and now she would lose another day by coming here to see how the DPU worked, but she considered the sacrifice more than worth it. She'd make up the money by working longer hours for a couple of months.

The DPU sitting room was empty when she entered, so she took a moment to stand in the doorway and look around to take it all in. Sofas and armchairs with brightly coloured cushions and throws scattered on them were set around three edges of the light, airy room, with a large square coffee table in the centre and side tables placed so people could put their drinks down within easy reach. Set in the far corner was a beech wood cabinet on which sat a filter coffee machine. Straight ahead of her, the top half of the wall was a single pane of glass, so the very large conservatory beyond was visible.

She could hear chatter coming from behind the closed door to her left, so she opened it carefully and found herself in a narrow kitchen where women were moving around each other as if in a well-rehearsed dance. Pam, the supervisor whom she'd met during the induction training, spotted her and called out to her.

"Welcome, Kallie! I hope you don't mind, but everyone will have to introduce themselves to you as we go along. We're one short, so your help today will be invaluable, but it means there simply isn't time to ease you in as I would've liked. Could you write your name up on the chalk board over there please? It's a health and safety requirement so we know which volunteers are here each day, so please remember to scrub it off before you leave. Right, let's go through to my office to get a bit of paperwork done and then you can get started."

The office turned out to be a tiny room with no windows, into which Pam had squeezed a small desk, a swivel chair on castors and a three-drawer metal filing cabinet. Kallie had to go almost up to the desk to make enough room to close the door behind her.

The two walls either side were covered in corkboards with bits of paper pinned to them and whiteboards with different coloured writing on them, and on the far wall, behind the cluttered desk, was a large holiday chart with square and round stickers all over it.

"Here's your name badge, Kallie, and this plastic folder tells you everything you need to know about setting up the DPU." She handed the items across the desk. "I know you may not be volunteering with us after this as you'll be busy giving your lovely therapies, but you might find yourself willing and able to help out now and then so do please take it home. An enterprising volunteer a couple of years back created this, taking photos to show how each area should be set up and describing how things work in the Unit. So useful for anyone new. But you'll be shown everything today, or almost everything, it does get very busy. And if you're not sure, someone will help.

"Now, most of the people who come here are receiving hospice care in their own homes, but perhaps one or two might come from the inpatient unit if they feel up to it, but all are referred to as guests, not patients. If you have any questions at any time just ask one of us, okay?"

Kallie nodded her head, taking Pam's quick glance at her wristwatch as a signal that they both needed to get out of the office and get to work helping the others get the DPU ready for that day's guests.

Pam asked her to deal with the coffee maker first. "The instructions are on the wall behind it, and your manual will show you how things should be laid out. You'll find everything you need either in the cabinet or in the kitchen."

Following the instructions line by line, Kallie spooned the required amount of ground coffee into a new filter, added sufficient water and switched it on. She found paper napkins, plates, cups, saucers and teaspoons in the cabinet and laid them out, then, after further consulting the instruction manual, she went to the kitchen to collect the biscuit tin and a glass jar containing an assortment of wrapped sweets, making sure everything was set out so it looked just like the photograph.

Through the window into the conservatory, a recent add-on to give the DPU sufficient space with lots of natural light for arts and crafts, she could see Fiona, a permanent member of staff she'd also been introduced to during the induction training.

The short, plump woman with an untidy mass of auburn hair streaked with blue and a multitude of rings and studs in her ears and eyebrows had explained to the group all the craft activities that were available, including pottery as they'd recently installed a small kiln. Now she was setting out materials for the afternoon's session. When she glanced up and saw Kallie she gave a wave and a cheery grin, mouthing, "See you later."

Kallie wondered what kind of creative activities Fiona had planned for that afternoon, very much looking forward to joining in.

As it was such a lovely day the conservatory was open to the gardens. Kallie could see volunteers deadheading roses and weeding flower beds, and patients and visitors sitting on benches here and there, including a man with a portable IV drip by his side who was reading a newspaper and tucking into a giant bag of crisps.

From here she had a much wider view of the extensive gardens than the one she'd had from the small, sheltered patio of her grandad's room, and she was delighted to see the Rainstones sculpture again. She never had found the opportunity to go to the sculpture to see how the quartz sparkled and the little copper bells tinkled in the flow of water, but now she would easily be able to do so.

A woman with a tanned, heavily lined face and thick blond hair styled in a modern spiky cut, came teetering in on sky-high heels, carrying a cake on a foil-covered board.

"Kallie? Lovely to meet you. I'm Monica, practically a veteran in the DPU, and I do Tuesdays and Thursdays." She held up the cake. "This is for Bob, one of our guests. Would you be a dear and make room for it on the table by the coffee machine, and see if you can find some candles? Oh, and matches to light them, of course. I know we have some in the kitchen somewhere. Obviously, we can't put eighty-nine candles on a cake, even if we had that many, but if you can find enough to make a good show that won't set off the sprinklers or smoke alarms that'll do."

Before Kallie managed to say a word, Monica bustled away, laughing at her own joke. She made space for the magnificent rectangular cake as asked, careful not to dip her fingers in the thick chocolate butter frosting, and found a box of candles and matches after rummaging through every drawer in the kitchen. With that mission accomplished, she was about to go in search of Pam for further instructions, when yet another volunteer came in, introduced herself, and asked Kallie to go to the dining room.

"Pam asked me to finish things in here. You'll find Trish in the dining room and she'll show you how we set up for lunch." She patted Kallie on her arm, and leaning forward and lowering her voice as if sharing a confidence, she said, "You're going to be very, very tired by the end of today."

Her head already spinning with the whirlwind of activity she was participating in, Kallie found the dining room by following the smells of hot food. Hospice inpatients had their meals in their rooms, and she'd never come here during the time her grandfather had been staying in the hospice, as she had made use of the small kitchen facilities near his room. Food and drink had been taken in the seminar room during the induction training, so she'd only seen the dining room once very briefly when they'd been given the grand tour of the whole hospice on the Saturday.

"Hello! Your badge gives you away as a volunteer, are you a newbie, Kallie?"

Kallie smiled, liking the cheerful, open expression on the woman's face. "Actually I'm a therapist. I'm going to be working in the treatment rooms on Thursdays starting next week, but I'm here to help out today so I can learn how the DPU works."

Trish indicated her own badge saying, "Mine says Patricia but everyone calls me Trish. Delighted to meet you. I'm afraid it's always a bit of a mad house before the guests arrive, but things do calm down once we're all set and everyone's settled."

"I was told how much is involved, but you really have no idea until you're part of it, do you? What would you like me to do?"

"We need to lay out our three tables over there so we can bring our guests straight in at lunch time, which is usually about half past twelve. All the other tables are for staff and visitors." Trish handed Kallie a tray of cutlery.

"We leave the chairs as they are, but be ready to whip a couple out of the way for those in wheelchairs, and offer to help anyone with sticks or walking frames. Everyone tends to want to sit in the same places every week, but Pam likes us to encourage them to move around a bit so they get to know each other better. Now, I'll pop the tablecloths on and fill the water jugs, if you would please set each table with six places. That cupboard over there, the one with the dark blue doors, is ours, and that's where we keep everything: cutlery, serviettes, water glasses and wine glasses."

At Kallie's raised eyebrows, Trish said with a wide grin, "Oh yes, drinks are always on offer, provided they're not on meds that bar the consumption of alcohol, of course. We've got wine, beer and spirits, mixers, the whole works. You should have a peek in the drinks cabinet when we go back, it's pretty impressive; there are bottles of booze in there that I've never even heard of!"

The two women talked and worked companionably together to get the tables set, and Kallie remarked how lovely it was to see how much care was taken to make it look so nice. Trish agreed, replying that she always thought the tables looked as if they belonged in a lovely little bistro, not a hospice canteen.

"Do you do any other kind of work, Trish?"

"I work in an engineering factory three days a week where they make things like iron railings and oil tanks, so it's always rather grubby, as I'm sure you can imagine. I have a tiny little office all to myself there, though, and I love the job almost as much as I love being here."

83

For the last task in the dining room Trish fetched two clean cotton tea towels. Handing one to Kallie, she said, "We've just got time to polish all the glasses, and let's give the cutlery a bit of a shine as well. Then we'll go back to the DPU as Pam likes to give us an update before the guests arrive."

With less than ten minutes still to go until the Unit opened and admitted the guests, Pam called everyone together. As they gathered round Trish explained quietly to Kallie that this was an opportunity for the volunteers to sit down and draw breath while Pam went through the list of expected guests, giving brief outlines of their illnesses and current treatments. Kallie saw Kevin with another tunic-wearing therapist and waved.

Pam addressed Kallie. "You'll be working in the therapy rooms after today, but it's worthwhile for you to come and listen to this bit if you can so you'll know in advance what's going on medically with anyone who comes from here to you for a treatment. If you are asked to give a treatment to anyone from the dementia wing you'll be told what you need to know by whoever brings them over."

Pam ended by telling them of one recent death, all in the matter of fact manner that was the way of the hospice. At last all was ready, and the guests started to arrive, brought by friends, family members or volunteer drivers. There was a flurry of activity as everyone was welcomed into the room and seated. The volunteers organised coffees and teas and passed round the tin of biscuits, and when everyone was settled and comfortable Pam asked that all the volunteers sit down again so she could begin.

"Let's get the sad news over with first," she said. "I'm sorry to tell you that Alfred died on Monday. He was at home with his family, and it was very peaceful. I don't yet know the funeral arrangements, but as soon as we hear I'll let those of you who wish to go know when and where it's to be."

Pam paused to let the news sink in, and Kallie felt the atmosphere in the room sink a little. This was a necessary announcement, she supposed, otherwise people would notice that a guest was missing and would be wondering and asking where they were. It was right and proper that Pam tell them straight away, for this was a hospice and anyone attending the DPU knew that their own deaths would likely occur within months, a year, or maybe two years at the most.

Pam rustled the papers on her lap and, with a much lighter, happier voice, she gestured first to a young woman in a wheelchair then to Kallie herself. "I'd like you all to welcome new guest Louise, and also Kallie Harper, our new therapist. She'll be here every Thursday, so if you'd like a treatment from her there are leaflets on the coffee table listing everything she offers, which includes massage, Reiki healing and aromatherapy. Kevin and Chris are here today, so just let someone know if you want to see them and we'll get you booked in."

There were murmurs of appreciation, and Kallie heard a woman, whose head was wrapped in a colourful scarf, say to the person sitting next to her that she would love a head massage because her hair was growing back and her scalp itched.

Pam waited a moment, then said, "And finally, let's all wish our Bob over there a very happy birthday! We'll have the lovely cake his niece made after lunch, so do please leave a little room for it."

After a few more items of news covering general hospice matters, including a night-time fundraising half-marathon that Kallie thought she might like to sign up for, it was time to top up the hot and cold drinks, offer more biscuits, go round with the lunch menu and take orders and, when all that was done, sit and chat with the guests. She headed for Bob, opening the conversation by asking about his birthday plans.

He chuckled and replied, "I think the family will insist on taking me out to dinner tonight, though I don't have much of an appetite these days and am happy with scrambled egg and bacon. I thought I'd be gone by now because of the damned cancer eating away at my insides and here I am at eighty-nine and still breathing. Ridiculous."

Liking the twinkle in the old man's eyes, Kallie said, "Why is it ridiculous, Bob? It's quite an achievement, surely?"

He was a tiny man, almost swallowed up by the high-backed armchair he was sitting in. He grinned, showing a row of crooked teeth with a front one missing, and nodded towards the cake, saying with a broad Wiltshire accent, "Tell you what'll be an achievement, and that's if I can blow them candles out without needing to be resuscitated and then eat any of the cake without getting most of it down the front of my shirt."

Kallie sat with him for five more minutes, enjoying the warmth and charm, the sparky humour he displayed. Bob was entertaining and funny and she would have liked to stay with him, to hear his whole life story, but he tapped her on the wrist and said, "You'd best work the room a little, love, or I'll be accused of monopolising the prettiest volunteer in the place. Go on, now, someone else'll soon be over to keep me company."

Giving him a playful tap on his arm for his delightful compliment, which she was sure he used on all the ladies, Kallie glanced around to see where to go next. Her eyes alighted on the new guest, Louise, but Trish was sitting with her and didn't look like she was going to move on to someone else. Louise had the most beautiful hair, dark brown with coppery streaks, thick and wavy, and so long it spilled down the back of the wheelchair almost to the seat. Trish was chatting to her quietly, and Kallie thought back over what Pam had said about Louise's condition. The young woman was unable to talk, yet Kallie could see that Trish was giving her every ounce of focus and attention, as if she was having the most riveting conversation ever.

As if sensing she was being watched, Trish glanced up and smiled warm encouragement to Kallie before offering Louise a plastic beaker with a straw in it. Kallie decided to go over to a very handsome man who she thought might be in his early forties, who had the deepest blue eyes she had ever seen.

When he introduced himself Kallie recalled Pam saying that he had an inoperable brain tumour. During training, she'd been told not to talk about their illnesses unless they mentioned it first, but to concentrate instead on who they were and everyday things they liked to try and keep things light and cheerful. She asked John if he joined in with the afternoon arts and crafts sessions, and he told her he had trouble with his co-ordination and preferred to stay in the lounge, but sometimes he brought his guitar and played for everyone.

"For some reason I can still play well," he said. "I used to be able to sing pretty well, too, but nowadays I can't hold the tune and I forget the words. I miss singing almost more than anything else."

The smile never left his face as he answered Kallie's questions about his music and his family, and everything was explained to her without any self-pity or anger, just a matter-of-factness that she really admired.

At half past twelve it was time to take everyone to lunch, so Trish took Kallie under her wing again as they helped move guests to the cafeteria. Pam indicated which table the volunteers should sit at, and Kallie had to admit to herself that she was relieved none of the guests in her care would need her help with eating or drinking. She was quite capable of doing it, but these people didn't know her and she wouldn't be with them next week, so it seemed best to let the regular volunteers undertake such an intimate task.

Trish stayed with Louise, as they had already formed a bond during the morning. It was a lovely, congenial forty-five minutes, with good conversation and lots of laughter, and then it was time to go back to the Unit and everyone except John went straight into the conservatory to spend a couple of hours being creative with Fiona.

About halfway through the afternoon, the birthday cake was served with more hot drinks and after that it seemed no time at all before the guests had gone and the DPU had been set back in order for the following day. Kallie used the blackboard eraser to rub out her name and was on her way back to reception to sign out of the visitors' book when Trish caught up with her.

"How are you after your baptism of fire in the DPU?"

Kallie laughed. "Absolutely exhausted but deeply satisfied with myself. I woke up in the early hours feeling really nervous, and I honestly wondered if I'd be up to it, but I loved every minute of it. Everyone's so positive, aren't they? Amazing people, all of them. I'm so looking forward to being in the therapy room next week, today really helped me prepare for it."

"I'm glad you feel that way. This is such a happy place, which comes as a major surprise to many, let me tell you! But, as you probably found out, not everyone makes it through the training course, and the reality of working or volunteering here can prove too much for some. Most of us volunteers come here because we've had family members looked after here. In my case it's because my dad's in the dementia care wing. I saw posters about volunteering in the DPU and here I am!"

Kallie replied, "I'm sorry about your dad, it's a dreadful disease. My grandfather was a patient here and told me about the DPU, how much he loved it when he was well enough. I miss him dreadfully, but I knew I wanted to be part of this and grabbed at the chance to do this one day a week. I love the salon where I work, it's a pretty building in the most beautiful country setting, and now I've got Thursdays to look forward to in this fabulous place as well."

Trish regarded Kallie with steady, light brown eyes. "Patients really appreciate the treatments you give, especially things like aromatherapy. Even acupuncture is popular; I've never tried it but I'm told you really can't feel the needles.

They're so used to painful injections and blood tests and pills and all the other not-so-pleasant stuff they have to endure, that spending time with someone like you is just the tonic they need." Her eyes sparkled as she said, "Did they tell you that volunteers can have treatments as well? If you do hot stones massages I'll be forever your friend."

"I do," laughed Kallie. "So book yourself in! Are you parked outside? My car's way over in front of the dementia wing."

"In that case you may as well walk with me through the building and go out through the dementia wing exit. I'm going to sit with my dad for an hour. Not that he'll know I'm there. He's a hundred years old and fast heading to being one of the oldest surviving dementia patients."

She explained to Kallie that her father had been married three times and that she, his youngest, had been born when he was in his sixties. "My mum looked after him for as long as she could, but she's thirty years younger and it didn't seem fair to keep her tied to someone who no longer even recognised her. Mum adored him and he was the best of dads; the diagnosis hit us all hard, but especially her. I'm happy to say, though, that she has found happiness with a new partner who we all love. I'm the only one of the family still local so I sit with him just about every day. Come on, I'll show you the way; it's safer than weaving your way through that car park at this time of day when so many cars are coming and going."

Kallie confided as they walked along that she didn't know who her father was, and her mother had been nearly forty when she had her. "So that makes us both the product of an older parent, though I'm an only child. I suppose being raised by your dad was a bit like me being brought up by my grandparents? Age means nothing, though, does it? It's all about how young we are inside."

Feeling she had made a new friend, Kallie said goodbye to Trish and trudged wearily to her car. By the time she got home she was so tired she fell asleep on the sofa for an hour, only waking up because she was hungry and thirsty.

The room was in semi-darkness, for she hadn't even switched on the lights when she'd come in. With a groan, she swung her legs off the sofa and headed for the kitchen, switching on the lights as she went. They flickered, on-off, on-off, on-off, on.

Chapter 12
Alex

Alex took his seat on the plane and buckled the seat belt. When this trip was being organised by Eselmont Productions he had declared that he would prefer to go by train, not minding that it would be a long journey starting at six o'clock in the morning, with a change along the way. Eselmont had offered him a first-class ticket but he had refused it, saying he was perfectly happy to take the first empty seat in second class and read a book and enjoy some time just being by himself. On arrival he would get a taxi at the station to the location and meet up with the film crew who had travelled there the previous day to scope out the site and plan the shoot.

But then Paul had scuppered his plans for a peaceful journey by deciding to visit his parents the day before, stay overnight, and travel to Manchester with him. There would be no crack of dawn starts or train journeys for Paul, first class or otherwise; he insisted that they fly out of the nearest airport.

"Why take four hours when you can get there in just over one?" he'd said. "I'll arrange a limo to take us to the airport."

Alex had known it would be no good arguing.

It was a short, uneventful flight, landing in Manchester slightly ahead of time thanks to a good tailwind. Alex handed down Paul's bag from the overhead locker before grabbing his own. Paul, as always, was in a hurry. He wanted to get through the domestic arrivals checks and find the driver that Eselmont had organised so they could get going straight to the film location. The same driver would pick them up and take them to their hotel afterwards, and be available for any other places they needed to be taken to during the day or evening.

Alex followed more slowly, looking with interest around the terminal concourse, at the milling crowds, the shops, the cafés and bars, careful to keep his psychic senses closed as he always did when moving through public spaces. If he didn't protect himself he'd be bombarded with information about those around him, begged by those in spirit to pass on messages to people who were total strangers to him. He couldn't cope with that, wouldn't dream of just walking up and tapping someone on the shoulder as they went by and saying, "Hey, your long-dead Uncle Harold/John/Wilbert wants you to know that they're okay."

When he caught up with Paul in the Arrivals area, he had already located the driver and was standing with him by the barrier, waiting impatiently for Alex to get a move on. The driver took their bags and led them to the car, stopping briefly to pay for the parking ticket. As soon as the doors had been unlocked, Paul was in, sinking into the back seat and immediately getting to work on his mobile phone. Alex simply looked out of the window, blinking as they emerged from the harsh strip lighting of the car park to softer daylight outside.

He was so deep in thought about what was to come that he didn't know how long they'd been travelling before the car turned into a cul-de-sac and then the driveway of a substantial house. This was where the bones had been discovered, and the couple who owned it were apparently very excited at having a film crew in their back garden.

A well-built man with a red baseball cap visible under his hard hat, clutching a clipboard, came through a side gate with a beaming smile and a cheery, "Hi, great to see you again."

Alex grinned back and shook the proffered hand, trying not to wince as his bones were squeezed in a very strong grip.

"Hi, Marcus. Good to see you too. How are you?"

"Oh, you know, busy, busy! But delighted you're back with us again, it was great working on your previous programmes."

Marcus glanced at Paul who had his phone to his ear and merely raised a finger to indicate he'd be with them when he finished the call. From the one-sided conversation Alex could tell he was talking to Marcia, and it seemed a celebrity that Paul had been after for some time had finally signed up for Paul's company to represent him.

Alex chatted to Marcus, a man he really liked for his perpetually sunny nature and his professionalism when filming. Marcus had been moved to tears when Alex had taken him to a private corner after completing a show one day and delivered a very important message to him from his late mother.

"The light is good this morning, Alex," Marcus said, leading him back through the gate where the rest of the crew were setting up. "We'd like to film as you take a look around, just to get some shots, but no commentary from you is needed. The digger driver who uncovered the remains is working somewhere else now but we can call him if you need to talk to him. The couple who own this place are longing to meet you." He winked. "Between you and me I think the missus is a bit of a fan. But the detectives leading the investigation want nothing to do with us. They're total sceptics, but we'll see if we can change their point of view, won't we? They only have to see you in action."

Alex made no comment. He'd come up against police officers before who didn't want to hear what he had to say. He understood their stance, of course he did. They wanted and needed hard proof, evidence they could see and touch, not information from a psychic medium like him that couldn't always be proved. Still, his hit rate was excellent.

It wasn't public knowledge, but he'd proved himself on the cold cases and missing persons he'd been asked to work on, and so Eselmont had in their possession genuine police testimonials, and these had helped to get agreement, they could come here and film as long as they didn't interfere in the investigation.

The investigating team had now finished with the area and had released it back to the owners, but the swimming pool firm had started a job elsewhere and wouldn't be back for a fortnight. That meant that the burial area would remain uncovered for that time before they restarted the work, giving Alex and the Eselmont team plenty of time.

By now Paul was off the phone and Marcus led them to a very pretty summer house, explaining that the owners had offered it to them to use as a base while they filmed.

"Hard hats, boots and Hi-Vis jackets are mandatory at all times, I'm afraid," Marcus said. "Meals have been arranged for all of us back at the hotel, which isn't far from here, but if you want anything to eat at other times we can send a runner out. Since I've been here, though, there've been endless offers of coffee and cake from the owners."

Once suitably attired to meet the health and safety requirements for being in a private garden with a huge crater in it, they left the summer house and walked across the lawn to where there would soon be a very large swimming pool.

"This area was once a street of Victorian terraces," Marcus explained. "It was marked for redevelopment years ago, and these executive houses were built in their place. They're about ten or eleven years old now, and if the owners hadn't decided they wanted a swimming pool, the bones could have lain undiscovered for years, if not forever."

Alex felt a shiver as he stood looking down into the hole. He glanced around, taking in the well-kept, landscaped garden around this ruined area, noting the piles of bricks and glass that would eventually enclose the pool. When he looked at the house, two faces were watching him from one of the upstairs rooms. The owners, he presumed.

Marcus was right. If not for them, the bones might have stayed buried forever.

"Of course," Marcus continued, "all work had to stop and the police were called in. The body had been wrapped in a sleeping bag, of a type used by the army, so I understand, and put in a shallow grave, making it obvious that it had been buried there not too long ago so was of no interest to archaeologists. Pathologists have the remains now and we're waiting to hear what they find out, though the police are likely to keep that to themselves while the investigation is ongoing. How much do you want to know, Alex?"

Alex, once more staring into the hole gouged into the dark earth yet not seeing it, brought his focus back to Marcus and told him he didn't want to know any more than what he'd just told him.

"I don't want to see any pictures, either, though I might want to see photographs of the recovery of the remains at a later stage when I've made contact with whoever was buried here. Tell me nothing more, Marcus, nothing at all."

"Okay. So, what now, Alex? How do you want to play this?"

He could tell that Marcus was excited and intrigued, but his senses also picked up that Marcus wanted justice for whoever had been buried here. It was hardly a big leap to conclude that this was a murder, and this was why Eselmont was so keen to cover the case.

Alex asked to be left alone for a short while. "I know you need to film, but if the camera crew could please stay as far back as possible, that would really help. I just want to get a feel for the place to begin with, then I'll have a better idea of how I want to proceed."

He waited until everyone had gathered in front of the summer house then focused his attention on the grave site, opening his psychic senses ready to receive any communication that might happen. He didn't have to wait for long.

Chapter 13
Flora

As the greyness surrounding her began to dissipate, Flora slowly became aware that she was back once more at the place where her body had been buried. After she'd died and been placed there by the big man with the greasy black hair she hadn't known what to do, where to go. Then a tall lady with huge black eyes had appeared and taken her hand. She'd said her name was Grace and that Flora had nothing to fear. Flora had cried a lot, but Grace had been patient and explained things over and over until Flora had calmly accepted it and Grace had led her away to the pretty place where she lived now.

She'd visited her grave many times since then, sometimes with Grace but mostly on her own, watching with curiosity as the terrace of houses had been demolished and transformed. Once the rubble had been cleared the area had been fenced off for quite a while, with nothing happening, and then heavy equipment had come and cleared and levelled the land, followed by builders who shouted a lot and liked their radios loud. Eventually the large houses had become occupied, their gardens transformed, and yet throughout all that disruption, her bones had been undisturbed until now.

The day her remains at last unearthed, still wrapped in the now ragged remnants of the big man's sleeping bag, Flora had looked on while lots of people came to see, to dig, to examine, measure, mark and photograph. She'd recognised policemen and women because of their uniforms, and white vans had arrived and people covered head to foot in white protective clothing and masks that made them look like spacemen. Her bones, her clothes and trainers, the little pink torch, had all been removed from the dirt, labelled, put in plastic bags and taken away, she didn't know where. The people had all gone and for a while nothing more had happened, then, a few moments ago, she had been alerted to activity near her grave again and had arrived to see people in jeans and heavy boots with cameras balanced on their shoulders crowded around the hole where she'd been discovered.

She could see one of them, the one she'd heard called Marcus, who wore a red baseball cap underneath one of those hard hats. He was pointing his camera at a man she hadn't seen before. He was dark-haired, with a nice face. A kind face. He was standing by himself on the lip of the hole.

He'd been talking to Marcus before he'd walked to the very edge, and something about him held her interest. He was tall and nicely built, his face smooth and handsome, not at all like the huge, scary man who had come crashing into the house when she'd been alone, waiting for her mother. Was this the man Grace had told her about, the one she could trust? She wished Grace would come now and hold her hand, for she was a little bit scared.

"I can see you."

For a moment Flora thought the handsome man was talking to someone else. Not one of the hundreds of people who'd come before had ever spoken to her. But he was looking straight at her. Could he really see her?

"My name is Alex. Will you talk to me?"

Oh, yes! She wanted to talk to him, but she wasn't sure how.

"You only have to speak to me with your mind. Just think the words and I will hear them. I'm a medium, do you know what that is? No-one yet knows who you are or how you died, but you'll be able to tell me and I'll be able to tell everyone else. Will you start by telling me your name?"

Her thoughts were jumbled, confused, and still she didn't know how to talk to this man. He seemed to understand, because he smiled at her and kept talking.

"No-one should be buried without a name. They're making a clay model of your face in the hope someone will be able to identify you, but in the meantime they are calling you Tabitha, because this street used to be called Tabitha Gardens. Did you know that?"

She thought about it. Tabitha sounded like a fancy name, but she preferred her own name. And going to the trouble of making a model of her face? How on earth did they do that? She was aware that she'd had no schooling and so was pitifully ignorant of so many things. But those bones, *her* bones, meant nothing to her.

She was happy in the other place, which was like a favourite story of hers, with Grace and friendly deer and rabbits, and yet she'd found herself being dragged through the fog time and time again against her will. But as she'd watched the whole excavation she'd felt like giggling at the care taken to remove her broken skeleton, care the like of which she hadn't really known when she was a flesh and blood person. And they wanted to know who she was?

She didn't know how she felt about all that now, but she did know that she liked this man. Alex. A nice name. A warm name she could trust. She formed it in her mind and sent it across the crater.

"That's right, I'm Alex."

She studied him, reaching out with senses brand new to her, feeling her way to him with her mind as he'd told her to, feeling the connection as her senses met with his. She encountered nothing but warmth, kindness and compassion, something she'd not had much experience of, only from her mum, and she liked it so she edged a little nearer. What was he doing here? A medium? What did that mean?

He definitely wasn't wearing a uniform, she could see blue jeans below the bright yellow jacket he wore, and he had no medical instruments. He wasn't digging with a trowel or taking soil samples, he wasn't scribbling notes or taking hundreds of photographs.

Looking past him she could see others standing with Marcus, one with a microphone on a long pole that looked like a fluffy grey animal, reminding her of the cat at one of the places she'd stayed in. Flora had loved that cat, because it curled up on her lap and let her stroke its lovely soft, thick fur while it purred. That, in turn, reminded her of finding the cat curled up on her slippers once, the slippers she'd loved because they were pink and girly and cosy, but they'd been left behind when she and her mother had been forced to make yet another night-time escape from trouble.

She turned her attention back to Alex and lifted her hand in a wave. He waved back, a wide and friendly grin that showed his even, white teeth. He really was very good looking. And he really could see her.

She felt something else besides compassion in him as their senses continued to unite and merge. She felt sadness, regret. For her. She knew it was for her, and wanted to cry for the knowledge that someone cared. Someone cared about her, just as her mummy had before she had gone away and left her.

She felt determination in him, too, an iron will, and that he had come here for a reason that wasn't the same as all the others. The others just wanted to identify her and get the answers they needed so they could get on with their jobs.

What did he want?

She glanced down into the pit at her feet then back at Alex as he spoke again.

"Please tell me your name. I can tell you don't like Tabitha, but that's what I'll have to call you if you don't tell me what you're really called!"

She smiled shyly and whispered, *"Flora. My name is Flora."*

"Oh, I like that name! When I was a little boy, probably not much younger than you, my Granny Mairi used to sing 'The Skye Boat Song' to help me to go to sleep. Do you know that song?"

Flora shook her head.

"There's a lady called Flora in it." Alex took a breath and softly sang,

> *"Rocked in the deep,*
> *Flora will keep*
> *watch o'er your weary head.*
> *Speed bonnie boat*
> *like a bird on the wing,*
> *onward the sailors cry."*

Across from him Flora, pink-cheeked, was giggling.

Alex laughed too. *"I know, my voice is terrible, isn't it? Be glad I didn't sing the whole song to you! It's a story about a dangerous sea journey, and this lovely lady Flora is keeping a royal prince safe from harm. Will you talk to me, Flora? It would help you to tell your story, it really would. And then you can go back to the lovely place you've come from and never have to come back here again. It is lovely over there, don't you think?"*

She wondered how he knew about that, about the place where everything was pretty and it was always warm and never dark, always safe. She thought for a long moment.

All right, she would tell him.

She described her life, her not very happy life. It had always been just her and her mother, Rachel, going from place to place, living with men for as long they tolerated having a 'brat' like Flora hanging around, Rachel stealing food and clothes, something Flora hated her doing but she always said there was no other way if they were to survive.

She described how they had broken into the abandoned house that had once stood here and the night they had spent on a horrible, musty-smelling mattress. Of her mum going out in the pouring rain to get some food and Flora falling back to sleep, then waking up again, shivering, teeth chattering, scared because Rachel hadn't come back.

She'd been told not to leave the room, but she'd heard sounds downstairs and thought it was her mum. She described the strange taste of the piece of cold and congealed pizza, the delicious taste of the fresh, cold milk.

100

"And then the man came. He was very big. He had a scarred face. I thought he was angry to find me there, touching his things. But I hadn't stolen anything. Only the pizza and a little milk. I was trying to run, to get out of the house and find my mum. I'd thought that she had brought all the things in there, that she would light the fire and we would sit in front of it. I ran straight into him, that man, knocking the wind out of him and he pushed me away. I fell against the fireplace, hitting my head on the corner. The man was so very sorry, he hadn't meant to push me so hard, but I had frightened him. I could hear him talking to me, trying to get me up off the floor, but I felt funny and couldn't talk. He hadn't been angry with me, he'd been scared! He told me that over and over and then everything went black."

Alex sighed and said she was a very brave little girl to tell him all that, and Flora felt strangely relieved to have shared it with him.

"So, it was an accident, the way you died? The big man didn't mean to hurt you?" Alex asked.

"No, he really didn't. He cried so much and he didn't know what to do. He was going to leave me there, I think, but then he didn't want to because of the mice and rats, so he wrapped me in his sleeping bag and put me in the ground. When he carried me outside in the rain I saw him start to dig the hole, and then I wasn't there any more. Grace came and I wasn't scared. I was in a different garden and the sun was shining."

"So you've met Grace?"

Flora nodded her head and leaned forward, telling Alex as though it was a big secret that she was a little scared of Grace.

Alex chuckled. *"She scares me a little, too. Now then, tell me Flora, have you been able to find your mum?"*

Flora's expression dropped. *"Yes, but she doesn't see or hear me. And she's so sad."*

"Of course she is, she must miss you very much. But I'm going to help you. What's your last name, Flora, so I can find your mum?"

Flora told him.

"Okay, that's good. You've done well, Flora. I have to leave now because my wife's mum is very ill in the hospital and I need to go there. But then we're going to find your mummy and I'm going to talk to her

and tell her what you've just told me. Okay? And when I do that, you'll come, won't you? I'll need you, you see, to tell me what to say so she knows it's really you. Will you do that? You'll know when, I promise."

Flora nodded. She didn't want the kind man to leave, but he'd promised he'd go and see her mum and tell her everything. She was excited about that.

She so wanted him to stay and talk some more, but she felt she was being tugged backwards. The distance between her and Alex grew larger, until Alex seemed very far away. In the blink of an eye she was back in her dappled wood, and Grace was waiting for her.

Chapter 14
Alex

Alex and Beth couldn't linger in conversation over breakfast as they usually did because they needed to get across town to pick up Simon. Two days earlier Simon had managed to damage his car by reversing into a bollard in the hospital car park and now refused to drive it even though it wasn't at all serious; he could still close and lock the boot and the car was perfectly okay to drive. It had really knocked his confidence though, so now they or Anna collected him and took him to the hospital, or he went by taxi.

Sylvia was showing no signs of recovery and Alex felt sad that Beth's world had painfully shifted yet again and she faced the heartrending possibility of losing her beloved gran.

Beth looked so tired, he hated seeing the dark shadows under her eyes again as she said she wished she could crawl back into bed and stay there for a week. Every time the phone rang he saw how she flinched and if it was her mum or grandad, she had to visibly brace herself to answer it and hear the latest news.

Yesterday, she had answered a call from Simon, who'd been at Sylvia's bedside all morning, saying that Sylvia was showing signs of waking up. Alex, Beth and Anna had rushed there in high excitement only to find Simon had misunderstood the doctor and their hopes had been raised for nothing.

Anna tried to get Simon to come away from Sylvia's room for a short while, to have a drink and something to eat, but he wouldn't leave her bedside, so Beth and Alex offered to go and find something for him so he could stay near her. Anna had followed them out, and as soon as they were out of

Simon's earshot she said that she had never seen him look so haggard, and she was worried about his frequent memory lapses and refusal to drive.

"It was such a little accident, something any one of us could have done under all this stress, but maybe at Dad's age he shouldn't be driving any more anyway? He's always been so sprightly I find it hard to think of him as old, but he's really aged since Mum's been in here. I want him to come and stay with me and Felix," she'd said. "But he point-blank refuses. I'm sure he's not eating properly, and he really shouldn't be alone. Beth, darling, see if you can talk some sense into him, will you? He won't listen to me at all!"

That was yesterday. Today was a new day and maybe, just maybe, Sylvia would come back to them after almost two weeks in a coma. Even the word stopped Alex in his tracks. How could 'coma' have anything to do with the lively, vibrant, young-at-heart Sylvia? Come to that, how could 'heart attack' have anything to do with her either? In the years he'd known her she'd not had a day's illness. Yet it was all too real and he had to help Beth and his in-laws deal with it.

Beth's mobile started trilling in her handbag five minutes after they'd started the journey.

"It's Pops," she told Alex. "I wonder why he's calling, he knows we're picking him up."

Alex listened to the one-sided conversation.

"Hi, Pops… What do you mean? Is everything all right? You sound annoyed… No, we're on our way now. Pops… Pops, listen to me! We're not late. No, listen… are you there?"

She looked at Alex in surprise and said, "He hung up on me! He says we're late."

"He just wants to be there as soon as possible; I'm surprised he isn't camping outside the ward. He's stressed, Beth, that's all. You'll have to have another word with him about going to stay with Anna and Felix, it would be much better for all of us if he did."

Clenching his jaw at the prospect of another distressing visit to Intensive Care, he wondered with despair why no-one at the hospital could answer why Sylvia had lapsed into a coma following the bypass surgery. It was very rare, but it happened, they said. Neurological damage, lack of oxygen to the brain, adverse reaction to anaesthesia, and they used medical terms beyond the average person's understanding. They would keep conducting tests, they told them, and her vital signs were good, so no-one was to give up hope.

A light rain pattered the windscreen as Alex turned the car into the street where Beth's grandparents had lived for the best part of forty years. Her mobile started to ring again, and he could see Simon standing at the end of the driveway with his phone pressed to his ear. Was he calling her again? He tooted the horn as he pulled up to the kerb, and for a strange couple of seconds Simon looked straight at him with no welcoming smile on his lips. In fact, he looked furious. As he pressed a button on his phone, Beth's stopped ringing.

They both got out of the car and Alex was relieved when Simon's face at last relaxed and he hugged her and warmly shook Alex's hand.

Beth spoke gently, "Were you ringing me again? I said we were on our way."

"I was worried. You're so late."

Beth checked her watch and told him they were, in fact, almost ten minutes earlier than they'd said. "So, are you going to get ready?"

"What do you mean? I *am* ready. I've been waiting for you!"

With a sidelong glance at Alex, she pointed down at Simon's feet. "You're still wearing your slippers, Pops."

Rather than laughing, as Alex expected him to, he heaved a heavy sigh of irritation and stomped back into the house. Within moments he reappeared with his shoes on and joined them in the car and Alex was happy to see that his humour had been restored as he said in a cheerful voice, "Maybe today's the day, eh? Paul's coming later. Sylvia's always loved listening to his voice. Maybe he'll be the one to bring her back to us, eh Beth?"

As he drove them to the city hospital, Alex mulled over Simon's quick-changing moods of the past few months and uncharacteristic tactlessness. After Simon's comment about Paul, Beth would be fighting against the exasperation and jealousy that stabbed her in the heart every time Simon held out the hope that it would be her brother who would make a difference in a way none of the rest of them could. Paul and Adele had cut their honeymoon short and come straight home, and were staying at Paul's small apartment in Bath so they could be close to the hospital.

The doctors and nurses said it was entirely possible that Sylvia could hear them so they all talked and read to her, for hours at a time, so it was insensitive of Simon to say that it would be Paul's voice that would be able to reach into the dark depths of wherever Sylvia had retreated to and not Beth's. Or Anna's. Did Sylvia really favour her grandson over all the other members of the family? Of course she didn't.

They were all there as much as they could be, even Felix who travelled so much for work, had cancelled some trips and his quiet strength was a steadying influence on Anna, Beth and Paul.

Paul didn't show his emotions often, but he was as emotional once he'd seen Sylvia as he had been when Amber, his little niece, had died. Alex could also see that Beth, just like that harrowing time when Amber died, was not comforted by it. She preferred it when Paul was his usual self, rather arrogant but always endearing, covering his deeper feelings with sarcasm or silly jokes, not red-eyed, quiet and bewildered as he was now.

Sylvia had always been at the centre of their lives; none of the family could imagine life without her, and seeing the stress Anna was under at the thought of losing her mum but trying so hard to be a rock for Simon only added to everyone else's

106

stresses. As for Simon… well, he clearly wasn't coping at all, and that should surprise nobody.

While the family gathered around Sylvia's bed, Alex suggested to Adele that they go to the restaurant and have a cup of coffee.

When they were seated with their drinks, Adele stared down at her hands wrapped around her cup and said, "What if she doesn't wake up?"

Alex blew out a sigh. "It doesn't bear thinking about, does it? Simon would be utterly lost without her, and Beth… Well, I don't know how Beth would cope, having to deal with another death of someone she loves so much. It's bringing back all the dreadful memories of losing Amber and she's not eating well and hardly sleeping at all. What about Paul? How's he holding up?"

Adele shrugged. She looked tanned and glowing with health from her short safari honeymoon, but the tension showed in the stiff way she held her head and her shoulders.

"He doesn't say much. He's using work as a crutch, of course, but, well… You and Beth both forewarned me and I've seen for myself that Paul does not readily show his emotions, but he does feel them, and strongly. And Alex, I don't know how to say this, but I'm so sorry you all have to face another tragedy. I never knew your baby daughter, of course, but since becoming an aunt to darling little Hope it breaks my heart to think of what you both must have gone through." She hesitated, and Alex sensed what she'd say next. "Do you still see her, your little girl? And Scott? Lily misses him so much, but she draws strength from little Hope."

He smiled. "I see my little girl a lot, because she's with my father. Scott, well, I don't see him, but I know he's fine where he is, and he's bound to be watching over your sister and their daughter until they find their way to live without him. I'm sure he'd come through to me if Lily wanted it. I talked to her briefly at your wedding, but she didn't raise the subject."

Adele put her elbow on the table and rested her chin on her hand.

"Hmm, Lily doesn't say much, she's like Paul in that way, but I think she's come to terms with it, as far as one can come to terms with losing the love of your life. And her coping with it is thanks to you, Alex. I'm so glad you were there for her at that torturous time, though I know you were badly hurt in the accident too. She still has some awful days, but she's focused on being the best mum she can be to Hope."

Alex smiled. "That's good to hear. Now let's change the subject and talk about you and your new husband. Did Paul actually manage to relax on honeymoon? It's such a shame it had to be cut short, because he's always glued to his phone— working, working, working—and a long rest would have done him good."

Adele laughed. "Yes, that blasted phone was a bit of a problem to begin with. I threatened to chuck it out of the jeep and let an elephant trample it to pieces, but as the days rolled by in all that sunshine he gradually relaxed until he was only calling Marcia once a day. And she gave him short shrift, let me tell you, refusing to update him on anything no matter how he begged and then threatened to fire her! I think Paul is actually a little afraid of her."

"Everybody cowers before Marcia! But actually, away from the office and the almost impossible job of managing Paul, she's delightful company. Paul couldn't hope for a better PA and Marcia knows he would no sooner fire her than fly to the moon."

He was about to say something more when a strange and totally unexpected sensation overwhelmed his entire body, pushing all coherent thought from his head.

"Alex? Alex! Are you okay? Goodness, you've gone white!"

Fighting to keep his breathing steady and controlled Alex managed to reassure her that he was fine, but he needed to get away to somewhere he could be on his own. The sensation of being zapped by lightning, or how he imagined that would feel, utterly shocking and yet it was familiar. He couldn't just up and march away from Adele, but at least he could explain to her what he'd felt because she'd seen first-hand how he worked and what he was capable of.

"I'm sorry, Adele, I felt for a moment… well, something just hit my psychic senses rather hard. A bit difficult to describe, but it knocked me off balance for a bit. It could be Dad trying to reach me, but it doesn't feel like him. I don't like leaving you on your own, but do you mind if I go outside for a bit? I need some fresh air and somewhere quiet to concentrate."

"Of course I don't mind! I'll go back to the ward and tell Beth where you are if she comes looking for you."

Relieved to be alone, Alex strode away, wondering how many miles he'd have to walk along corridors that all looked the same before finding the way out. Exiting through the main doors at last, he ignored the huddle of smokers in their dressing gowns and slippers, some of them with portable IVs on wheeled poles, and headed across the car park to a small grassy area behind the bus shelters. Days of sunshine had dried the greenery to a crisp surface, so Alex sat down on the warm ground, closed his eyes and opened his mind.

"Dad? Was that you calling me?"

He listened with that mysterious part of his mind that connected to people who had crossed over, but he sensed immediately that his father was not there. Someone was with him, though. Flexing his psychic senses to the max, he reached out to the energy trying to connect with him. With so much power, he wondered if it could be Grace.

"Hello?"

Whoever it was moved in really close to him, but he couldn't yet tell if the person was male or female. He could feel their energy now, but it was weak and soft, not at all like the powerful force he'd felt inside. He surmised that whoever it was, he or she was having difficulty communicating with him. If only his dad was around to strengthen the connection! He tried again to initiate a better link.

"I don't know who you are, but if you can hear me then please don't give up."

There was a sensation of a hand brushing the side of his face, fingers stroking his skin in an affectionate way, leading Alex to believe that it was someone he was close to.

He concentrated even harder, straining every fibre of his being to hear a voice, no matter how faint, how fragile. Still nothing. The hand remained on his cheek and Alex felt a different sensation now emanating from the person in spirit. A frisson of fear, soon replaced by puzzlement. Experience told him that whoever it was could only recently have passed over, and as Sylvia was still alive he didn't know who it could be.

At that moment he felt the energy leave him, a hesitant and gentle withdrawal, but Alex had only seconds of respite before the energy that had struck him inside the hospital hit him again and he almost gasped at the sheer power of it. He forced himself to relax so his psychic senses could expand fully, because now he recognised this immense power.

"Hello, Grace."

She inclined her head in acknowledgement, her eyes, black as the darkest night, were fixed on him and he found his own gaze locked onto hers. Her lips did not smile, her face was totally impassive. His heart sank.

"Grace, are you here for Sylvia?"

Grace merely looked at him, her astonishing eyes never wavering, never blinking. What did that mean? He asked the question again, but she was fading now. Fading and then gone.

Alex kept his eyes closed, breathing deeply and evenly, until he felt himself entirely back in the present, just a man, a visitor to a hospital, sitting on a grassy bank behind some bus shelters, the sun warm on his face.

110

Chapter 15
Sylvia

Sylvia looked on as her family sat in vigil by her bedside. Simon held her left hand in both of his, turning her wedding ring and stroking her fingers one by one, over and over. Anna was next to him, reading aloud from the day's newspaper. Sylvia didn't want to hear what was happening in the world; she only wanted news of her family. How was Simon coping at home? Had he been for the tests and the scan? What did they all do when they weren't at the hospital? Surely Paul and Adele hadn't cut their honeymoon short because of her?

She was at a loss to understand what had happened. One moment she was a spectator in the operating theatre as the surgeons worked to bypass the blocks in her struggling heart with veins taken from her arm and leg, the next she was watching Simon, Beth and Alex walking up a corridor.

She'd thought of returning to her body but immediately there'd been a tremendous jolt and she'd found herself back in the theatre. Just reflecting on that took her thoughts back there now, seeing it again like an action replay.

There was some commotion going on, but she regarded it all impassively from where she hovered just below the ceiling, impressed by the surgeon's skill with needle and suture but wondering how bad the scars would be. It took a moment before she realised that the body below—her precious body—had gone into cardiac arrest again.

The medical team fought hard to bring her back and she fought even harder to return to her body, but it proved impossible. She was shocked to the core to hear it declared that Sylvia Savarese had slipped into a coma. The lead surgeon had noted the date and time, peeled off his gloves, and walked out of the theatre.

A little while after that, she'd trailed after her own body as it was wheeled to Intensive Care and hooked up to various machines, machines that would keep her alive while they tried to work out what had happened and how to treat her. IV lines and tubes were inserted in various parts of her body, a ventilator forced air into her lungs, a cannula taped securely to the back of her hand awaited drugs to be administered, and sensors were stuck on her chest either side of the narrow dressing that covered the long line of neat black stitches, feeding their data to the monitor above her bed.

With a glance at that monitor she was back in the present moment, feeling even more frustrated. How could she force herself back in so that her body would function on its own again? What did she have to do?

It didn't matter how hard she tried she remained separate from her physical self and so had to endure seeing Simon, Anna, Beth and Paul weeping over her, reading to her, pleading with her to wake up.

Sylvia wanted to shake them, to yell into their ears that she could hear them, that she was in the room with them, but it seemed she was powerless to do anything other than observe, unheard and invisible.

Even when Alex was in the room, her handsome, enigmatic grandson-in-law who could talk to the dead, she could not make him aware of her presence. In fact, she admitted wryly to herself, maybe it was a good thing that he couldn't see or hear her, because it was surely proof that she was still alive!

She smelled Paul's strong, expensive aftershave moments before he arrived, worry etched into his tanned face. He kissed first Anna, then Beth, before hugging Simon. Anna asked if Adele was with him.

"We saw Alex outside as we came in," Paul replied. "He and Adele have gone to the café. It's a shame they won't let all of us in here together."

Sylvia agreed, it would be far better if they could all be here together, but the space around her bed was tight and the number of visitors rigidly restricted. Alex and Adele, not being direct members of the Savarese family, had little choice but to wait nearby, only popping in if one of the others left the room for any reason.

Felix flitted in and out too, never staying long so as to allow Sylvia's nearest kin to spend as much time with her as possible. She was grateful that he and Alex came so often, grateful that their warm, calm presence was so supportive to Anna and Beth. How lucky she was with her family, she thought.

Her partnership with Simon had been joyous from the beginning, their fall outs had been few and far between, nothing more than the usual minor spats between a happily married couple. When Anna had been born Sylvia hadn't minded that Simon had fallen so deeply and irrevocably in love with their little girl, because she felt the same. They had become a close-knit family of three until Anna had grown up and married Felix, and they had embraced him lovingly. A year after the wedding, Paul had been born and a year and a half after that Beth had come along, both of them making Sylvia and Simon the proudest of grandparents.

Ah, the grandchildren. Felix, like Anna, was an only child and his parents lived abroad, so she and Simon had truly appreciated all the time they'd been able to spend with Paul and Beth as the only grandparents on the scene. Beth had brought Alex into the family, and now lovely Adele had joined them too as Paul's wife. She stopped her reminiscences there, wondering why she was thinking about it all now, and not wanting to relive the pain of losing their first and only great-grandchild, darling little Amber, the agony of seeing how Beth had suffered. Paul was speaking and she brought her lapsed attention back to hear him.

He was standing behind Simon, keeping his eyes averted from the various tubes snaking in and out of her body. He was a little squeamish, she knew, but of course he must appreciate that all the medical equipment, intrusive as it was, was necessary to keep her alive until she could breathe on her own.

"Any change?" He asked the same question every time he came.

On the first day, when he'd rushed straight from the airport, he'd sounded hopeful, almost eager for news, but the passing time had brought no change and it had dulled his optimism. Today it was obvious he had no expectation that the news would be any different, and his shoulders sagged when Anna said they would be conducting more tests that afternoon.

Sylvia had heard the doctors discussing her, saying that some change had been detected in her condition and they were very concerned, and knew that Anna and her family would be very worried and frightened when they heard this.

Once more Sylvia tried with all her might to force her way back into her body so she could feel her husband's hand grasping her own, make her lungs breathe without aid of the machines so she could speak to them all, tell them she was fine. She wanted so badly to hug and kiss them all. But her efforts brought no result. In fact, she mused, she was feeling more and more divorced from that thing of flesh and bone lying on the bed. The very idea of it was heavy and restricting, and she'd begun to like the being of pure energy she had become since leaving her body.

"Sylvia."

The voice was in her head, but she felt someone behind her. She turned slowly, initially afraid of who, or what, she might see, but she relaxed as a soothing warmth enveloped and embraced her.

The walls, floor and ceiling of the room slowly disappeared as if being painted out by a brush held by an invisible hand. Sylvia reached out to touch the sparkling pinkish mist that was all around her, feeling as if she was floating in candy floss.

A figure was approaching, too far away to make out any features, but Sylvia could tell that she was unusually tall in stature and her voice, though very soft, was unlike any she had ever heard. The figure stopped and beckoned to her and one word rang clear and compelling:

"Come."

Come where? Why? What if she followed this figure, whoever or whatever it was, and couldn't find her way back? But wait… Did she *want* to find her way back? As the realisation dawned just how much she wanted to go to that tall figure she panicked, for how could she so willingly walk away from her family after all her struggles to re-join them? Oh my God! Was she…

"Am I dead?" Sylvia asked, her voice merely a rasping whisper.

"Come."

This time the voice was deep inside her mind and, as if tethered by an unseen but benevolent force, Sylvia wanted nothing more than to go where she was led.

Chapter 16
Kallie

Averting her eyes from the things that had been her gran's favourites and wondering if she'd ever forget the small details, Kallie briskly pushed the trolley up and down the supermarket aisles.

After Walter had died she'd struggled to get used to shopping for just her and Gran, but then Verity had passed away within months of Walter and even now Kallie did not enjoy shopping for one. Putting a packet of pasta next to the potatoes, chocolates, sweets and peanuts already in the basket, she headed for the dairy section.

A man about her age, medium height and good looking, an empty basket on his arm, was browsing the shelves and when she selected the butter she wanted he asked her if it was good for frying with. For a brief moment she wondered if it was a chat-up line, but he didn't even look at her face; he genuinely wanted her opinion on the attributes of a particular brand of butter and that was all.

Suddenly depressed, for here she was, still in her twenties and no romance since the love of her life had announced that she was not the love of *his* life, Kallie ignored the low-fat yogurt she had been intending to buy and headed for the freezer section. She selected a large tub of salted caramel ice cream, hoping that it might, just might, make her feel better. She chose the self-checkout to pay for her purchases, glad that for once she got everything through without having to call for assistance, and left for home.

When she pulled up in front of the tiny cottage that had been her home since she'd been born, she switched off the engine and stared at the white-painted house that she adored.

But would she ever get used to this, coming home to an empty, silent place? Verity had always made sure Walter and Kallie were given a good welcome home, the gentle tones of Classic FM or BBC Radio 4 playing in the background, the delicious smells of their supper wafting from the kitchen. They would eat together at the kitchen table, crammed between the fridge freezer and the back door, Verity wanting to hear all about their day.

After Walter's death her gran had tried to keep things going as normal for her and Kallie, but in her last few weeks Kallie had not had a welcome home when she got in from work for lunch or at the end of the day, finding instead that Verity had spent most of the time sleeping.

With a deep sigh, she grabbed the bags of shopping and her handbag and marched up the short path and through the door, stepping straight into the living room. Kicking aside the local paper and the post lying on the mat, most of it probably junk mail, Kallie carried her purchases to the kitchen and put everything away.

Checking the kettle had sufficient water, she switched it on then changed her mind and poured a glass of cold white wine instead. Holding the glass by its stem, she stared out into the garden, a small square patch of lawn edged with flower beds in serious need of attention. Her gran had mostly tended the garden, with Kallie joining her sometimes at the weekends to potter rather uselessly about, but she hadn't had the heart to do more than mow the grass and pull a few weeds since Verity had died. She must get out there soon. She didn't have the gardening skills to return it to its former glory, but she was determined to try both for her own satisfaction and to honour the memory of her grandparents.

The phone rang and she dashed back into the living room to grab it before the answering machine switched on, wondering if it would be her mother. Celia was the only one who used the landline, all her friends and salon clients called Kallie on her mobile.

"Hello?"

Instead of her mother's clipped greeting there was nothing but crackling on the line, and she waited for someone to speak. Nothing. She placed the receiver back on the cradle, noticing for the first time the blinking red light. There were six new messages. Six! She pressed the button, listening to them one by one just long enough to know there was nothing but the crackling sound, and then she deleted them, cursing all call centres, for that was surely what was going on here.

Kallie sipped her wine, thinking she ought to call her mother, *ought* being the operative word, because they were no more than duty calls and she found her mother very hard to talk to. She hadn't seen Celia face to face since the day of Verity's funeral, when they had rowed, as usual, and her mother had flounced out in a huff.

For the millionth time, Kallie thought to herself, why, oh why, can we not be in the same room for longer than five minutes without arguing?

She thought of the mother and daughter who had come to the salon that morning. It was their first visit to Kallie and she had quickly seen how close they were from the way they finished each other's sentences and laughed easily together as they regaled everyone in the salon with tales of hilarious shopping trips and shared holidays.

On automatic pilot Kallie had smiled and made the appropriate responses as she gave them their chosen treatments one after the other, wondering all the while how the two women would react if she were to tell them how she hardly even knew her mother and they barely spoke to one another. It had made her wonder just how long it had been since they'd had one of their stilted conversations on the phone.

Too long, no doubt.

The old carriage clock on the mantelpiece chimed the hour, bringing Kallie out of trying to decipher their difficult relationship, and she decided she'd call Celia some time over the weekend.

She made some supper and placed it on a lap tray so she could eat while watching television. She was halfway through a sitcom that actually made her laugh out loud when the channel suddenly changed. Surprised, Kallie wondered if she was sitting on the remote but, no, there it was on the cushion beside her.

Putting the lap tray and her half-eaten dinner on the floor, she picked up the remote, shook it, and pressed the buttons hard in an effort to get back to the channel she had been watching. As if it had developed a mind of its own, the TV switched back and forth between the channel she wanted to watch and one showing a documentary about deep sea fishing that she wasn't the least bit interested in. Thoroughly exasperated she pressed the off button on the remote and the screen went blank.

"Oh, so you'll turn off but you won't let me watch my programme? I can't afford to replace you, you know!" she said to the blank screen.

There was a faint click and the television came back on to the right channel.

Bemused, Kallie picked up her supper again. "It's just an electrical glitch," she muttered under her breath. "Just like the lights. This old place probably needs rewiring."

For a couple of weeks the lights had occasionally flickered, and now with the TV playing up as well, she knew she would have to get an electrician in. She hoped it wouldn't cost too much.

The television behaved itself and she was able to finish her meal uninterrupted and watch the programmes she wanted to see. Deciding to wash-up her dishes and then do some ironing, Kallie carried the tray through to the kitchen.

The lights flickered.

Feeling a little silly, yet compelled to speak out loud, she said, "Grandad? Gran? Are you two playing games with me?"

She had never given any serious thought to the possibility of communication with loved ones who had passed away, but her grandmother had constantly claimed that Walter was with her in those last months she was alive. He was keeping them company, she'd insisted, and Kallie hadn't questioned it or contradicted her because it had cheered Verity immensely to think he was always around, and it cheered Kallie too.

Thinking about it now, though, she wondered if both of them really could be watching over her and rather welcomed the idea of it even if she couldn't really believe it. Many other holistic therapists she knew believed fervently in life after death and fairies and the power of crystals and angels… Oh, there was quite a list. Kallie herself admitted that she simply wasn't sure about such things.

When she'd been a little girl, Walter had made up stories to scare her about the cottage being haunted because of its great age and its close proximity to the thirteenth century church and its graveyard.

But when she'd stared wide-eyed at him, her little body beginning to tremble, he'd taken her in his arms and told her that there were no such things as ghosts and she had nothing to be afraid of, ever. He explained that the noises she heard in the dead of night were nothing but the skittering and scratching of little furry mice in the thatch that wouldn't harm her and the old floorboards creaked because of changes in temperature. These were normal things that one expected in a place that was hundreds of years old. Walter had always made her feel safe.

Kallie called out, "I'd love it if it is you two trying to make your presence known, but I'm going to need a little more convincing please!"

The landline started ringing again and though she was tempted to let it go through to the answering machine she answered it. All she heard was a crackling sound.

Thoroughly unnerved now, she decided the only remedy was a pamper session. She had a long, hot bath in her most luxurious bath foam, her shampooed and conditioned hair wrapped in a towel, her face covered with a home-made face pack and slices of cucumber on her eyes. Bliss!

When her skin started to pucker from the hot water she washed her face and rinsed her hair, towelled herself dry and smothered her skin in lotions and creams before going upstairs to get ready for bed.

The room was so small there was barely room to move around her double bed and open the wardrobe doors, and although it would make sense for her to finish clearing out and move into her grandparents' room, which was much bigger, she couldn't bring herself to do it.

After Walter's death, Verity had said a couple of times that they should clear out his things, but they never even made an attempt as Verity had noticeably begun to fade day by day. Besides, Kallie rather thought that it had been comforting for her to have her husband's personal things around her.

Now, even after all this time, her grandparents' possessions were still there: the flower-sprigged comforter on the double bed, Verity's make-up, the silver compact and powder puff on the tiny dressing table, a bunch of bluebells, the flowers fresh when they had been placed there, now colourless and desiccated in a crystal rosebud vase on the window sill, Walter's old and well-worn slippers by his side of the bed, their dressing gowns hanging from a hook on the door.

The bed itself was strewn with clothes and shoes where Kallie went in every now and again intending to sort through them, but it always upset her so much she'd leave the room and close the door without making much progress.

In her own room she plugged in her hairdryer and sat cross-legged on the bed against the pillows, running her fingers through the honey-brown tresses and reflecting on her gran's love of having her hair done and how she'd taken real pleasure in dressing well and always looking feminine and smart. What a shame she was five inches taller and a size bigger than her gran, otherwise she could have worn some of her stylish clothes, most of them made so beautifully by Verity on her old sewing machine.

It occurred to her then with a bit of a jolt that she, a trained beautician, was letting herself go a bit. The face pack and deep hair conditioner had used to be a weekly treat for her and for Verity, but before this evening she hadn't done it in ages.

Of course, her face was always carefully made up and her nail polish never chipped because it was important in her job, and she always wore a smart plum-coloured tunic with light grey piping and dark grey or black trousers when she was working, but she'd got into the habit of scraping her shoulder length hair into a band rather than keep it in the loose, layered style that suited her so well. It was too long now and she noticed as she dried it that she had some split ends, so she definitely needed to get it trimmed, and maybe a few highlights would be a good idea.

She'd also not been eating properly, relying far too much on microwave meals for one and tubs of ice cream. She was fortunate that she had the kind of metabolism that kept her slim no matter what she ate, but her diet was far from healthy.

"Gran would have something to say about you, Kallie Harper. Time to get yourself sorted out," she said to her reflection in the mirror.

Humming cheerfully at her decision to take herself in hand, she ironed two of her tunics so she would have one to wear for tomorrow's stint at Rainstones House and a spare in case of spillage or accident.

Thursdays were fast becoming her favourite day of the week. She felt she was part of an important team there, and the Day Patient Unit guests who came to see her, mostly for gentle massages with aromatherapy oils, were so cheerful and always telling her how much they loved coming to see her. Plus there was Kevin, who she liked enormously. He made her laugh, and it didn't hurt that he was single, good-looking and seemed to like her too.

Fancying a mug of hot chocolate while she read the latest issue of the holistic therapies magazine she subscribed to, Kallie skipped back downstairs to the kitchen. Just as she was pouring the hot milk over the chocolate powder in her favourite mug, a loud bang had her instantly on alert, ears straining.

She thought it had come from upstairs, but couldn't be sure.

Pondering on the episodes of the TV switching channels, the phone calls with no-one at the end of the line, and the lights flickering, her mouth went dry. She carefully put the saucepan down and walked into the living room. It sounded like something had fallen from quite a height, or a window had flown open and banged back against the wall, but there was no wind this evening. Creeping into the living room she grabbed the poker from the hearth and wondered where she should investigate first. Should she go upstairs, where she thought the bang had come from, or check out the back?

Biting her lip, she moved stealthily back through the kitchen to the bathroom, making sure that the windows were secure and the kitchen door bolted. Returning to the bottom of the staircase she switched on the light and peered upwards. Did electrical faults cause things to go bang? She really must call an electrician to come and check everything, she absolutely could not risk a fire in a thatched house.

She climbed the steep stairs, the poker gripped in both hands, more aware than ever how loudly the staircase creaked. When she reached the top she glanced to the open door of her bedroom, then the closed door of the larger room. She decided her own room should be checked first, but it took no time to see that all was just as she had left it not ten minutes before.

On tiptoe, she moved across the landing to the other bedroom. After all, she reasoned, as she'd been moving stuff and beginning to sort everything into piles for items she planned to keep, those she'd send to charity shops, and those she would discard, wasn't it possible that something had shifted, over-balanced somehow and toppled to the floor? She walked round the double bed but nothing had fallen. She looked out the window to check that her car was still there.

The skies were clear and bright, but it would be a full moon tonight, casting a silvery glow on the churchyard. It was a sight she found beautiful, not at all something to bother her like it spooked some of her friends. Why people thought graveyards, where people had been lovingly buried in consecrated ground, should be the source of so much fear at night was beyond her. If they were really under the illusion that dead people could rise from the grave and haunt them, then surely it was those buried in unconsecrated ground they should be afraid of.

She let her eyes rest on the garden wall at the spot where the graves of Verity and Walter were just over the other side, sending mental thought waves of love to her grandparents, telling them that she would bring fresh flowers on Sunday.

The bedroom was a mess, but as she quickly ran her eyes over the piles of clothes and shoes strewn across the bed she could see that everything was just as she'd left it the last time she'd been in here.

The smell of her gran's perfume was very strong, though, and she couldn't think why this would be. Crossing to the dressing table, Kallie let out a gasp of surprise, because the crystal bottle wasn't where it should be. Working so much with aromatherapy oils she didn't wear perfume, but the beautiful bottle and its contents was something she had no intention of getting rid of. Just the sight of it helped her recall lovely memories of watching her gran hold her finger over the top of the heavy crystal stopper and tip the bottle once, twice. Verity would then take the stopper and stroke it behind her ears and on her wrists, perfuming her pulse points.

When Kallie had been very young and allowed to play dress-up in her gran's clothes and shoes she had been forbidden to touch the bottle as it was heavy and she might have dropped it. But her gran had sometimes given her the stopper so she could dab herself with a tiny drop of the lovely floral scent.

The bottle was not there and Kallie stared in bewilderment at the clean circle in the fine layer of dust on the dressing table surface. The circle in which the crystal bottle should have been sitting.

She felt the first prickle of fear as she wondered if someone had broken into the cottage while she'd been at work; the perfume bottle was vintage and probably worth several hundred pounds now.

Rushing to the drawer where her grandmother's jewellery was kept she yanked it open and quickly scanned the rings, pearl earrings and fine gold necklaces and bracelets that were neatly laid out on dark blue velvet pads. Nothing was missing.

"Come on, Kallie," she reassured herself. "The TV is still downstairs, the laptop is on the floor next to the sofa, there are no broken windows and you had to turn the front door key twice to open it so there's been no forced entry. Nothing downstairs or up here has been ransacked."

No, she hadn't been burgled. She must have moved the bottle and just forgotten about it. Maybe it was in her own bedroom, or in the bathroom? It was the best explanation she could come up with, though it rankled that she could be so forgetful, and she was still no nearer to understanding what had made that tremendously loud bang.

As she walked towards the door the smell of *Joy* got even stronger, forcing her to look back nervously over her shoulder. A shadow moved by the dressing table. She would swear it.

Trembling a little, she turned her body all the way round and brought the poker up in front of her, as if it were a samurai sword. She stared intently at the dressing table and the area around it. Nothing moved, but as her eyes scanned the area she spotted the perfume bottle on its side beneath the dressing table. The stopper had rolled a couple of feet away from it, and perfume had spilled onto the carpet making a dark stain on the cream wool.

Blowing out the breath she hardly realised she'd been holding, Kallie relaxed her grip on the poker and slowly lowered it. The bottle falling to the floor would not have made the loud bang she'd heard, but it did explain the intense smell of *Joy* and why it wasn't on the dressing table: she had obviously knocked it over when sorting through the drawers and simply not noticed.

She retrieved the bottle, pleased to see there was still a little scent in it, replaced the stopper, and put it back on the dressing table, positioning it so it sat exactly in the circle in the fine dust.

"Gran," she said out loud, "Is that you?"

Of course, there was no response. What was she expecting, that her gran would answer? That she would write a message in the dust? Whatever that noise had been, she convinced herself it couldn't have been anything electrical and must have come from outside. It could have been something as innocent as a car door being slammed shut in the church car park or the lane, but because she'd been in such deep thought she'd not recognised the direction or cause of the sound.

The ringing phone made her jump and sent her hurrying back downstairs. Would it be yet another of those calls where no-one spoke? She glanced at her watch, saw it was getting on for nine o'clock.

A friendly voice asked to speak with Miss Kathleen Harper.

"Yes, that's me."

"And could you confirm for me please that you are a relation of Celia Harper?" More curious than alarmed because the tone of the caller did not seem to indicate that she was about to deliver bad news, Kallie said, "Yes, she's my mother."

When she'd understood who the caller was and the reason for the call she had to sit down on the floor and ask for it to be repeated.

Chapter 17
Alex

Alex idly wondered how often he saw Paul without a phone glued to his ear. Surely it must get tiresome, he thought. Now he was sitting across from Paul's desk, waiting while he handled a phone call with a client who clearly was very happy and excited about something.

Tuning out from the one-sided conversation, Alex let his eyes roam across the gallery of framed photographs of the celebrities that Paul represented. He didn't consider himself a celebrity, but his own photo hung on the wall, the same one Beth had insisted on having a copy of, because, she'd said, he looked so 'broodingly handsome'.

Paul at last managed to end the call. "Sorry, Alex, my latest signing has just landed a real gift of a role and is obviously over the moon about it. Now then, let's talk about—"

He was interrupted by his mobile ringing again, and, telling Alex it was Adele and he'd deal with it quickly, he answered the call. Just as Paul said hello to Adele, Alex's mobile trilled.

"Hi, Beth. Everything okay?"

All he got in reply was a sob, and his heart sank. It had to be about Sylvia.

"What's happened?"

"C-can you come? Please, c-come to the hos… hospital. Gran's…" She couldn't finish the sentence.

"I'll be right there. You hear me? I'm on my way! Paul too."

Paul was pushing his mobile into his jacket pocket and Alex noted the tell-tale reddening of his brother-in-law's eyes as Paul asked, "Was that Beth calling you?"

"Yes, but she could hardly speak. What's happening, do you know?"

Paul nodded, his expression grim. "There were tests done this morning and now doctors are saying we should consider switching off life support."

Dammit. Why did they have to be in Paul's London office? It would take at least a couple of hours to reach the hospital and Alex could sense that this was urgent. He'd come by train, but Paul's car was in the underground car park.

Though he didn't show his emotions, Alex was aware that Paul felt them deeply, and would be very distressed at the news that his beloved gran was possibly dying. He said, "Do you want me to drive?"

Paul shook his head and went round to the driver's side. "No need. Besides, I know my way round London much better than you do. Did Beth tell you anything at all?"

"No. She was crying too hard. I'm so sorry, Paul, what a horrible situation."

Alex saw Paul's jaw muscles tighten and hoped he could stay focused in the busy traffic to get them to the hospital in one piece. He decided it would probably be best to stay silent, unless Paul wanted to talk, and was glad when Paul turned the radio on. Luckily, it was a smooth ride out of London and they were soon cruising on the M4 towards Wiltshire.

It was late afternoon as Paul's sleek Mercedes pulled into a space near the exit barrier in the hospital car park. Alex called Beth to let her know they'd arrived.

Paul found a space close to the exit barrier and Alex had to lengthen his stride to keep up, as Paul was practically jogging towards the main entrance.

"She's still alive, isn't she?" Paul demanded. "You'd tell me if she wasn't, right? I mean, you'd *know*."

His mind conjuring up that one appearance of Grace, an event he had shared with no-one, not even Beth, he kept his voice low as he replied, "I really don't know, Paul. Let's go and find the others, then we'll know what the situation is."

As they entered the corridor leading to Intensive Care, Adele was heading their way, clearly on the lookout for them. When she saw them she hurried into Paul's waiting arms.

"What's going on?" Paul demanded. "Is Gran okay? They haven't…"

"No, no, try and stay calm, Paul. I'm not sure what's happening, but a nurse asked to speak to immediate family members and took them to a private room. Beth came out briefly to tell me they'd been asked to prepare themselves because the doctors were considering asking to let them switch off Sylvia's life support. That's when we called you, and Felix is on his way, too. They're talking things over and I told them I'd wait out here for you, and send you in, Paul, as soon as you got here. Alex and I will wait outside."

Alex nodded. "Of course. We'll be right here if we're needed."

Paul asked where the family room was. Adele led him to the waiting area and showed him where to go. When he'd walked away she visibly sagged and Alex put his arm around her shoulders and pulled her to him. All the time she'd been talking to Paul he'd been able to sense that she was holding something back.

Letting her go he said, "Right, so tell me now, what's really been going on in there?"

"God, Alex. It was pandemonium. I'd just walked in and suddenly all kinds of alarms were going off and nurses and doctors came running, pushing us all out of the way. A nurse asked us to wait out here. It seemed ages before anyone came out to tell us what was going on, and then, as I said, they asked the immediate family members to go into that private room. They really only wanted to talk to Simon, as he's next of kin, and Anna, but Anna insisted that Beth stay with them and Felix and Paul join them as soon as they got here. I've not seen anyone since Beth called you so I've had no more news."

"How about Simon? Have you actually seen him today?"

"Oh yes, but only briefly because, as I say, I hadn't long arrived when all these alarms started going off. I understand that he came with Anna first thing, and Beth arrived shortly after I did. The poor man is beyond distraught and won't hear of the machines being switched off. He got really angry, and at one point it looked like he was going to take a swing at the doctor! None of them want life support withdrawn, and of course I understand that, but if the doctors think there's no hope…"

Alex sighed and gently guided Adele to a chair, taking the one beside her, thankful that the seats were padded and quite comfortable.

"It might not come to that yet, but there's no point in asking because they won't tell us anything as we're not immediate family. All we can do is wait."

Adele clasped his hand. "You're not keeping anything back are you? You'd know if Sylvia was already dead, wouldn't you?"

"Paul asked me that. I don't think she is, because I don't sense her. But the thing is, she's being kept alive by machines. Maybe she'll breathe unaided if they do switch off, but only time will tell. We have no choice but to trust and rely on the medical staff looking after her."

"I know, but oh my goodness, it's awful beyond belief. I know you believe Sylvia is going somewhere wonderful, the same place Scott went, but still, the family will suffer so much when she's gone." She leaned forward and touched Alex's hand. "We've never really talked, you and I, but one day I hope you'll tell me, explain to me, what happens to us when we die, and what it is you see."

Alex promised that he would, and Adele offered to go and find them some coffee. When she'd gone he leaned back into the chair and closed his eyes, silently reaching out for his father.

"I'm here, Alex."

"Dad, they're talking about switching off Sylvia's life support. Do you have any idea what's happening to her?"

There was a long silence and Alex sensed the brief absence while his father checked. He returned and said, *"I'm sorry, it's not looking hopeful for any sort of recovery. Her vital organs are shutting down. I can sense her, but it's very, very faint. Do you remember when you crossed over for that short time after your accident? It feels similar to that. She's here, but not completely. Her time is close, though, I'm pretty sure of that. You know you'll have to be strong for Sylvia's family, for they don't know as we do the wonders she will see when she's here."*

At that moment Adele returned, carrying two plastic cups of coffee, and Felix came dashing in, demanding to know where the others were and what was going on with Sylvia.

Adele offered to take Felix to the family room.

"I warn you," she said, "emotions are running really high, especially Simon. He's been quite aggressive today, which is only adding to Anna and Beth's distress. They'll be glad to see you, Felix."

Alex took a sip of the coffee, surprisingly good considering it was instant from a machine, and watched the two of them walk away. What an awful situation. For him, knowing as he did what awaited Sylvia when she left them, it was an easy choice. If her body was no longer functioning and there was absolutely no hope of recovery, then it was pointless keeping her alive by machines.

But that was the crux the matter. Could they be certain, one hundred per cent certain, that Sylvia would not recover if given more time?

What a terrible, terrible decision the family had to face.

Chapter 18
Kallie

The alarm went off at six thirty and for a while Kallie lay in her bed feeling dazed, knowing she had to do something different today, but not remembering what.

Then it came to her. The phone call. The patient voice explaining that her mother had experienced a bad fall at her home and was in hospital with some broken bones and other injuries. She had been there for a week and they were ready to discharge her at the weekend, but she had to be released into someone's care. Her daughter's telephone number was the only one Celia Harper provided, so could Kallie please come and collect her on Saturday, as her mother would not be allowed to leave unless accompanied.

Once the call had ended and Kallie had gathered her thoughts in order, she'd texted Kevin to explain the situation and say it was unlikely she'd be back from Cambridge in time for their date. He'd immediately replied, telling her not to worry, that they would fix another time. Maybe Sunday lunch? That had made her smile, and she'd offered to cook a roast.

But on this Saturday morning she had far more serious things to consider than her budding romance. How strange that only yesterday evening she'd been thinking about her mother and pondering their difficult relationship, and now here was Celia, slamming back into Kallie's life in a most unexpected fashion.

Though she was reluctant to see her, of course Kallie would go to Cambridge. What choice did she have? She knew it was about a three-hour drive away, but she'd never been there so she had better get the full address of the hospital and key in the postcode to the GPS on her phone. But when she got there, what then? What on earth was she going to do once her mother had been discharged? She hadn't been told what bones Celia had broken, but Kallie fervently hoped her injuries didn't mean she wouldn't be able to manage for herself.

So, the plan was for Kallie to take her mother to her home in the centre of Cambridge, make sure she had plenty of food, and be back home in the cottage by late evening. Then she would have Sunday to look forward to, spending a day with Kevin. Maybe it would stretch out to the evening… the night perhaps? She felt a little shiver at the thought, a frisson of excitement that she might, at last, have met the man with whom she could be herself, and they would make each other happy.

Within an hour she was ready to set off for the hospital. She grabbed her handbag and dipped her hand into the ceramic pot on the shelf by the front door for her car keys.

They weren't there.

Exasperated, she wondered how many times lately she had put things down and when she went to pick them up later they weren't there. When she eventually found the item it was always somewhere she knew she hadn't put it.

For a moment she just stared down at the crudely painted pattern on the bottom of the empty dish, not believing her own eyes. She could swear she had thrown the keys in that dish when she had come in from work yesterday, just as she always did. But they weren't there, so the only conclusion she could come to was that she must have put them down somewhere else.

She went from room to room searching, then, when she didn't find them, replayed in her mind her return home, picturing herself coming through the door with the keys in her hand. There'd been no post on the mat, no flashing light on the answering machine. She had switched on the television as she always did, just to fill the empty house with sound. She knew she had placed the keys in the pot, a rather ugly thing that Verity had treasured because Kallie had made it for her at primary school many years ago.

She really needed to be on her way to Cambridge, but she searched everywhere again, including pockets, drawers and under the furniture. She'd tipped the contents of her handbag onto the floor and put everything back item by item.

No keys.

Baffled and beginning to feel a little tearful with frustration, she went to get a glass of water, and there they were, by the sink. Unable to explain it other than a complete memory lapse after she'd come in yesterday evening and then developed a blind spot this morning, she grabbed them and ran out of the house.

After a horrible drive in pouring rain, Kallie at last slipped her car easily into a space a Range Rover had had to pass up. She quickly and neatly reversed into the bay before another circling car could grab it, and sat for a moment once she'd switched off the engine to calm herself before going in to face her mother. That dreaded moment was all too near now, for Celia was lying in a ward in the enormous building that Kallie was staring at through the windscreen.

It took a minute to get her bearings but she was soon following the signs to the right ward, marching along with her mind on the meeting to come. What were her mother's injuries? What would she be like when she saw Kallie walk in?

Her musings were interrupted painfully when she collided with a tea trolley being pushed out of a side ward. Hobbling, Kallie had to stop at the first seating area she came to and rub her bruised shin bone. The trolley-pusher had apologised, but Kallie felt ashamed of her own, rather graceless response, especially as it had been more her fault because she hadn't been paying attention to where she was walking.

Besides that, it was bad form to take out ill temper on other people who had nothing to do with the cause of your bad mood. She wished she could track down the trolley-pusher to apologise properly and explain to him that she was in a temper thanks to the nightmare journey to Cambridge in her slow little car, getting snarled up in heavy traffic, all the while worrying about dealing with her difficult mother.

She forced herself up and carried on until she was in the doorway to the ward. At first, she didn't recognise any of the women in the six beds and hesitated; she'd spotted Celia's name written on the whiteboard by the entrance and all the beds were occupied, but she couldn't see her. Not sure what to do, she was relieved when a nurse came to her and led her over to the bed on the left-hand side, in front of the window.

Kallie wondered if the nurse had made a mistake, for she could hardly reconcile the image she held in her mind of her mother with the elderly lady that lay with her eyes closed and mouth open.

Her long, wiry, wild hair, usually held back from her face with clips, was spread out messily on the pillow, shades of dark and light grey against starched white cotton. Her left arm was in a plaster cast from elbow to knuckles, leaving bruised and swollen fingers and thumb free. Celia had been provided with a pale blue hospital gown, one that fastened at the front with a bow tied at the waist rather that one of those horrid, undignified things that tied up at the back, and Kallie saw that her clothes, in the usual shades of olive green, beige and black, had been neatly folded and placed on a chair beside the bed.

Celia must have heard her approach, because she slowly turned her head and Kallie audibly gasped at the sight of the livid purple bruise that almost covered one side of her face. It was difficult to look at the blackened and puffy eyelid, stitched and crusted with dried blood, without wincing. Celia mumbled something, then her head rolled back on the pillow and she appeared to fall asleep again. The nurse came back then and beckoned Kallie to follow her to the nurses' station.

"There's no need to worry," she said. "Mrs Harper had difficulty sleeping last night and is catching up now that her pain relief has kicked in. I know it looks as if she's been in a boxing match, but apparently she slipped and fell down some steps outside her home. Her wrist is broken but there should be no complications once it's healed, and her eye looks far worse than it is; luckily, she hasn't got any damage to the socket. She really banged her head as she fell, though, and was in a lot of pain and a bit disorientated, so we kept her in for observation just in case of concussion, and of course we couldn't send her home by herself anyway."

The nurse stopped talking, giving Kallie the opportunity to speak, but Kallie didn't know what to say, not even to correct the nurse in her assumption that Celia was or ever had been married.

"Right, then," continued the nurse. "She's ready to go home as far as I'm concerned, but that needs to be confirmed by the doctor. She will need some assistance at home as she's going to have to be very careful of her wrist until it completely heals. Obviously." The nurse waited again but Kallie still said nothing. "Does she live alone, your mother?"

Kallie, not missing the slight emphasis on *your mother* and feeling stung by the manner in which it had been said, nodded. "Yes, she does. And I live in Wiltshire."

"Hmm. You've had quite a journey to get here, then. Well, the doctor will be doing his rounds in about fifteen minutes and I'm expecting that he'll be happy to formally discharge her now that you're here, so if you'd like to think about arrangements for her care during her recovery and come back for her in, say an hour?"

Not knowing what else to do Kallie left the ward and went to find some strong coffee and a large slice of cake to fortify herself while she considered the options.

She certainly couldn't stay in Cambridge and she couldn't imagine having her mother with her in the cottage even if it was the best solution for both of them in the short term. She didn't know if Celia had any friends she could call on, nor if she could afford to pay for someone to look in on her several times a day and help her, for she would certainly need help. How could she prepare and cook food, wash and dress herself with her arm in plaster?

The nurse had said she'd fallen down a few steps, but with those injuries surely it was an entire flight of stairs she'd tumbled down? Kallie tried to imagine what it would be like to have a broken wrist, but she'd never been injured other than grazed knees when she was little or the odd cut to a finger so she really didn't know. She didn't, in fact, know very much at all at this stage.

She reached for her phone intending to text her friends and ask for some advice, but stopped halfway through composing the message. This was her issue and no-one else's, so she must put her practical head on and deal with it.

Checking her watch to ensure more than an hour had passed, she forked up the last piece of coffee and walnut cake, grabbed her bag and headed back to the ward. It seemed even further going back, the building was simply enormous, and she felt as if she were walking the bustling corridors for miles before she was once again standing beside her mother's bed.

Celia was awake and sitting up, a couple of pillows piled behind her back. She rolled her good eye towards Kallie as she approached the bed and said, "Take me home, Kathleen."

No hello, no lovely to see you, or, how are you? Not a single thank you for coming all this way, and she called her Kathleen, a name which Kallie hated and had discarded many years ago. She felt her temper rise and pressed it down hastily. Her mother was injured and in pain, she must remember that.

"Yes, I'll take you home, but what then? You know you can't stay there alone with your injuries, how will you manage? And I can't stay in Cambridge to look after you because I need to work." She sounded sharper than she'd intended, but this was the effect her mother always had on her.

"I will manage just fine. If you would be kind enough to…"

She was interrupted by the arrival of the same nurse who had earlier spoken to her, and disapproval was written all over her face. She must have heard what Kallie had said and the way she had said it, and her estimation of Kallie had fallen even lower.

"As your daughter says, Mrs Harper, you simply cannot be home on your own. You will be quite unable to dress or undress yourself with that broken wrist. You will need help washing yourself, preparing food, all the things we take for granted until we can't do them." She turned to Kallie. "Please assure me that your mother will not be left to fend for herself?"

Biting back what she really wanted to say in reply to this obvious criticism of her lack of daughterly compassion, never mind that it was the truth, Kallie found herself saying that she had already decided to have her mother come and stay with her in Wiltshire.

Her own words surprised her, because she certainly hadn't made such a decision until that very second, and her mother looked equally dubious, though she mercifully kept silent. If they were to start arguing, as they usually did, she wouldn't put it past this nurse to call in Social Services to sort out this clearly dysfunctional mother and daughter.

The nurse drew the curtains round Celia's bed with a sharp swish and Kallie, marvelling that the curtain hadn't been torn from its rings, waited in the ward while Celia was helped to dress in her own clothes. She could hear her mother fussing and objecting, the nurse's firm responses that she needed her to co-operate or she'd be going home in the gown.

When the curtains were swept back again, Celia was sitting on the edge of the bed, her arm in a sling, being ordered by the nurse not to move because she would need a wheelchair.

"A wheelchair? Don't be ridiculous. It's my arm that's broken not my leg! I'm perfectly capable of walking and I'll be just fine on my own at home too."

The nurse, the hospital gown bundled in her arms, flashed Kallie a quick smile as if she at last understood the difficulties she faced in caring for her.

"Mrs Harper, it is quite a distance to the main exit and it is hospital policy that patients be taken by wheelchair. Now, your daughter has your medication and discharge letter." She turned to Kallie. "I'm sure you won't want to travel all the way back here to have the stitches removed or for check-ups so I suggest you get in touch with own doctor's surgery and ask for advice from them. Ah, here's the wheelchair."

Celia was expertly manoeuvred into it and Kallie, still in a state of shock and disbelief at the whole situation, followed the cheerful porter as he wheeled Celia to the main exit.

When she had paid the exorbitant fee at the ticket machine outside the exit doors Kallie realised with extreme irritation that she had no idea where she'd left the car in what was a very large car park. She scanned the area, trying to locate a memorable landmark, but she had been in such a state when she'd arrived... oh, wait... yes! She spotted a sign she remembered seeing, and leaving her mother seated on a sheltered bench, she set off to get her car, thankful when she eventually found it.

She drove round to the pick-up area and once they were both belted in, Kallie having to help Celia pull the seat belt across and under the plastered arm, Kallie prepared to drive away.

"We'll need to go to your place first to get your things," said Kallie, getting her phone out and opening the GPS app. But then she realised, with an emotion that was a cross between exasperation, wry amusement and disbelief, that she had absolutely no idea of her mother's address. It had been Verity who'd sent the birthday and Christmas cards; Kallie hadn't even signed them.

Celia, recognising the dilemma, gave her the name of her street and Kallie quickly keyed it in and slotted her phone on its dashboard mount so she could see the map as she drove.

After what seemed an age driving along really busy roads with numerous traffic lights that seemed to go red as soon as she approached them, Kallie at last saw the little chequered flag on the screen and heard the female voice announce that she had arrived at her destination.

Celia instructed Kallie to park in a visitors' space in front of a modern apartment building with a plain brick facade, and it came as another surprise to Kallie to realise her mother lived in a flat and not a house. She'd never given it much thought, but she supposed she'd imagined Celia living in something similar to the cottage, or at least somewhere with a bit of character.

They went up to the third floor in the lift, Celia ignoring her reflection in the mirrored sides of the elevator. Once inside the apartment, Kallie admired how light and airy it was, despite the floors and every surface being piled high with books and papers. It was far from homely and Kallie could see that her mother never bothered with dusting and maybe didn't own a vacuum cleaner. She hoped the bathroom would be clean because she really needed to use it.

When she came back out, determined not to comment on her mother's lack of basic hygiene, she found Celia in her bedroom trying to take some underwear from a chest of drawers.

It was obvious that her stitched eye and sore arm were bothering her, so Kallie offered to do it if she would tell her what she wanted. Celia told her to get a suitcase down from the top of the wardrobe, which Kallie had to stand on a chair to reach, then she sat on the bed while Kallie gathered the clothes and shoes she wanted.

There weren't many things, and it cheered Kallie a little to see that her mother favoured skirts with elasticated waists and loose, button-front blouses that would be easy to take on and off. She folded and packed the items neatly, then went to the bathroom to collect her mother's wash things in a small zippered bag that had been in the case.

All the while, Kallie expected her mother to raise objections to coming back with her to the cottage, but since leaving the hospital their desultory conversation had skirted round the subject.

Celia said she wanted to take some books with her, but she gasped and winced as she made an attempt to stand up and inadvertently jogged her arm. Kallie helped her, surprised at how light Celia had become since she'd last seen her. Her mother had always seemed so much larger than dainty little Verity and Kallie herself, but that could have been the sheer force of her personality.

Celia said, "Are you sure about this? I can't say I'm not grateful because I have no-one else to call on to help me in my predicament, but we both know this isn't going to be easy."

She didn't sound grateful and there wasn't a hint of humour in her voice but Kallie was glad to have it out there at last, and agreed that it would not be easy, but that they would both have to make the best of it.

"Right, it's a three-hour drive. It's time for your painkillers, which will be a help, and we'll stop on the way for something to eat, though it'll have to be quick because I need to get back and clear out the big bedroom for you because it's still full of Walter and Verity's stuff."

Celia raised an eyebrow as she said, "You haven't done that yet?" Then, catching Kallie's expression and seeming to realise how unsympathetic that sounded, she indicated her bandaged arm and said, "I'm sorry that I won't be able to help you much, but I think you'll feel better when it's done."

Kallie nodded. "Yes, you're right." She smiled at Celia, attempting to hide her trepidation at what the next six weeks would bring, and said, "And now I have a good reason not to put it off any longer."

Thinking of just how much there was to do, Kallie was concerned at the short time she had available to get her mother installed in that room, because by the time they got back to the cottage it would be evening.

And what about her date tomorrow with Kevin? Well, all that was ruined now. She'd have to call him and cancel.

Disappointed, she told herself firmly she could only take it one step at a time.

Chapter 19
Kallie

Back at the cottage more than four hours later due to heavy traffic and another downpour, Kallie preceded her mother across the threshold and into the living room of the cottage, clumsily manoeuvring the cumbersome suitcase and putting it down with a thump at the bottom of the stairs.

Celia followed behind, closed the front door and then stood in front of it as if awaiting further instructions. Sighing, for her mother had been like this since they'd left Cambridge, Kallie apologised for the chill and said she'd boost the heating a bit.

She eased Celia's coat from her shoulders, mindful not to jog her arm in the sling, and invited her to sit down. Her mother chose Verity's armchair, the one she'd died in, but Kallie wasn't sure if Celia knew that and she wasn't going to tell her.

Celia perched on the edge of the cushion with her knees and ankles together, her one good eye looking round the room, and Kallie was amazed again at just how different her mother's physical appearance was to Verity and to herself. For the first time she realised how much she resembled Walter.

"Well now!" exclaimed Kallie in a forced jolly voice that was the opposite of how she felt inside. "I need to go and clear Gran's room and make up the bed, so would you like a cup of tea? Shall I put the telly on for you?"

Celia said, "No, thank you" to the tea and, "Yes, please" to the telly, so Kallie switched it on and handed her the remote so she could choose something she'd like to watch. She had quite a collection of DVDs but had no idea what her

144

mother's tastes in films might run to. She rather thought romance, which figured high in her own preferences, would rate very low on her mother's list.

She went to pick up the suitcase to take it upstairs, but, having more books than clothes in it, it was too much for her to lug up the stairs with its sharp turn at the top. Quickly, she opened it and removed the books, placing them in a tidy pile on the floor against the wall, her mother watching her with her one good eye. Able to manage the case now, she carried it quickly upwards, chewing her lip as she thought how hard the next six weeks or so were going to be.

They'd hardly exchanged a word on the journey back, Celia not even wanting to listen to the radio or one of Kallie's classical CDs Kallie had kept in the car for Verity's pleasure. This woman, this untidy, grey-haired person who looked more eighty-six than the sixty-six she actually was, was a stranger to her.

They had not been alone together since after Verity's funeral when they'd had that row, but before that? Kallie had to think hard. Really, had they ever been entirely alone together before that day? Very possibly they had not, because Verity had always been there during Celia's visits as Kallie was growing up. When Kallie had reached her teens and they'd had that heated argument about how she dressed and wore make-up and did her hair, then her mother's outright refusal to ever divulge her father's identity, she had declared she no longer wanted Celia to visit.

This had saddened Walter and Verity very much, but Kallie would not be moved. Celia had continued to come, for she and her parents still wanted to see each other, but she came less often and Kallie always kept out of the way. Verity had made a point of phoning Celia every other Sunday, half-past ten in the morning on the dot, but Kallie had not been interested in hearing any of the news Verity tried to pass on.

When Verity died, Kallie had really not minded that she would most likely be permanently estranged from her mother without Verity there to keep that tenuous link between them. But now this unfortunate circumstance had forced them together and only time would tell if they could form a friendly relationship with each other. And if they couldn't, well, they only had to put up with each other for six weeks. Just six weeks until Celia's broken bones healed, and then Kallie would take her back to Cambridge and they could go their separate ways again if that was how things had to be.

If ever there was a woman who should never have been a mother, Celia was it as far as Kallie was concerned. Her best friend Rosa had asked her once if Celia had ever hit her or abused her in some way.

"Absolutely not!" Kallie had said but she had struggled to find the right word to describe their relationship. She'd tried 'indifferent' but that was wrong because indifference meant a total lack of emotion, and that had never been the case.

They'd got on well enough when she'd been a little girl, perhaps something like the way distant cousins got on, but mostly because Verity had always been there to calm the waters.

Celia hadn't been at all happy when, at nine years old, her daughter had declared she wanted to be known as Kallie and not Kathleen from now on, and had chosen to ignore it. All too often, though, once Kallie had entered her teens, their encounters led to explosive arguments. The one they'd had after Verity had been laid to rest had been the last straw for both of them.

Ah well. It wouldn't do to dwell on the past. Better to put all that out of her mind and hope that Celia's stay would give them a fresh start and they'd find a way to be more like a mother and daughter should be.

Kallie put the suitcase down, opened the window for fresh air, and contemplated the piles of clothes on the bed.

Walter's things were destined for charity or the dustbin, so she stuffed his things into large bin liners and put the charity bags on the back seat of her car and the others in the wheelie bin. She then did the same with Verity's clothes and shoes, keeping back all the things she felt were too lovely to get rid of in a hurry. They would have to go back in the wardrobe and drawers they'd come out of until Kallie decided what to do with them. As long as there was enough space for her mother's few things then that would have to do.

Swiftly, Kallie carried the rest of the bags downstairs, placing them by the front door ready to take out to her car.

She hung her gran's good dresses, jackets, skirts and blouses on the padded hangers that Verity had always insisted on using, and put them away. As she paired her gran's shoes and neatly lined them up on the floor of the wardrobe, she couldn't help a wry smile at the chaotic way her mother treated her own clothes.

Next, she fetched a tray on which to load all the items from the dressing table and carried them through to her own room, then she cleaned, dusted, vacuumed and put fresh sheets on the bed, a clean cover on the duvet.

In just over an hour the room was ready and Kallie was hot and tired, but she had yet to unpack her mother's things and make them something to eat so she had no time to rest. Dinner would have to be something she could pop in the microwave and she mentally ran through what she had.

There really wasn't much in the suitcase, Celia being far more concerned with having a good supply of textbooks than outfits, so it took no time at all until Kallie had them put away, frowning at the dull colours and shapelessness of everything alongside Verity's smart, colourful outfits.

She draped her mother's plain nightdress and gown over the dressing table stool and placed her slippers beneath it. All the while she was thinking incredulously that, just as she knew nothing about her mother, Celia knew nothing about her daughter either. Or did she? What had Verity told her in those fortnightly telephone conversations?

She would find out soon enough, but she'd quickly have to learn what Celia liked to eat, what her taste in music was, though Kallie rather suspected her mother was tone deaf, what she read for pleasure—or were those heavy textbooks that seemed full of scientific formulae and diagrams her pleasure? Did she like to take walks, go to the theatre?

On her trips downstairs she'd noticed that Celia was watching a documentary, a programme that described the forensic science used to solve crimes, so that was no surprise. She quite liked those programmes herself, so that was one thing they had in common! She hoped they'd find other things too.

She and her grandparents had rubbed along so easily together, and when Walter had died she and Gran, so stoic and determined not to be miserable, had soon settled into a contented routine with it being just the two of them.

When Verity had died peacefully in her armchair, which was just the perfect way to go in Kallie's mind, Kallie had dreaded being alone. But she had adapted, and although she missed her grandparents deeply every single day because she loved them so much, she was gratified to find that she was comfortable with her own company. So, how could she now share this small space with someone she wasn't sure she even liked? How was that going to work?

She heard a creak on the stairs and a moment later Celia was in the doorway.

She sniffed the air. "I can smell Mum's perfume."

Kallie started to tell her about the spilled bottle, but Celia seemed not to hear her because she carried on speaking. "I was born in this room. Mum hadn't wanted to have a hospital birth so she didn't tell anyone she was in labour until it was too late to take her there. The midwife wasn't happy as I was her first and she was so tiny they were worried she might need a caesarean. But I arrived quickly and with no complications. Did you know that?"

Kallie did know because Verity had told her. She had also confided how sad she and Walter had been that there had been no more children, it just hadn't happened for them.

148

Kallie decided not to let her mother know that she and Gran had ever talked about such things and so mutely shook her head.

Celia came further into the room and looked around her.

"This house is so small and dark," she said. "And too quiet. That view of the graveyard never appealed to me, I was glad my own bedroom—your bedroom all these years, of course—didn't overlook it. That's why I've always lived in modern places, you get more space and light and I'm happier with a view of a busy street and the sound of traffic."

Kallie bit the inside of her cheek. If her mother didn't want to stay in this room she'd have to move all her stuff out of her own and that would take ages. She couldn't keep the edge out of her voice as she said, "Are you saying you'd prefer the other room? I thought you'd *like* to have this one."

Her mother regarded her steadily, and Kallie detected an angry spark in the one-eyed gaze, although it was difficult to tear her gaze from the swollen and garishly coloured lid of the other eye.

"Did I say that I'd prefer your room? I don't believe so. As you have gone to the trouble of arranging this one for me, this is where I shall stay."

Feeling at a disadvantage having Celia glare down at her, Kallie jumped off the bed and went to close the window and draw the curtains. If her mother didn't like to look at the graveyard she could just keep them closed the whole time she was here, but her mother surprised her with a smile and her next words.

"I apologise. I did not mean to sound as if I was complaining. I have nothing to complain about, because you are doing all this for me and I'm sure you're not at all happy about it. But please believe me, I am very, very grateful and I will try to keep out of your way as much as possible."

Managing to give a small smile back, Kallie said, "I'll just take your wash things down to the bathroom." She grabbed the plastic zippered bag and sidled past onto the landing,

149

adding, "I need to get dinner started, so come down when you're ready. I hope you like chicken curry and rice? I always make it quite mild."

Before her mother could answer, Kallie fled downstairs and into the kitchen. She leaned on the kitchen sink, looking at her reflection in the darkened window.

They'd only been in one another's company for less than a day and were already rubbing each other up the wrong way. Okay, her mother had just made the most amazing apology, but how long would the truce last? She knew what her gran would say to her, for Verity's way had always been to go softly, softly.

She could almost hear Verity's voice echoing in her mind, saying to her, "You're going to have to learn patience and tact, my girl, and learn fast. Remember my golden rule: always placate, never retaliate."

Straightening herself and pushing her shoulders back she went into the bathroom and placed the toothbrush and paste alongside her own into the holder on the shelf above the sink. The idea came into her mind that she'd enjoy a long, hot soak in the bath before bed to ease the tensions of the day, but that soothing image was quickly replaced with another one that horrified her: would she have to help her mother take a bath?

And then she thought of something else, and her spirits dropped even further. She had to call Kevin and cancel tomorrow's lunch.

Chapter 20
Sylvia

The sun was so warm, so soothing. Sylvia sat on the grass with her face tilted to the sky and her eyes closed, not worrying at all about the strange situation, she was just mulling it over. To begin with she'd thought it was all a dream, but now she knew it wasn't. It was real.

A light breeze ruffled her hair and somewhere close by a solitary bird sang its heart out, its notes so sweet, so poignant.

Since following the tall, enigmatic figure she'd been here, alone and content in this wonderful place. She didn't mind at all, in fact she enjoyed the profound peace and the freedom to move this strange dream gave her. So much nicer than the confinement of her hospital bed in the ward with its constant noise. She had thought intensive care wards would be quiet, but they weren't. Far from it.

She was dying, she knew that, but the ferocious need to hang on to life was dissipating. She knew she would miss her family, but when she thought about them it was in a strangely detached way, the details of their faces and their voices seeming to drift away from her. Time seemed not to matter here, and all the raw emotions she'd experienced after the heart attack to the moment she'd been brought here felt as if they had happened to someone else.

She was sure she wasn't yet dead, so how long, she wondered, did it take to die? And once she was dead, would she still be here?

"Sylvia."

Her eyes snapped open and she gasped at the sight of the tall woman standing in front of her, the same one that had led her here. Only now she could see her very clearly for the first time and her huge black and silver eyes drew Sylvia to her feet as she stared into their depths, finding herself unable to look away or speak. She waited.

"It is time."

Time? Time for what? With a start, Sylvia realised she must have been away from the hospital for ages. The last clear memory she had of being there was of Simon reading to her. There'd been an annoying sound, one of those frightening alarms going off, and some kerfuffle around her bed. Nurses had come rushing in and ushered her family out of the room, and she'd fallen into this dreamlike state.

Now she was back in the hospital, the tall figure beside her, and this was surely a nightmare.

Sensing with horror yet not understanding how she was sensing it, she knew that her kidneys, liver and heart were struggling, their signals to her brain getting weaker as they began to shut down. The serenity of just moments before abruptly left her and she fought desperately to get back inside her body.

But no matter how she struggled, just like before when she'd tried and tried, it was no good. Which way round was it, her body rejecting her soul, or her soul rejecting her body?

As minutes ticked on, she had no idea how many, she perceived that the only sensation she had through her strange connection with her physical self was the air being forced in and out of her lungs by the ventilator. But her lungs were tired too, they wanted to rest, to stop functioning like her other organs, and the equipment she had relied on to keep her alive now felt callously intrusive.

Sylvia turned to the being with the unblinking night-sky eyes.

"Am I dead?"

The beautiful face and fathomless black eyes continued to look impassively down at her.

"Soon. Your physical self is beyond saving. The technology can keep you alive indefinitely, but being tethered to a machine when there is no

possibility of recovery is not living. If there was a chance, the merest chance that you could recover, I would not be here."

Sylvia turned to the figure and asked, *"Who are you?"*

"I am Grace. I am one and I am many. I am here and I am everywhere. I am here to help you."

Grace reached out and placed her long-fingered hands on Sylvia's shoulders. She felt the tension, the fear, drain away as she hovered by the hospital bed, watching as a doctor examined her, and then a couple of nurses began the task of removing all the technology.

When the ventilator was finally switched off Grace took her by the hand and said, *"There is nothing to fear. Your family will be coming soon to say their goodbyes. It will be distressing. Do you wish to stay?"*

Biting back tears, Sylvia could only nod.

"It is done. Come, Sylvia. Walk with me."

Chapter 21
Kallie

"Kathleen, I'd like to take a bath by myself. I think if you put a plastic bag on my arm and tape it in place so there's no danger of getting it wet I'll be able to manage."

Gritting her teeth at her mother's insistence on calling her Kathleen, Kallie quickly ran through the logistics of what her mother was asking.

"Are you sure that's a good idea? Well, let me find Gran's rubber mat to make sure you don't slip. I think it's still in the airing cupboard."

"I do not require a rubber mat; those things are horrible to sit on. I'll be extra careful getting in and out. I know you don't enjoy bathing me any more than I enjoy you having to do it, and I most certainly don't want to be continually treated as if I'm an invalid. I'm sure I'll be fine."

Having no choice but to agree, and relieved to not have to see her mother totally naked again, Kallie got the bath ready and put a nice thick towel within easy reach, then returned to the kitchen to hunt down a plastic bag. She didn't have any of the thin plastic supermarket bags that would have been ideal so her mother suggested they try cling wrap.

Kallie used large sticking plasters round the top of Celia's arm above the plaster cast then wound the wrap all the way down and totally enclosed the hand so it stuck to itself and formed a good seal.

"Okay? I'll leave you to it then. I'll make a start on dinner so just shout if you need me."

Celia went into the bathroom and shut the door and Kallie waited until she heard the splash of water as her mother climbed into the bath. Wearily, she started to peel some

154

potatoes. She hadn't slept well since Celia had arrived because she was too aware of her sleeping in Walter and Verity's bed across the landing. Their meals together were difficult, and not because her mother couldn't manage to eat, because she'd proved quite deft at forking up whatever Kallie served, but because they found it so damned hard to talk to each other. It was a relief for them both to leave the table and sit in front of the television until Celia announced she was tired and going to bed.

With the potatoes coming to the boil, Kallie lowered the heat and tapped on the bathroom door.

"Are you alright, Mum? Do you need any help getting out?"

Celia replied that she was already out and coping just fine and it wasn't long before she came into the kitchen, dressed in her nightie, dressing gown and slippers. Her hair had curled in the steam.

"Would you tie the belt for me please? That's the only thing I can't do."

Kallie did so and said, "Wow, I can't believe how much you've managed to do by yourself! How on earth did you get your nightie on?"

"I told you I could manage. Could we eat soon so I can have an early night?"

Kallie, secretly delighted that she would have the evening to herself, quickly got their dinner served up. As soon as she'd finished the mashed potato, vegetables and roast chicken, which Kallie had cut up into bite-size pieces, Celia said she was going upstairs and would read until she fell asleep.

"I hope you sleep well," said Kallie. "Oh, I need to be at work early tomorrow, so shall I help you get dressed before I go?"

"There's no need." Celia indicated her nightwear. "I'm sure I can dress myself from now on. I've been independent all my life, Kathleen, so if I can at least be trusted to do that I think it'll suit both of us, don't you? I don't think you need

155

to leave me breakfast or lunch, either, though I appreciate that you have always thought to do so."

Kallie wanted to dance a jig round the room now that getting Celia bathed and dressed had come to an end, and not just for her sake, of course she was well aware how humiliated Celia felt at having to be helped this way.

Every morning so far Kallie had got up extra early to make her mother some breakfast and a lunch that would be easy for her to manage and then she'd helped her get dressed. The embarrassment they had both felt would always be painful to recall. After the first time, Celia had insisted on putting on her skirt by herself for modesty's sake before Kallie came into the room, but Kallie had still to put Celia's knickers on.

Celia, almost in tears, had said that she would do without tights and a bra, so Kallie had very carefully eased her blouse on, starting with Celia's bad arm, keeping her eyes averted from her bare breasts, and finally draped a cardigan over her shoulders.

Once assured that her mother had everything she needed and would be fine on her own with her books, Kallie happily escaped to the salon where she could immerse herself in aromatherapy oils and beauty products as she made her clients feel good and relaxed. Unfortunately, it didn't make herself feel good and relaxed, for she dreaded going home. She'd got so used to coming in, switching on the TV, getting changed into jeans and taking it easy with a mug of tea or coffee. Now Celia was there and her routine had had to change quite drastically to accommodate her. At least there had been no incidences of flickering lights, mislaid keys and a TV that seemed to have a mind of its own!

She would be able to escape to the salon tomorrow without even seeing her mother. Kallie said goodnight and promised to keep the television volume down low so she wouldn't disturb her.

"It won't disturb me. I prefer noise to silence, that's why I live on a busy road."

Once Celia had gone upstairs Kallie decided to watch the sitcom she'd been missing because Celia didn't like it, keeping the volume low no matter what her mother said about not minding noise; the monotonous sweep of passing traffic was quite different to the lively sound of a television.

An hour passed and Kallie contemplated making some hot chocolate with marshmallows on top, wondering if she should pop up and see if Celia wanted some. Suddenly, though, as if thinking about her had somehow caused her to materialise, there was Celia about halfway down the stairs. Barefoot, in her long white nightdress and with her wild grey hair she looked quite ghost-like and Kallie wondered for a horrified moment if she was sleepwalking.

She called out, "Mum? Are you okay? Do you need something?"

Celia came all the way down. "I was asleep. Something woke me."

"Oh, sorry, it must be the TV, though I've got it down really low."

"No. Someone spoke to me, called my name. I thought it must be you."

Kallie shook her head and said her mother must have been dreaming. "I haven't called you. You're still on strong painkillers, and you said you were really tired, so perhaps you were dreaming. I was about to make some hot chocolate, would you like some?"

Celia smiled then, a smile that reached her eyes and softened her face, and she said she would love some hot chocolate as long as Kallie wouldn't mind if she stayed down with her to drink it. Hiding her surprise, Kallie agreed and went to make it.

When she came back, her mother was sitting on the couch, her legs tucked up under her, her plastered arm resting on her lap.

"You must be cold. Let me get you something to keep you warm."

"Thank you, Kallie, that's very kind."

Kallie! Her mother had called her Kallie! She thought it could very well be the first time that word had ever passed her mother's lips. She fetched a blanket and arranged it over Celia, ensuring her feet were covered. She switched off the television, thinking they might have a go at conversation as her mother was being uncharacteristically sweet.

Celia had already shown that she could be very entertaining and witty, because Kevin had insisted that the three of them have lunch the day after Celia had come to stay with Kallie. Kallie had tried to talk him out of it, not wanting him to meet her oh so difficult mother, but he wouldn't be budged and had turned up with a bottle of good red wine and two bunches of flowers.

Somehow he had managed to coax things out of Celia that Kallie had never managed to do, and Kallie realised that day that she would be an idiot to let such a lovely and special man go.

Now Celia was that person again, regaling Kallie with some of the student exploits and pranks she'd witnessed over her many years of working at the university.

Watching and listening to this woman sitting across from her and making her laugh Kallie wanted to say, "Okay who are you, and what have you done with my mother?" Of course, she didn't. She didn't dare say or do anything that might spoil the mood, break the spell. It was so nice!

When they'd drunk the hot chocolate Kallie hoped that their companionable evening would continue, but Celia's face suddenly went quite blank and she looked around her as if not quite knowing where she was. Announcing she should be in bed, Celia got up abruptly, letting the blanket drop to the floor in a heap, and she was gone, with no more than an abrupt, "Goodnight, Kathleen."

Stunned, Kallie could only wonder what the hell had just happened.

"Well that was surreal," she muttered to herself as she washed up the mugs and the milk pan. It was gone eleven o'clock, far later than she'd intended to stay up, so she went to bed too, setting the alarm for seven the next morning.

It's only for a few more weeks, she said to herself. I've just got to get through a few weeks and then we can go back to our separate lives and our irregular, awkward, five-minute phone calls.

Once settled in bed, she quickly sent a goodnight text to Kevin. He replied immediately, and Kallie, who'd thought her evening was going to end on a sour note, went to sleep with a happy heart.

Chapter 22
Alex

He wasn't sure if this was the right time to be doing this, so soon after Sylvia's death, but Alex had made a commitment to Eselmont and, more importantly, to Flora, so here he was, with Marcus and Virginia. The three of them were standing in a line, craning their necks to see all the way up at the East London high rise, hoping there would be a working lift. There wasn't. Virginia offered to carry what she could and the men set-to lugging between them the heavy box of video recording equipment.

Slowly, they worked their way upwards, stopping for a breather halfway, Marcus moaning that the place smelled like a public toilet that hadn't been cleaned in years.

When they at last reached the twelfth floor they had to negotiate a long balcony open to the elements and strewn with abandoned bikes, skateboards and a couple of used cat litter boxes, until they were standing outside a scratched and battered half-glazed door. They were all out of breath.

Marcus said, "Remind me again, Virginia, why this couldn't be done in a hotel?" He removed his red baseball cap and wiped his forehead.

Virginia, puffing out her reddened cheeks, grinned. "Now, I thought you were a super-fit gym bunny, so why are you complaining? That was nothing more than a light workout for you!" Her grin faded as she explained, "Rachel suffers from agoraphobia. She suffers from panic attacks and only goes out if she absolutely has to, usually for food, and she goes in the dark. She insisted we do the interview here, where she feels most comfortable, and I had no choice but to agree."

She rang the doorbell.

Alex listened to it reverberate inside the flat, an electronic rendering of a tune he couldn't identify. A figure appeared, blurred by the frosted glass panel, until the door was pulled open to reveal a skinny woman with greying hair hanging loose and straggly down her back. Her eyes were red-rimmed and shadowed. Haunted.

Virginia, who'd met her before when she set up the interview, introduced Alex and Marcus and asked rather anxiously if she was still willing to be filmed. The look she gave the three of them spoke a thousand words and Alex half expected her to close the door in their faces and send them back down those twelve flights of stairs empty-handed, but with a sigh of resignation she stood back, and Virginia led the way in.

The four of them had to cram into the tiny sitting room. Sparsely furnished, there was only a small cabinet in the corner, one armchair and a sagging three-seater couch with an arm missing. The mismatched fabric of both was faded, stained and ripped in places where the material had worn thin. The only other seat was a dark green plastic garden chair. The walls were unadorned with pictures or hangings of any kind, the thin curtains were too short, the carpet threadbare, and everything seemed to be in varying shades of grey. Even the damp stains in the corners where the ceiling and walls met were grey.

It was cold and uninspiring and he felt conspicuous in his clean blue jeans and blue and yellow rugby shirt. Even Rachel, who'd taken the garden chair, was dressed head to toe in grey, as if trying to disappear into the drab surroundings.

She leaned back and crossed thin, bruised, bare legs, the higher leg swinging from the knee in agitation, as she watched Marcus setting up the camera and sound equipment. She was nervous, Alex didn't need his special senses to know that, but he could feel a mix of impatience and curiosity coming from her too.

At a nod from Marcus that he was all set, Virginia moved out of camera shot and Alex was given the nod to begin.

He wanted Rachel to speak first, and it took an uncomfortably long time, but finally, with a quick sideways glance at Virginia before looking back at him, she said, "So, you're a psychic medium from the telly? I'm sorry, I've never heard of you."

"Have you ever seen a medium?"

Rachel shook her head. "Why would I? I don't believe in all that stuff."

Alex smiled at her candour. "So, why did you agree to see me?"

The look Rachel gave him was keen, penetrating, and she replied that the information Virginia had provided had made her wonder. "The stuff she told me, personal things you could only have got from me or from Flora. It got my attention, so here you are." She shrugged her narrow shoulders, her eyes sliding to a scattering of burn holes in the carpet at her feet. "Anyway, what the hell have I got to lose? Things can't possibly get any worse for me, can they?"

"Let me ask you this, Rachel." He waited until he was sure of her attention. "Even if the worst thing should happen following the investigation, and no-one should be under any illusion that I can help you there, wouldn't it at least help you to know what actually happened that day, even if the police couldn't be convinced?"

He could see how she flinched at the mention of the police. Virginia had told him how Rachel had seen the image of the reconstruction that had been made of Flora's face from the skull in an old newspaper and had called the number given. They'd taken samples from her to check against DNA taken from Flora's remains and then the interrogations had begun. Why hadn't she been in school? Had she ever seen a doctor or dentist? Why hadn't she been reported missing? Had she killed her daughter?

Rachel's reasoning that she would hardly have come forward now if she'd anything to do with Flora's death seemed to fall on deaf ears, and she thought it only a matter of time before she was arrested and charged.

"Rachel," Alex said, "Flora is fine, absolutely fine, she just needs to tell you what happened, and she needs to know in return what happened to you that day. She loves you very, very much, but she's confused. You can share the information through me, and then... well, you'll know the truth, and that can only be a good thing."

As if she'd been prodded, Rachel suddenly leapt up, looking wildly around her as if she wanted to bolt from the room, but then she apologised and collapsed back into the chair as if all the strength had drained from her body.

Virginia told her to try and relax and that she'd already explained to Alex about the panic attacks. "You can stop the interview at any time, just tell us if you can't carry on."

Rachel nodded and addressed Alex. "I'm sorry. I'm always on edge. All this... so long not knowing what happened... well, it drove me to drugs, just to escape my own thoughts. My guilt. Now I'm clean, but I still get wired, you know? It's been so hard. All these years of wondering, not knowing, and then when I heard about you... the truth is, I've been longing for this day ever since, for you to come and tell me, even though I don't really believe you can." She pinched the bridge of her nose. "Can you really see her?"

"Yes. She's here now, standing beside you. She's been visiting me often since I met her where she died. She's a delightful little girl."

Unlike most people would on being told someone from spirit was standing next to them, Rachel did not look around. Alex could sense that she didn't believe him, at least not yet, and her attitude was, why make a wasted effort?

Alex described Flora as he saw her, then said, "But you know that her image, the clay model of her face, has been in all the newspapers and on the TV news and I have seen it too

163

so I can't offer that as evidence. But I can offer this. I know they didn't get her hair and eye colour quite right, they had to make assumptions about those. And she has freckles across her nose, just as you do."

Rachel, her voice a mere whisper, said, "When I first saw the photograph in a newspaper I almost fainted. To see her face again! Yes, some things weren't accurate, but they wouldn't know it all from a pile of bones, would they? How on earth were they able to make that model of her face though, so life-like?"

"I've seen how it's done, it is amazing. But I still need to give you evidence that you can accept, because of course you could say I was guessing the colour of Flora's hair and eyes by looking at you. I need to provide you with proof that I'm communicating directly with Flora, it's vital if this is to work for you. What exactly was it that Virginia told you that made you agree to this meeting?"

Rachel glanced at Virginia then gave a long, slow blink before looking back at him. Her front teeth, one of them with a corner chipped off, bit down on her lower lip and she nodded again with a quick dip of her head.

He sensed that she'd like to light a cigarette, but Flora told him she'd given up because she had a bad chest and they were too expensive. Alex relayed this and Rachel nodded her head, picking at fingernails that were bitten to the quick.

Rachel said, "Virginia showed me a tape of your programme. She said you would prove yourself. She said you'd given her a message from her father, something that only he could have told you."

Alex, remembering that very message he'd received for Virginia, opened his psychic senses wider and asked silently for Flora to give him more information, more evidence, that he could relay to her mother, telling her how important it was. He listened and spoke at the same time, his eyes closed to concentrate.

"A grey cat. Pink fluffy slippers. You had to leave the slippers behind and Flora was upset about that. Hemp? She's saying hemp, though I don't know what that means. A mattress… it's spread with clothes, yours and hers. You slept on them, but she packed them away while she waited for you. She says you always used to kiss the tip of her nose, you called her Munchkin and you liked to say hallelujah when things were going well. You said it when you broke into that house, because it was much easier than you'd expected. She's showing me a birthday cake, with pink icing, you both ate it all in one go. She likes pink, she says, because for a while you made her dress like a boy so the bad men wouldn't notice her, but they still did and it made you angry and sad at the same time."

Flinching, Rachel put her hand up. "Enough! Is she still near me?"

"Yes. She's stroking your right hand. Close your eyes and concentrate. Really concentrate. She says to turn your hand over and remember how, when she was really little, you used to trace a circle in the palm of her hand while you said a rhyme that ended in a tickle under her arm. She wants to do that to you. Maybe you'll feel a tingle in your hand and up your arm? That's her energy making contact with you. She's so happy to see you."

Turning her hand so it was palm upwards, Rachel closed her eyes and tears pooled beneath her lashes. She let them fall. She spoke so quietly Alex had to strain to hear her say that she thought she could feel something, like the stroke of a feather, in the centre of her palm, but she was so desperate she couldn't be sure. Alex almost had to look away from the naked anguish in her face.

"Did she… did she suffer? Oh my God, I just didn't know what had happened to her! I got back and she wasn't there, just this pool of blood by the fireplace. I looked everywhere, but I couldn't find her, I thought she'd been taken and I couldn't bear it!"

Her last words ended in a wail and Alex went to her, gathered her in his arms, ignoring the stale smell wafting from her skin, her hair and her clothes.

"She didn't suffer, Rachel, I promise you. I know it's what people always say, but she insists she felt nothing more than a short, sharp pain as she fell and hit her head on the corner of the hearth. It was an accident, a tragic accident. The man didn't mean to hurt her."

He hesitated, listening as Flora said something else.

"She's telling me that she thinks you're the best mum anyone could have and she loves you very much."

Rachel's face went chalk white and she looked as if she was about to faint.

"Oh my God, oh my God!" Rachel started to rock, her arms wrapped around her stomach.

"Rachel, do you need some time?" he asked.

The expression in her eyes, the way her hands moved in her lap. Had she done something terrible after all? He opened his seventh sense, the one that enabled him to read the true nature of people, and was relieved to feel no harm, no malice in her.

He said, "What will you do now she's been found? The story must come out."

Rachel nodded, shredding the tissue in her lap, her agitation growing. "I know!" she cried. "The police believe my little girl was murdered and I can't convince them I didn't do it. I would never have harmed my Flora, I *protected* her!"

Deciding to say nothing yet and feeling they needed to wait until Rachel had calmed down, Alex returned to the couch with a quick nod first to Marcus and then to Virginia, who was sitting on the equipment case. Alex didn't know where Virginia had worked before joining Eselmont, but this kind of interview was very likely new to her. Marcus, who'd filmed things far worse than this show of raw, desperate emotion, showed no expression as he concentrated on filming the exchange.

166

"I know you loved her, Rachel, I know you only wanted to protect her, but I'm sure you understand why they'd think as they do. I have no hope of convincing them otherwise, but I felt it important to tell you in person that I know they're wrong. They can only work with hard evidence, something I cannot provide. As far as they're concerned, because it looks as if Flora died from a blow to the back of her head and was buried in a shallow grave, she must have been murdered and you are the most likely person to have done it. But Rachel, Flora tells me it isn't so. You weren't there, and she says you would never have harmed her, not in a squillion years." He paused as Rachel gasped.

"She always used that word," she whispered. "Squillion. Anything bigger than she could understand wouldn't be a million or a billion, it would be a squillion. My God. So, what did happen to my baby?"

With Flora's help, Alex described those last moments, how she'd heard noises and come downstairs, thinking Rachel had returned with some breakfast, but instead there was a big man with a scarred face and long, stringy hair, and she'd tried to run past him but his huge body had filled the doorway and she'd run straight into his stomach, winding him.

"The man was as scared as she was, and he shoved her away from him in a reflex action. She fell backwards, hitting her head on the hearth so hard it cracked her skull. He tried to help her, to save her, but there was nothing he could do. He panicked. He didn't want to leave her, so he wrapped her in his sleeping bag and buried her, crying and begging her forgiveness as he did so."

"Is there anything she can tell us that might get him caught? Because unless he is I don't have much hope, do I?"

Alex couldn't answer whether or not the man would be caught, but he rather thought the police wouldn't even bother looking on the say so of a psychic medium.

"Why didn't you report her missing, Rachel? If you'd done so at the time there would still have been evidence in the house."

She sighed. "Oh, all sorts of reasons. I'm the type they don't like to put themselves out for, a shoplifter and a prostitute, a down and out with no fixed address. I knew I'd get into trouble for dragging Flora from place to place, not putting her in school. Child neglect, they call it. I didn't neglect her, I looked after her in the only way I could! If I'd gone to the authorities for help they would have taken her away from me. But I didn't know what had happened to her! What could I have told them? I was in such a state, so scared, I just wasn't thinking straight. So I ran, and I kept on running until I ended up here."

Alex, keeping to himself that his idea of what constituted child neglect was markedly different to Rachel's, replied, "I know, and I'm sorry. But I don't see how the man can ever be located. That entire row of houses was destroyed before her body was discovered and any chance of finding fingerprints or DNA in the fabric of the sleeping bag or the scraps of Flora's clothing was lost after years in the earth. It would never have been discovered at all if it wasn't for the building of a swimming pool in what is now a private garden. There's the remotest possibility that the man will see the publicity and come forward, but I really think the chances of that are next to zero. Flora says she doesn't want you to go to prison but neither does she want him caught, because the whole thing was an accident and who would believe him, a tramp that looked the way he did, and not quite right in the head? Those are her words, not mine."

"But it would get me off the hook!" Rachel cried. "Doesn't she care about that? Oh God, what am I saying? I don't want an innocent man punished. I'm sorry. I really don't care if I go to the nick, I deserve it." She indicated the shabby room and cheap furniture with a wave of her hand. "At least I'd be warm and dry and fed three times a day and people wouldn't spit at me in the street. Ever since my name's been in the papers everyone around here thinks that I'm the woman who murdered her child. But I didn't do it, I swear I didn't! I could never have hurt Flora!"

"Rachel, Flora has her arms around you. She doesn't want you to cry because she's absolutely fine where she is. She's happy!"

But Rachel, her head in her hands, was rocking to and fro and crying as if she'd never be able to stop. Alex stayed where he was, smiling reassurance at Flora who was stroking Rachel's hair, deciding it was better to let her cry it out now.

He thought it highly likely that Rachel would end up being charged and sent to prison, and there was absolutely nothing he could do about it. The type of evidence he could offer would hardly stand up in a court of law. But if she could at least believe the truth, that Flora hadn't been murdered and that she hadn't suffered, she could surely put her guilt about that part of this tragic story to rest.

Prison would be far from an easy ride for her, despite the heating and the regular meals she'd made that weak joke about, for as far as her fellow inmates would be concerned she would be the worst kind of child killer, a mother who had murdered her young daughter and left her to rot in a shallow grave behind a row of condemned houses. Not knowing the truth, the whole truth, they would make her suffer for that in all sorts of ways, far more devious and nastier than spitting in her face.

Alex despaired for her, but he knew beyond a shadow of a doubt that he could do nothing to help her if, indeed when she was arrested.

But, Flora reminded him, there was still more that needed to be said.

"Rachel? Flora's waited all these years to tell you what happened, now she wants to know what happened to you. Why were you gone so long?"

At Rachel's howl of despair, Alex assured her that Flora held nothing against her, she simply wanted to know because she'd been so worried for her.

"She was worried for *me*? Oh God! Flora, Flora! I'm so sorry!"

She steadied herself, and Alex could feel her resolve strengthening. He agreed with Flora that Rachel needed to tell her part of the story, so Flora could finally go on in peace, and grow up on the Other Side just as his own Amber was. He was resolved that he wouldn't leave this sad, dingy little flat until it was all out in the open.

Rachel took a shuddering breath and started her explanation, speaking in a low monotone as she relived that day.

"It was pouring. I mean, pouring so hard you couldn't see a yard in front of you. The streets were practically flooded and I only had light shoes on and my coat was soon soaked through. I walked a long way with no sign of any shops and thought I must've picked the wrong direction. I walked up street after street until I could hear cars passing up ahead, and I found a small high street. I went into the first grocery store I came to to get some food. I was tempted to nick a few things to try and save what little money I had, but I couldn't risk it in case I got caught and couldn't get back to Flora. The bloody irony of that, eh?"

Her voice dropped to a whisper. "It was still pouring when I started to head back, and I got lost! I hadn't been able to keep my bearings because of the rain, so I just didn't know the way back. I don't know how many wrong turns I must've made. I was so cold my teeth were chattering, and I was in a panic, which just made things worse. I could hardly ask for directions to a street of condemned houses, even if there'd been anyone to ask, so I walked and walked, going up and down streets and roads, so desperate but unable to find where Flora was waiting."

Eyes closed, she stopped speaking for a little while. Alex glanced at Marcus and Virginia, signalling that the story wasn't finished yet and they should keep quiet.

Rachel took a breath. "Finally, I recognised where I was; I was close. I ran the rest of the way, climbed through the window and pounded up the stairs. Flora wasn't there, but she'd packed all our clothes in the plastic bags, and there was an empty water bottle and biscuit wrapper on the floor." Rachel swallowed hard. "I ran all over the house calling her name. The front room downstairs was quite dark because of the boarded-up windows, but I lit a candle. I'd bought some you see, and some matches, because Flora had reminded me we needed them. I saw a dark stain round the hearth. I… I touched it. There was nothing else in that room, just that horrible pool of blood, and I didn't know if it was hers, but she wasn't in the house, so…"

Alex stopped her. Flora was getting distraught and Rachel, who'd gone alarmingly white, was clearly bordering on exhaustion.

"Let me get you a drink," Virginia said. "Water? Or do you need something stronger?"

Rachel gave a quick smile, a mere twitch of her bloodless lips. "Whisky please, if there's any left. Over there." She nodded to the small cabinet and Virginia quickly located the cheap whisky. She poured what was in the bottle, having to drain it to get a mere half inch in the glass.

"Here. Drink it down. This is hard for you, I know, but getting it all out in the open will be cathartic, both for you and for Flora." Alex waited a beat while Rachel drank it down in one swallow.

"Flora says she doesn't need you to talk any more. It's enough for her that you hadn't been hurt, because that's what she'd been worried about, that you'd been in an accident or something. She's so happy that wasn't the case."

The whisky restored some colour to Rachel's cheeks and lips, and Alex was relieved that their session had indeed been cathartic, for he could feel a marked difference in both mother and daughter. She and Flora both knew all the facts about each other now, everything that had happened on that dreadful day, and they could go on from here without being shadowed by the appalling doubts that had hung over them for years.

But Rachel wasn't quite finished.

"I ran. I ran through every inch of that house, the garden, the other houses, screaming for her. The ground was muddy, I remember that, but you couldn't see very far and I didn't notice anything. I mean, I still couldn't see much because of that bloody rain! If not for that I might have seen—he might have still been there! But I had no idea, how could I? I searched everywhere for her, but then I had to go. I heard people and machines, workmen coming to demolish the houses. I grabbed our things and bolted, thinking my heart would break.

I even went back to Hemp and asked him if he'd taken her to spite me for leaving him. All I got for that was a black eye and this chipped tooth for taking some money from him and running away. When I realised I had no hope of finding her, and that she was likely dead anyway, I left everything and I walked and walked until I came to a railway line."

She stopped a moment, turning the empty glass between the palms of her hands. "I thought of ending it. How could I go on without my Flora? Especially not knowing what had happened to her! God knows I hadn't given her the life she deserved, but I loved her! Oh, how I loved her. She meant everything to me. I felt bad about the way things were going for us, but I couldn't stand the idea of her being taken into care."

She swallowed and her voice dropped. "But if I had let that happen, she'd be alive, wouldn't she? She'd be safe, with a family. So, I wanted to die, I really did. But then I thought, what if she wasn't dead? What if she'd been taken somewhere and one day she'd get away and come looking for me? I had to stay alive."

Rachel squeezed her eyes shut, reliving every painful second, and the glass tumbled from her hands. "Oh, Flora, my sweet little Munchkin, I'm so sorry! I wanted to keep you safe and I failed. I hope you can forgive me. I don't care what happens to me now, it's enough that I know the truth and that you are happy where you are."

Alex grinned as Flora managed to lift a strand of Rachel's hair away from her scalp so that Rachel could feel it. Marcus and Virginia both gasped as they watched it happen.

"Is that her?" whispered Rachel. "Is Flora playing with my hair?"

Alex nodded and in a moment Rachel was on her knees crawling across the carpet to him. She wrapped her arms around his legs, saying over and over, "Thank God for you, Alex. Oh! Thank God for you!"

***

"Wow, that's really powerful stuff!"

There was a long silence, the atmosphere in the Eselmont conference room electric following the first viewing of the as yet unedited version of Alex's interview with Rachel. Everyone was stunned by the raw emotion captured in the footage.

Alex let out a breath and leaned forward, his hands palms down on the table. "I want that last bit cut. No-one should see her crawling to me on her knees like that. She hasn't been formally charged yet, and she's lucky not to be under arrest, but it's surely only a matter of time. The situation for her is really serious; at worst she'll be charged with murder and at best it will be child neglect and not reporting her daughter missing. It pains me deeply to know the truth of what happened and yet be unable to do anything about it."

He put one hand to his chest. "I would willingly go to the court and speak up for her, but no-one there would take my evidence. If ever there should come a day when mediums like me are one hundred per cent believed and can take the stand in a criminal case, I shall be long gone."

Virginia was the first to speak. "It's an incredible interview. I knew it would be as I sat there next to Marcus and watched it unfold. I know you're concerned that you can't prove anything, Alex, but your audience will see it and the media will run with it, and the public will have the chance to make up their own minds. After all, the chance to tell her side of the story is what Rachel wants and she's signed the authorisation to go ahead, no matter what happens to her. Seems to me she doesn't *care* what happens to her."

"Yes," agreed Alex, "she's so full of guilt and confusion, she feels prison would be a just punishment. But although I *feel* that Flora is telling the truth, we all know that unless the man who buried her comes forward, there will always be too many questions. For instance, how did he dig a hole so deep?"

"Hmm." Paul leaned his elbows on the desk. "She could be covering for her mum, but even if she is, how did Rachel manage to dig that hole?"

A gravelly voice spoke up then, and all heads turned towards the Creative Director. Strangely for one working for a production house that specialised in all things paranormal, Nathan declared himself a 'devout sceptic' and 'the voice of reason' in an otherwise crazy company. Everyone absolutely loved Nathan, knowing that he was really only playing devil's advocate for the fun of it; he was as firm a believer as the rest of them, he just wouldn't admit it.

"Most of you weirdos believe in Alex's psychic skills." He winked at Alex. "But can you imagine how the press are going to react if, and let's face it, it's more likely to be *when* Rachel is locked up for the murder of her daughter? Alex's credibility could be shot down in flames."

Marcus gave a snort of exasperation. "Alex was able to give the girl's name and lots of personal details to the police about Flora long before Rachel came forward."

"That's as maybe, but we can't substantiate anything," declared Nathan. "Alex, you can't prove that what Flora told you is the truth, can you?"

There was a collective intake of breath at that and everyone waited for Marcus to explain.

"For the sake of argument, how do we know she's not lying to protect her mother?" Nathan held his hand up to forestall any interruptions and turned to Alex. "Set aside your own emotions for a moment. Isn't what I've just said feasible, that the girl would want to protect her mother? It could well have been an accident as she says it was, but it could have been Rachel that did it, not some tramp. None of the stuff Flora says belonged to that man was left behind, Rachel would have seen it, so there's not a trace of anyone else ever being in that house. Rachel did herself no favours by living the way she did and by not going to the police straight away when Flora went missing. Even when they created an image of Flora's face and plastered it all over the media she still took her time coming forward."

He held up his hand again as objections were raised by Virginia and Marcus. "I know she told you it was because she doesn't read the papers or watch the news and it was only by accident that she saw it, but try convincing the general public of that. No, she might well be a nice girl who fell on hard times through no fault of her own, but I don't think she did right by her daughter, dragging her from pillar to post, keeping her from an education and healthcare, and that's what everyone is going to home in on."

Alex admitted that he had thought of the possibility that Flora might be lying about the big, scarred man, and so had been very careful in his questioning of her. When people lied they usually found it difficult to keep to the details and something seemingly insignificant often gave them away, but

Flora's story never wavered, even when he eventually challenged her outright. At no time did his senses pick up anything of deceit or guile from her or Rachel, and he wholeheartedly believed that Rachel hadn't had anything to do with Flora's death.

Nathan continued, "As I said, the media could have a field day with this. Aren't they already sniffing around?"

"I'm not bothered by the media," Alex replied. "Some continue to vilify me since the show first aired and there were a few journalists who were downright cruel when Amber died. Well, I'm still standing!" He paused. "A little girl died in miserable and suspicious circumstances and the wrong person is going to be found guilty of killing her. I know that she didn't and for the sake of common humanity we owe it to both of them to broadcast their story with honesty and integrity and allow people to make up their own minds."

There was a murmur of agreement, except from Nathan, who tutted and shook his head.

"A fascinating story with a paranormal twist," he said. "Yep, that's what we do, folks!"

The head of Eselmont, who'd not joined in the exchange, despite having plenty to say before they'd watched the interview, slapped the table, his signal that the meeting was concluded.

"Right, let's get a press statement prepared, and I'd also like some blurb to start and end the programme when it's broadcast. I was thinking to slot it in with one of the programmes like we're doing with the one-to-ones but now I've seen this I think it deserves to stand alone. You all know the kind of thing that's needed. In the meantime, we need to get to work in the editing suite. It's a brilliant interview, Alex, brilliant."

Chapter 23
Sylvia

This was the most peaceful place Sylvia had ever known, a place where she could quite believe the most damaged of souls could be repaired. Her own soul was intact and she was grateful for that, she was merely surprised and confused about her new state of being and sad at leaving her family.

Grace, the strange figure with the impassive face and astonishing black eyes had commanded her to follow, and she'd wanted to tell her family that she had to leave them even though she didn't want to, but Grace had taken her away. Even Alex, who she was sure had sensed her presence and felt her touch on his face that time as he lay on the sunny grass bank outside the hospital, had not understood that it was her trying to communicate with him.

There was no sign now of Grace, so she waited on the cool, lush grass of a vast lawn that spread around her as far as the eye could see, thinking about her family.

How were Simon, Anna, Beth and Paul coping? Were they looking after each other? Was Felix taking care of Anna and Alex looking after Beth, both of whom would feel Sylvia's loss so deeply? Thank goodness Paul had Adele by his side now.

Her deepest concern was for Simon. She had no idea if any other others were aware that he had a problem, that he might have a brain tumour or dementia. Had he been for the brain scan?

She had so many questions about them, but also about herself, only those were so immense she couldn't dwell on them for long. She was dead and she hadn't expected it to be like this. It was just like a dream, and in the way of dreams the lawn had shrunk while she'd let her mind wander and she was now sitting beneath an oak tree, resting comfortably against its warm, solid trunk.

She slowly became aware of feeling an energy pulsing against her back and instinctively knew it to be the tree's life force. Her own energy began to synchronise with the pulse and she sighed with utter contentment.

Before her was a beautiful landscaped garden that seemed to exist in all seasons at once. Sylvia could look at a beech tree and see it lush and green, and then in the blink of an eye its leaves would be russet and falling gently to the ground. Another blink and frost rimed the branches.

Perfume and sweet birdsong filled the air. Tinkling water could also be heard close by, although she couldn't see a stream or a fountain from her vantage point. The warmth of the day was pleasant and soothing, but the disc hanging low in the sky was not like the sun. There was a purplish haze over and around it, so she could look straight at it and not be dazzled.

Yes, it was like a dream and it was so lovely, so restful, she wanted to stay here for a little while. But the scene changed again and she became aware that there were many other people in the garden, standing around in groups or alone. They hadn't been there just moments before so who were they and where had they come from? Why had they invaded her garden and disturbed her peace?

She rose to her feet and headed towards the nearest group, but she didn't recognise anyone and no-one acknowledged her. They talked in low voices, but not in languages she understood so she walked on, stopping within hearing distance of each group, or moving close to individuals standing apart.

No-one seemed to notice her at all until one young woman, skin the colour of honey and a thick plait of blue-back hair hanging down her back, looked at her with enormous, thickly-lashed brown eyes and spoke a stream of

178

lilting words. They meant nothing to Sylvia, but the woman's expression and the intonation of her voice indicated that the woman had asked a question.

Sylvia shook her head. "I don't understand you. I'm sorry."

The woman frowned, gesticulating with her hands as she talked rapidly, not taking her eyes from Sylvia's face.

Sylvia shook her head again and smiled. "I don't know who you are or where you're from. Maybe you're like me, new to all this?"

The woman turned from her and hurried away, trying to catch up with one of the groups. Her feet were bare, Sylvia noticed, with brown swirly patterns painted on them. Her slender arms wore bracelets and bangles.

Everyone was moving purposefully in the same direction. Incredibly tall figures with dark eyes appeared amongst them as if from nowhere, laying slender, long-fingered white hands on shoulders, murmuring softly to the people they seemed to be guiding. They were just like Grace. Were they angels?

Sylvia found herself caught up amongst the milling crowd and so had no choice but to go with them. But she was curious now as to where they would take her, so she willingly fell into step and marched forward with the throng of strangers.

And then they were gone.

Incredulous, Sylvia swung around in a full circle and back again, but she was totally alone.

A little frightened she decided to go back the way she had come, to the safety of the great oak tree, but when she turned about she was further astonished to find that her way was barred by a high stone wall. Running to it, then going first to the left and then doubling back to the right she eventually came to an ornate wrought iron gate set in a high Gothic archway.

A large padlock secured the ends of a heavy chain which was looped through the bars of the gate and a metal ring set into the wall. She peered through the bars, half expecting the view in that direction to have changed as well, but the garden stretched away in the distance, the great oak tree she'd sat beneath just visible on the horizon. She once more contemplated the high wall and the gate. Barriers were meaningful in dreams, she was sure, but this was not a dream.

From somewhere behind her came sounds of young children at play drifting on the cool breeze and for the first-time thoughts of her great-granddaughter came flooding into her mind.

Oh Amber, she thought, your time was so short would you even know me? Are you somewhere in this place or have you moved on elsewhere?

As the words formed inside her head she felt a tug in the region of her solar plexus, a tug that wanted her to go and find the source of that lovely sound of happy children. But she was distressed by the gate, not liking that her way back to the oak tree was firmly held closed by that chain and padlock. It didn't look or seem right to have such an obstruction here, and she pulled at it with frustration.

She peered through the gate again, longing to be back under the tree, but she was startled by the appearance of a man who seemed to materialise from nowhere. He stood with his back to her, but she recognised his shape, the way he stood, the tilt of his head. She knew who it was.

"Simon!" she yelled, shaking and rattling the gate. "Simon! Over here!"

The man turned, and she had to hold back a sob at the look of utter confusion on his face.

What was he doing over there? She called over and over again, shouting until she was hoarse, but Simon didn't see her and in the space of a mere second he had vanished. One moment there, the next not there.

Bewildered, Sylvia spun about begging for help, then she swung back to the gate.

"I need to be over there!" she shouted. "I need to be with my husband!"

To her amazement the chain fell apart and the padlock dropped to the ground. She pushed the gate open and gingerly took a step forward, her eyes fixed on the place Simon had been standing just moments before. Another step. She felt she was doing a momentous thing, but had not the slightest idea what it might lead to. All she knew was she needed to be on this side of the wall.

Hoping she would catch up with Simon she started to run, but slowly the realisation crept over her that she would not find him. What she needed to do was wait for him, for she knew deep in her soul that he would return. She went back to the oak tree and curled up beneath its spreading branches, her hand caressing its rough bark.

She was no longer a purely physical creature, she was— what? She felt like she still had her body, that she was still Sylvia Savarese who had all five physical senses, but she also felt so much more.

She lay beneath the oak for a long while but no-one came and eventually peace settled over her once again. She let herself relax, listening to the birdsong and the rustling of warm, scented breezes in the leaves of the great tree, until she fell asleep.

When she awoke it was from a dreamless sleep, and she felt refreshed. She stretched herself and took in her surroundings again. The pretty daisies on the lawn drew her forward into the lush grass. Humming, she picked several handfuls and started making a chain. She had woven about half a dozen flowers when she noticed a young girl dressed in pink approaching her, her step slow and unsure.

The girl stopped several feet away, her eyes on Sylvia's hands as she pierced holes with her thumbnail and threaded the daisies together.

Sylvia smiled, and started singing, 'Daisy, Daisy, give me your answer do." She glanced up every now and then as the shy little girl, perhaps nine or ten years old, inched nearer.

"Want to join in?" asked Sylvia, waving her hand over the small pile of daisies beside her. "My name is Sylvia. Why don't you come and sit with me?"

The girl hesitated, her eyes flicking between Sylvia and the threaded flowers on her lap, then she came all the way forward and sat down, cross-legged.

Sylvia picked up the daisy chain she'd made and added a few more before joining the ends to make a garland. Placing it over the little girl's head she asked, "What's your name?"

"Flora."

"Well now, Flora, with a pretty name like that you must just love flowers! In Roman times Flora was the goddess of flowers and spring. Have you ever made a daisy chain?"

Flora, still a little hesitant, shook her head, causing her silky hair to swing forward, almost covering her dear little face with the smattering of pale freckles of her nose.

Sylvia selected two daisies and held them up. "Now then, watch me do a few and then maybe you'd like to make a garland for me to match the one I just gave to you, because a daisy chain is a sign of friendship."

Ensuring Flora had a clear view, Sylvia began to show her what to do.

"See? You pierce the stalk about halfway down, like so. Then you take the next daisy and push the stalk into the slit all the way through so the flower head rests on the slit. Got it? You go ahead and do some then, and when we've used up this little pile we can go and pick some more."

They worked companionably in silence, Sylvia sensing that Flora did not yet want to talk to her. But she wondered where the little girl had come from and why she had wandered into Sylvia's garden. It didn't take long before the heap of flowers she had picked were almost used up, so she pointed to a large patch of daisies and suggested Flora replenish their pile. She went skipping off, her shiny hair swinging.

Sylvia felt someone approaching from behind her and intuition told her who it was. Shielding her eyes she could only see a dark silhouette, but the height, the graceful stride and the flowing robes were enough to know that it was, as she'd thought, Grace.

When Grace came level with Sylvia she stopped, her incredible eyes on Flora, but Flora seemed not to be aware of her for she carried on daintily picking daisies, making sure to pick the whole stem of each flower as Sylvia had told her. Sylvia followed the black gaze, startled to see that the child had suddenly moved quite a distance away, as if the grass between them had been stretched so neither of them had moved yet they were further apart.

Grace seemed to read Sylvia's concern and reassured her. Her voice, spoken rather than implanted into Sylvia's mind as it had been in the hospital, was like music. "Do not worry. Flora knows me but she cannot see me just now. She can come to no harm here."

"But why is she so much further away? And why does she look like that... So slow in her movements?" Sylvia fancied she could hear the little girl humming a nursery rhyme, like a record being played at a very slow speed.

"I wish for her to take longer at her task so I may speak with you."

Sylvia stared up at the enigmatic being, the angel, whose great height from Sylvia's seated position made the difference between them seem immense.

Grace elegantly folded her limbs until she, too, was sitting on the ground, her robes spread around her.

For the first time Sylvia was able to study her face at close quarters. She had human features, but for her eyes. Her eyes were the strangest Sylvia had ever seen, black as black can be, with sparkles in their depths that gleamed like stars.

"Flora is waiting," said Grace, "Just as you are waiting, because you both feel you have something to do before you can fully cross over."

"I need to help my husband," Sylvia said. "But I'm sure you know that. So why is Flora here? She seems so young to be alone."

Grace turned her head and Sylvia was transfixed by those dark eyes as she said, "She has been here a long time waiting for the chance to help her mother. That has been done, and now she is going to help you."

"Help me how? I don't even know her."

Sylvia couldn't figure out any connection between her and Flora could possibly be. There was no family resemblance, and Sylvia, coming from such a close-knit family, was sure she'd know of this child. How had she died? Who was her mother?

The fathomless eyes, unblinking, were still trained on her.

"Tell me why you are here, Sylvia." With a sweep of her pale hand she indicated the gate set in the high wall behind them. "You were on the other side of it with all those other people, they were moving into the next realm, but the power of your determination to return here released the gate and you came back to this side. Tell me why."

"I saw my husband."

Sylvia waited, hoping Grace might make some acknowledgement or give some explanation, but neither was forthcoming.

"I saw Simon and I just knew I had to be here, to wait here, for when he comes again. And I *know* he will come again. Why was he here so fleetingly? Did I dream it?"

Grace still gave no reaction, but Sylvia's mind was whirling now and for the first time she allowed herself to really think it through. She certainly had unfinished business with Simon, for she didn't know if her family were aware of his condition, but what could she do for him from here? How could she make sure he was getting the help he needed? And how come she'd seen him here and knew with such certainty that he would come back?

As if she'd heard and comprehended Sylvia's thoughts, Grace asked, "Do you understand yet?"

Sylvia sighed and shook her head. "But I rather suspect that *you* know," she said, slowly. "Are you going to tell me?"

"I do not explain, I only guide."

Grace indicated Flora with a sweep of her hand, still happily picking daisies in ultra-slow motion.

Grace said, "Flora was helped by your granddaughter's husband."

"Alex?"

"When I first came for you, in the hospital, you briefly saw and touched him before leaving with me. Do you remember?"

Sylvia said that she remembered it clearly, how she'd seen Alex stretched out on the dry grass behind the bus shelters. She had no idea how, but she had been able to touch his handsome face, and he had responded but he had not known it was Sylvia.

She had not thought of him very often since, her mind being full solely of Simon, Anna, Beth and Paul. But why on earth hadn't she tried to make contact with Alex again, to tell him that she was worried about Simon? He could have passed on the information to Anna, and Anna would have ensured Simon had the tests and got the medical help he needed.

She wanted to slap herself with exasperation; she must have been lulled into stupor by this place not to think beyond that first and only sight of Simon. She knew why she had chosen to remain here, but now she also had a thousand questions.

However, Grace had made it clear she would give no answers. What had she said? She did not explain, only guide? So asking would get her nowhere, clearly.

"I don't understand what any of this means."

"It will all unfold as it should," Grace replied. "But I will tell you this, for it will have no effect on the outcome for Flora. Alex communicated with her, helped her and her mother to resolve what happened. He is the connection between you both and why I brought her here to ask you to watch over her for a while. She has been at her own waiting place, entirely alone, for a long time. She held information about her death that she needed her mother to know, and Alex was the conduit for that to happen."

"Oh my God, how did she die?"

Horrified at the idea that something dreadful had happened to the little girl she paused, hoping Grace would tell her. But Grace did not speak.

"Fine, you do not explain, and probably I am jumping to the worst of conclusions."

"Flora will tell you if she wants you to know. Her purpose now is to help you connect with Alex."

"Okay, but how is she going to do that? When I touched him he didn't know it was me, he thought it was someone else."

Grace smiled, the first time her impassive face had moved other than speaking, and Sylvia almost cried at the sheer beauty of it.

"As I said, that little girl over there knows how to speak to him. She will help you, but please know that you are equally important to her, Sylvia. She has no-one else." At that, she rose with a graceful, fluid movement to her great height.

Sylvia started to ask another question, but Grace was already walking away and Flora had skipped back, her hands full of daisies. Sylvia wanted to run after Grace and demand answers to the many questions she had, but Flora needed her now. She opened her arms and embraced the little girl, loving how the heart-shaped face grinned up at her with such trust. It reminded her so much of playing like this with Anna when she'd been little, and then with Beth, so proud to have a beautiful daughter and granddaughter.

186

She told Flora to look up at the sky and pointed out the animals she could see in the fluffy clouds sailing slowly overhead. Flora, chewing on a piece of grass, giggled at her suggestions of dragons and unicorns. Little by little, Sylvia coaxed Flora's story out of her, astonished to hear how she and Alex had met where Flora had been buried in a shallow grave and how Alex had relayed Flora's messages to her distraught mother.

At the back of her mind Sylvia asked herself why she had yet to communicate with Alex herself, and couldn't explain even to herself why she was so reluctant to do so. Perhaps it was because she didn't want to hear anything bad about her family, which was cowardly of her, or maybe she wanted to understand and so be able to ask him why she'd seen Simon for that fleeting glimpse.

"Who's that man?" asked Flora.

Sylvia gasped. "Simon! Oh, it's Simon!" She stood up and waved frantically. "Over here, over here!"

"But he's not dead like we are, is he? And he doesn't see us. Oh, he's gone."

Sylvia sank back down onto the grass. She didn't know why they could see him and he couldn't see them, but now she was sure they would learn the reason eventually.

"You miss him," Flora said, and it was a statement not a question. "I miss my mummy, but I feel much better now I've talked to her. I hope she doesn't have to go to prison."

Sylvia, now she knew the whole story from Flora, rather thought that was exactly what Rachel would have to do.

"Look at that cloud!" shouted Flora, bringing Sylvia back from her private thoughts. "It's a whale!"

"So it is. And spouting water too, how clever."

Lying there with this lovely little girl, so young and naïve, her small, trusting hand in hers, with the warmth of that strange sun on her face, Sylvia wished only that Simon was with them. But as her lazy mind formed a poodle out of a

187

particularly fluffy white cloud directly above her, something did disturb her. Something she could not ignore.

She pushed herself into a sitting position and looked around, but she and Flora were alone. There was an acrid smell on the breeze and she closed her eyes and inhaled deeply to better analyse it. Someone, somewhere, was having a bonfire.

"Do you smell smoke?" she asked Flora.

Flora lifted her face and sniffed the air. "Yes," she replied, wrinkling her nose.

Feeling an invisible, irresistible pull in a certain direction, maybe the direction of the fire where there might be people, she rose and told Flora to stay while she investigated.

"My mum told me to stay while she went off to get some food, but she never came back."

"I will come back, sweetheart. And you're perfectly safe here, you know that. It never gets dark and the angels are always nearby. I need to go and check something, but I promise I won't be long and I want you to stay put, okay? Keep looking at the clouds and remember what you see so you can tell me when I get back."

Flora nodded, reassured, so Sylvia set off through the long grass and wild flowers, not bothering to brush away the seeds that rose up and caught in her clothes and her hair.

As she walked, lightly brushing with her fingers the bright red nodding heads of poppies and marvelling at how the cornflowers reflected the blue of the sky, images of her childhood came to her of joyful times when she'd played with her friends in a country meadow just like this.

It seemed a long walk, until the meadow suddenly came to an abrupt end, as if an invisible line had been drawn along the ground from side to side as far as the eye could see. Her next step would take her onto a familiar, lush, close-cropped lawn, with beds aglow with roses and summer flowers.

It was her own garden.

And if it was her garden, then surely the house, her and Simon's house would be… yes! The French doors were open. Was he in there?

But wait… something was wrong. She started to run forward, but in the next second the wall, the very wall that should be way back behind her, blocked her view of the house. All she could see was the solid stone, too high to scale, stretching either side as far as the eye could see.

As she had when she'd first encountered it she started running, following the wall first one way and then the other in search of the gate. Where was it? As if the thought invoked its presence she saw it some distance away to her right. By the time she reached it, dismayed even further to find it padlocked, the smell of burning was stronger, more acrid, causing the first pang of anxiety to grip her stomach because it did not smell like a bonfire now.

Grasping the bars with both hands, bewildered that the gate was here, padlocked and blocking her way to her own home, her husband, she peered through and felt her senses reel even more as she saw that Simon was standing on the other side of the gate, on the lawn of their house, just a short distance away from her. Expecting him to disappear as he usually did, she was surprised when he remained there, his back to her.

"Simon?" Her voice was just a croak and she tried again. He did not turn; he couldn't have heard her. She called again, louder, "Simon! Over here!"

This time he did look her way, but his arms hung loose by his sides and his expression didn't change, so she couldn't tell if he'd heard her shouting or even if he could see her. She yelled again, jumping up and down and pushing and pulling the gate so the chain rattled, calling his name over and over.

The smell of burning was strong now, choking, terrifying, and she knew it had to have something to do with him, with his being here like this.

Then, suddenly, he looked directly at her. At first, he didn't register who he was looking at, because she was partially obscured by the vertical bars of the gate, but slowly his face broke into a smile which grew wider and wider in delight. He started to walk forward. Then, calling her name, he started to run.

Yet he seemed to get no nearer.

Frustrated, she looked up to see if she could get between the top of the gate and the stone arch above it, but it grew in height even as she stared upwards. Simon would have to open the padlock from his side; he could do it, just as she had. She looked back, ready to tell him what to do, and screamed with shock and frustration.

The smell and crackling sound of things burning and melting in raging flames remained, but her husband was no longer there.

Chapter 24
Alex

"Hi Mum. I'm in the car with Alex, we've just arrived in town... no, we were going to call in a bit later... well, maybe he's out? No, no, it's fine. Honestly... yes, we'll go now. I'll call you when we get there. I'm sure he's fine, Mum. He has to leave the house on his own sometimes, maybe it's a good sign... okay, bye."

Alex glanced across at Beth as she put her phone back into her handbag. "I take it our shopping expedition must be abandoned then?"

"Afraid so, at least until later. Right now we need to go and check if Pops is okay. Do you mind? Poor Mum's about to have a root canal and the dentist happened to mention that Pops has missed two appointments. She's left messages on his mobile and the answering machine at home and he hasn't called back, so now she's really worried. He has been acting really odd lately, hasn't he?"

Alex didn't want to answer that, because he had first noticed Simon's strange behaviour some time before Paul and Adele's wedding. He simply said, "Let's go."

He took a side street which would get them back on the main road heading in the direction of Simon's house. None of them were coping well with the loss of Sylvia, so long the linchpin of the family, but poor Simon was really struggling, as was to be expected.

He'd been utterly heartbroken at Sylvia's funeral, so heartbroken he'd been sedated by a doctor afterwards because he was near collapse. He seemed to have aged a great deal in a short space of time, and he was much quieter, more introverted, but he still wouldn't drive and steadfastly refused to stay with Anna and Felix even for a short while. However, if no-one called him regularly, he was soon on the phone to Anna, Paul or Beth, using any pretext he could think of to get them to go to his house and stay awhile to keep him company. This was why Anna was so concerned that he wasn't answering her messages.

They all offered to take him out somewhere, even offered to take him away for a holiday, but they could not prise Simon away from his home and his memories.

Less than twenty minutes after Anna's call, they were driving along Simon's street to be greeted by the chaos of two fire engines, a police car, an ambulance, and a small crowd of people who had gathered for the excitement.

Alex was unable to get close to Simon's house, so parked in the first available space alongside the kerb, wondering whose house was on fire, and if Simon was one of the spectators, which would explain why he hadn't responded to Anna's messages.

"Oh, my God!" cried Beth, opening the door the second Alex parked.

A large woman in a pink and white floral dress broke from the crowd and ran up to her. One of the fire engines roared past them, leaving the scene.

Alex recognised the woman as Mrs Keene, Simon's long-time next-door neighbour, and hurried to hear what she had to say, because, like Beth, he'd seen with a sinking heart just where the emergency was.

"Beth! Oh Beth, my dear, I'm so glad you're here. Your grandad set the kitchen on fire! I was pegging out the washing when I saw black smoke pouring from the window. I looked over the fence and he was outside, just standing there in the middle of the lawn staring towards the bottom of the garden. He didn't respond to my shouts so I called the fire brigade. I wanted to phone your mother, dear, but I don't have her number and Simon said his mobile was inside and he was in too much of a state to remember it. The police have been and gone, luvvie, and I think the fire is out."

Mrs Keene grabbed Beth's arm and started to pull her along. "He's in the ambulance, but I think he's not badly hurt. Some slight burns on his arms and face, but thankfully he got out before he could breathe in too much smoke. Come on now, come and talk to this gentleman over here, he'll tell you what happened."

Alex and Beth waited beside Mrs Keene as she explained to the fire officer that Beth was the granddaughter of Mr Savarese, the man whose kitchen had caught fire, and Alex was her husband. The officer tucked his filthy, flameproof gloves under his arm and shook their hands, reassuring them that the fire had been extinguished and they were just ensuring there was no chance of it reigniting.

"Is my grandfather okay?" Beth asked, not looking much relieved when he assured her that Simon was a little burned and had inhaled some smoke, just as Mrs Keene had said. She was asked to wait a few minutes as he was being treated in the ambulance, then she could go and see him and talk to the paramedics. He'd have to go to hospital, he said, because they'd want to give him a thorough check over.

"Do you know what caused the fire?" Alex asked.

"From what little Mr Savarese has said so far it looks like a forgotten chip pan, sir. Happens all the time." He looked at Beth. "We found a fire blanket in the drawer under the hob, but I suspect your grandfather panicked and threw water on the flames, which is absolutely the wrong thing to do. The fire quickly took hold and spread, and I'm afraid we've only added to the damage putting the fire out. But insurance will get it sorted, and I think Mr Savarese is more shocked than hurt. Which is lucky, let me tell you, because it was like a fireball in there by the time we arrived, and we were here within minutes of receiving the call from his neighbour."

Sounding dazed, Beth thanked him, then said she really must go to her grandad. The fire officer escorted her to the ambulance, and Alex watched as she was helped into it.

Mrs Keene fixed her friendly gaze on Alex. "Turns out that they're the same ambulance crew who attended Sylvia when she'd had the heart attack. They said they were sorry to hear that she hadn't survived it. It's a shame, but it has to be said that poor Simon is not coping at all well. It's only to be expected. He and Sylvia were such a wonderfully close couple, of course the poor lamb's finding it a real struggle on his own. I know how often Anna and Beth pop in. I go round when I can, take him a casserole or a fruit pie, and my Len offers to keep him company, takes him for a drink at the local when he's happy to go. But it's not us he wants, is it? Oh, here comes Beth, dear."

Beth said Simon was about to go to the hospital where his burns and smoke-seared throat could be treated, just as the fire officer had predicted.

"I can go with Pops in the ambulance, Alex. He's not badly hurt, I think, but he is in shock. Could you follow us in the car and come and find us at the hospital?"

Alex hugged her, reeling from the need for them all to go yet again to that hospital.

"I'll just check the house to see the extent of the damage and lock up, and I'll come as soon as I've done that."

Beth started to go back to the ambulance, and suddenly cried out. "I haven't called Mum!" But as she fumbled for her phone in her bag the paramedic called out that they needed to go.

"You go on. I'll phone your mum and leave a message, because if she's midway through a filling she won't be able to talk anyway."

When the ambulance had left, with no siren blaring or blue light flashing, which reassured Alex that it wasn't an emergency situation, his mind raced with what could have happened.

194

Simon had certainly been getting more and more forgetful, which the family put down to his grief and his age, but Alex knew the absent-mindedness had started well before then. Beth seemed either not to have noticed or she had decided to keep her worries to herself until now, but several times Alex had witnessed Simon become confused or unaccountably angry, and he had seen on more than a couple of occasions before she died the puzzled and concerned expression on Sylvia's face during some of the episodes.

When Simon had been told they wanted to turn off Sylvia's life support he'd become so agitated they'd all thought he would have to be sedated for his own sake, and since then those episodes had become more frequent and worse.

Had he put the chip pan on the stove to heat up the oil and then just wandered away, started doing some other task and forgotten about it? Was it simply a moment of forgetfulness like everyone suffered from time to time or was something more worrying going on?

He made the call to Anna and left a message assuring her that Simon was okay but to call him back as soon as she could. Within minutes she was on the phone, her speech slurred because of her numbed mouth, and she said she would go straight to the hospital.

"Thank you for checking the house, Alex, could you pack a couple of things for Dad so he's got what he needs if they keep him in? Pyjamas, shaving things, you know what he'll need. Obviously he's going to have to come and stay with us, he really won't have a choice now."

"I'm just about to go inside, Anna. I'll let you know the situation when I see you at the hospital later. He's going to be fine and Beth is with him, so take your time and drive carefully, okay?"

Alex had actually begun to think that Anna, Beth and Paul were in denial about the state of Simon's mind. They had always found a reason why he asked questions repetitively, forgot to shave, put on clean clothes. He'd mistaken Beth for Sylvia several times, and cried or become angry when he'd realised the mistake. And every time they had all put it down to grief. Alex had been working up to saying something, to suggesting that they get him to the doctor, and now reprimanded himself for not doing so.

The fire officer broke into his thoughts. "Sir? We've done all we can here, so we'll be leaving shortly. It's safe for you to go in the house, but I'd advise you to remove any valuables and make sure the property is secure before you leave. Here's a pamphlet explaining what needs to be done and how, but Mr Savarese needs to get onto his insurance company as soon as he possibly can. It looks worse than it really is, but the kitchen and hall will need a complete refit, and I'm certain they'll insist he's accommodated elsewhere while the work is carried out."

Within minutes it seemed that all the emergency workers had packed up and were gone. Mrs Keene had left to pick up her grandchildren from school, and the other neighbours and spectators had drifted away as the drama had come to an end. Alex stood on the threshold of Simon's house, the acrid smell of burning making his eyes water.

As he walked forward and trod on the doormat just inside the door, there was a slight splash; the whole carpet was sodden. Gingerly, he picked his way to the kitchen and peered in. The sight that greeted his eyes made him draw in a sharp breath with shock. He reminded himself that the fire officer had said it was 'not as bad as it looks', but it still looked really bad.

The walls and ceiling were black and peeling, as were most of the cupboard doors, some of which had warped and blistered. Everything that had been on the counter had charred and melted so they looked like sooty lumps, and only the electric kettle was still recognisable, though its flex and plastic base had liquefied and fused together. The window blind was a sopping, charred remnant of fabric. The linoleum floor was awash with filthy, black water, staining and making the edges along the skirting boards curl and lift.

Alex checked the rest of the downstairs rooms and apart from the sodden carpet in the hall could see no damage anywhere else. Upstairs too seemed to be fine; fortunately the fire had been contained in the kitchen, but the acrid smell throughout the house was awful and his throat was getting sore.

He gathered a few of Simon's things, thinking they'd have be washed before he handed them over at the hospital because of the smoky smell clinging to them.

He found a spare set of keys and left, locking the door behind him. Grateful to be outside in the fresh air he inhaled deeply. A man with a dainty little poodle on a red leather lead hesitated at the gate, then came forward.

"Alex, we have met before. I'm Len Keene, from next door. My wife told me that you might still be here."

"And she told me that you've both been looking in on Simon. Thank you for that, I'm sure he really appreciates it," Alex replied.

Len shook his head and something about his expression made Alex's psychic senses twitch. He waited, knowing that Len would eventually say what he'd specifically come round to say.

"Um, look, I don't know if I'm speaking out of turn, but, well, my wife thinks I ought to tell someone in Simon's family now that Sylvia's gone."

His curiosity piqued, and not in a good way, Alex asked him to go ahead and listened with growing concern as Len described the day he'd found Simon sitting in the pub garden, lost and confused.

"We've been neighbours and friends for years, and I just knew something wasn't right. Sylvia said it was high blood pressure medication affecting him, but I distinctly remember Simon boasting that he didn't have any of the usual ailments associated with his age. We know Sylvia got an emergency appointment and took him to the doctor that day," he said. "But not what the outcome was. There've been other things happening too. Sometimes it's as if he doesn't recognise me or the wife. We'd make arrangements to go out and he'd forget. Then, when Sylvia was in the hospital, he had that little accident in the car which he blew up out of all proportion and now this fire. Well, as I say, something just doesn't seem right with him, and hasn't done for a while. He wasn't right before Sylvia died and we think he's worse now. Of course, you might know all this already, maybe Sylvia told Anna or your wife and Simon's getting the help he needs, but if you're all unaware of how bad he is—we thought someone ought to know."

Alex decided to quickly go back into the house and see if he could find anything relating to treatment for Simon. They had a little office off the hallway, fortunately untouched by the fire, and his eyes landed straight away on a semi-folded letter on the desk. It was an appointment for a brain scan, and the date had already passed. Alex felt a shiver of alarm. Had Simon gone for the scan, or had he ignored it?

By the time Alex reached the hospital Simon had been treated for his burns and was in a ward with side rooms each containing four beds. Anna and Beth were sitting with him, and Beth signalled when she saw Alex that she would come out into the corridor.

"They're keeping him in. What did you find inside the house?"

Alex explained about the damage to the kitchen and hall. "There's no question Simon will have to move in with your mum and dad until it's fixed up. I hope the insurance company will pay out, as it looks as if he left a chip pan unattended and I don't know how they treat things like that. The smoke alarm was working though, so the fire officer told me. How is he?"

"I think Mrs Keene was trying to keep me from panicking when she'd said he wasn't badly hurt, but thankfully he's sleeping now. He was asking for you, though. Come in and sit with us, maybe he'll wake up soon. Mum will be happy to see you too."

Relieved that Simon was resting, because he knew that Simon would immediately ask him as he always did if he had yet made contact with Sylvia, he followed Beth into the ward and said hello first to Anna, whose mouth was still numb and lopsided, and then studied Simon.

His face and neck were reddened as if severely sunburned, his white bushy eyebrows entirely gone, and the bare skin shiny, whether because of burn or some sort of ointment Alex couldn't tell. Both hands were wrapped in something resembling cling film, but the doctor had been able to reassure them that he would heal with minimal scarring.

Beth explained to Alex that Simon had inhaled quite a bit of smoke so would have a sore throat for a day or two, and she'd lost count of how many times she'd heard someone say that he'd been lucky. But how had it happened? Sylvia had never deep fried anything, considering it unhealthy, and Anna hadn't known they even possessed a chip pan.

A nurse came by and checked the patient file hanging at the bottom of the bed and said, "He'll sleep on and off for a couple of hours, and he won't be up to talking much when he wakes as his throat will be very sore, so why don't you go on home? We have your number, but there's really nothing to worry about. He'll need a couple of days with us so we can manage his pain, but he'll be feeling a little better after a good long sleep anyway."

Anna wouldn't leave. A little stunned to find themselves in the hospital and sitting at the bedside of a family member yet again, Alex and Beth decided to stay a little while longer to keep her company.

Alex could see that Anna was tired and distressed but she insisted she wasn't in pain; that would come when the injections the dentist had given her had worn off. He would have to find an opportunity to talk to her in private about his conversation with Len Keene and the letter, because he was pretty sure that if she knew anything about Simon's mental state she'd chosen to say nothing to Beth, and there must be a reason for that.

Beth kept up a bright conversation, determined not to cry. Too many tears had been spent already, she said, and she was reassured to know that her grandfather would be fine once the burns had healed and now he would *have* to go and stay with Anna and Felix, which could only be a good thing. When she said she'd go outside and call Paul, Alex pounced on the chance to talk to Anna.

"Anna, there's no delicate way of saying this and I haven't said anything to Beth or Paul, but did Sylvia tell you that she had to take Simon to see the doctor?" He related what Len Keene had told him and the details in the letter about an appointment for a brain scan.

Looking shocked and upset, Anna shook her head. "No, Mum never said anything. But we all know something's wrong, don't we Alex? I mean, his strange behaviour can't all be down to grief, can it? Oh dear, I just haven't wanted to face up to it, which is utterly stupid of me. I'm going to have to do something, I just have to think what. I'll talk to Felix tonight. Thank you, Alex, I appreciate you telling me, and thank you for not telling Beth or Paul. I'd rather they didn't know until we've got all the information, although I'll understand if you're uncomfortable keeping secrets from Beth."

"It's fine, Anna. There's no sense in worrying her or anyone else until you have the facts. How about you talk to the doctors here? Maybe they can check him over with this new knowledge in mind and you can take it from there."

Simon's eyelids fluttered, and he came to with a startled groan.

Anna immediately ordered him not to move. "You're going to be fine, Dad, but you need to keep still and rest. Are you in pain?"

He shook his head slowly from side to side and tried to speak, but his throat was so sore it came out as if he were talking through gravel and they couldn't understand him. Anna held a glass of water to his lips.

"Don't try to speak, Dad, just sip some water. Look, Beth and Alex are here too. We'll be leaving shortly because the nurse is already making signals that we should go, but I'll be back tomorrow, okay? You're going to come and stay with me and Felix for a little while until you're better."

Simon fixed his eyes, shiny with unshed tears, first upon Anna, then they rested on Beth.

"Sylvia," he whispered.

The two women glanced worriedly at each other, but Alex felt a shiver go through him. Had the ordeal of the fire robbed Simon of the knowledge that Sylvia was gone? Simon switched his gaze to Alex and he tried to raise his bandaged hand towards him. His lips moved but Alex had to lean forward and put his ear close to Simon's mouth to hear what he said.

Simon whispered, "I saw her. I saw Sylvia."

Chapter 25
Kallie

Feeling like living with her mother for the past four and a half weeks had aged her a good ten years, Kallie called up the stairs, "That's the car loaded, are you ready?"

Celia's stitches had been removed and the plaster cast had been replaced with a lightweight, waterproof fibreglass one. Once she had found that she could look after herself in every way without difficulty, Celia was determined to go home. Kallie wasn't sorry.

True, there had been a few moments of fun, but most of the time it had been no fun at all, with some truly awful arguments, and Kallie feeling constantly wrong-footed by Celia's rapidly changing moods. She was looking forward to having the cottage all to herself again, and to seeing her friends, who she'd had to neglect rather than leave Celia in the evenings, as well as during the day while she was at the salon or Rainstones House.

Kallie wasn't yet sure which Celia she would be dealing with today, the mother she was most familiar with, the one who heard voices in the night, or the one who was a funny, kind and caring woman.

There had been no repeats of the phone calls, or the lights flickering, and the television had behaved itself, but Celia had insisted on a couple of occasions that the cottage was haunted. On one occasion, when she insisted that she'd heard someone call her name, she'd suggested that Kallie get the vicar in to exorcise it.

Kallie had said, "You're a scientist, surely you don't believe places can be haunted, let alone in exorcisms?"

Celia had just stared at her and left the room, and exorcisms hadn't been mentioned again.

Another time, though, Celia had come rushing downstairs saying that Verity's perfume bottle had fallen off the dressing table again, she'd seen it happen with her own eyes. Excited rather than scared, Kallie had said, "What if it's Gran and Grandad? After all, it's their cottage and they're probably very pleased that we're here together."

For a long moment Celia hadn't reacted at all, then she'd told Kallie that she was being ridiculous and childish. Kallie had heatedly retorted that Celia had not long before suggested an exorcism, so she must surely believe in ghosts, and her mother had amazed her by denying she'd ever suggested such a thing.

Kallie wasn't sure what she believed, but her mother's attitude rankled so much it had driven Kallie to declare that she positively *did* believe in life after death, that Verity and Walter *were* around and Celia would do well to poke her nose out from her rarefied world of laboratories and lecture halls now and then to see beyond the obvious. That had led to yet another of their fierce rows, which ended with the two of them not speaking for a whole day.

Fortunately that, too, had blown over and now here was Celia, a warm smile on her face.

"I'm looking forward to being back in my own home, as I'm sure you're looking forward to having the cottage to yourself again, but we've had some fun, haven't we?"

Ah, so it was the kind and caring Celia today, the one who used her chosen name with friendliness in her voice rather than calling her 'Kathleen' in her usual imperious way.

They got into the car, Kallie keyed in the directions, and they set off on the three-hour journey to Cambridge. Celia kept up a running commentary all the way to their stopping point for coffee, pointing out landmarks and talking more about her early life, and Kallie let her ramble on because it was pleasant to hear Celia talk this way. Besides, she was learning things about her mother, good things, and appreciating how smart she must be to have risen as high as she did in her field. She'd be retiring soon, though, and Kallie wondered how her mother would pass the time when she no longer had her beloved university to go to.

Kallie ordered a cappuccino for herself and a latte for her mother. Studying the pastries, cakes and cookies on display Kallie said, "Mum, do you want anything to eat?"

There was no reply and Kallie turned to find her mother wasn't behind her in the queue. The young man who was there said, "Your mother went off that way, to the shop I think."

"Oh, thank you."

Kallie bought two Danish pastries and carried the tray to an empty table. The shop was opposite but she couldn't see Celia; she must have gone to the toilet. Minutes went by and Kallie was starting to get worried, but at last Celia was heading towards her.

"Gosh, Mum, where have you been? You disappeared without a word and you've been gone ages."

"Can't I go to the toilet without being interrogated?" There was no humour in her voice, no sparkle in her eye.

Uh-oh, thought Kallie. *Nice taken-over-by-an-alien Celia has left the building and horrid mother Celia has returned.*

"Okay, sorry. I hope your coffee's still hot. I got you an apricot Danish."

Celia took a seat and ate the pastry as if she hadn't eaten for a week then drank the lukewarm coffee in a couple of noisy gulps.

"Can we go now? I don't like it here and I want to get home."

She marched off without waiting for a reply.

Kallie, with a sharp exhale, picked up her handbag and followed her mother to the car. The rest of the journey was made in silence, with Kallie seriously wondering if her mother was schizophrenic. These weren't just mood changes, they were whole personality changes, and it was most disturbing.

At last, they pulled up in front of Celia's apartment block. Still not speaking as the lift took them up, Celia stepped out as soon as the doors opened, leaving Kallie to follow with her suitcase. The place felt cold and sterile having been unoccupied for so many weeks and Kallie hoped her mother would open a few windows to let in some fresh air, but Celia just stalked in and out of the rooms as if checking everything was still as she'd left it.

"Wouldn't you like me to take you to the supermarket before I go? I'd feel happier knowing you had everything you need for at least a few days."

"I told you I'll be fine. I'll order online and get it delivered. I'm sure you want to get on your way, Kathleen, it's a long drive."

Heavens, so she was being dismissed, just like that! She decided to have one more try, though at the same time wondering why she was bothering.

"Mum, are you sure about this? I don't like to think of you being on your own with your wrist not fully healed yet."

"Kathleen, I have been alone all my life. It's the way I like it. I can manage just fine with this new cast, and as you haven't worried about me before I do not understand why you feel you must do so now."

"What? How can you speak to me like that? I—"

Celia put her hand up to stop Kallie continuing. "I know what you have done for me, and I'm very grateful. I will call you in a day or two just to reassure you. You have your own life to live, Kathleen, and I don't want to be a burden to you."

Verity had said virtually the same thing, about not wanting to be a burden, but she had said it and meant it with love. Her mother just wanted her gone and Kallie thought she would burst with indignation.

How dare her mother say such things, how dare she? But she knew that if she stayed a moment longer she would explode and they would be locked in one of their almighty battles and she didn't want to end their time together with yet another argument.

"I'll go. But please ring me tomorrow evening, don't leave it for days or weeks. We've spent almost six weeks together without killing each other, Mum, let's remember that, eh?"

She left quietly, the tears not coming until she was well on her way back to Wiltshire.

At least tomorrow, she kept telling herself, things will be back to normal. Tomorrow I can start enjoying my life again.

Chapter 26
Alex

"Are they absolutely sure, Mum? I can't believe it."

"Neither can I, Beth, darling, but the tests and scans have led to this diagnosis. We all admit now that we knew Dad was in bad shape even before Mum died. We refused for far too long to see it for what it was, but I am assured by the specialist that there was nothing we could have done that would have made any difference to the progress of the disease."

"Alzheimer's." Paul said the word as if it spelled the end of the world.

Alex was listening but not participating much in this family meeting, called by Anna after she'd learned Simon's test results yesterday. It had taken time, but eventually Anna had discovered that Simon had actually missed two hospital appointments that had been made before Sylvia's death. She had had to work hard to get his tests back on track as soon as possible because Simon proved far from co-operative.

Anna, Beth and Paul were naturally the ones most in shock, for the diagnosis, though not entirely unexpected, had rocked them to the core. Felix said they needed to think carefully about Simon's long-term care.

"Oh Felix, he'll stay with us! I will look after him."

"Anna, were you listening to the doctor? The behaviour he's exhibiting now is bad enough, but it will get a lot worse. We need to plan for his going into a care home eventually. His house will definitely have to be sold now."

Alex knew how Simon was going to take that. He was watching television in the living room, full from the huge lunch Anna had fed to everyone, and oblivious to the meeting taking place around the dining table. He'd been living with

Anna and Felix since his discharge from hospital after the fire, but it was fractious for all of them in the household.

Did Simon understand what was happening to him? Alex wondered. Quite likely he did, for he still had many lucid moments, and Anna had elected to be honest with him. He was sure that Sylvia must have known, because Simon's behaviour had been changing for quite some time, but why hadn't she told them?

There was a lot of heated discussion going on, and Alex decided it would be wise to keep his counsel while the blood members of the family argued it out, though he agreed with Felix that Simon's home should now be sold to contribute to the eventual care home fees. Insurance had paid out for repair and redecoration but it was obvious that Simon would not be returning to it.

Since the chip pan incident that had started this whole process, Simon was constantly insisting to them all that he regularly saw Sylvia. Alex had pondered long and hard on this, wondering why he was unable to communicate with Sylvia if Simon could do so. He had tried many times, hoping to learn how she was and to clarify things regarding Simon, but she did not come through and he could only surmise that it was because she didn't want to.

Eventually Anna closed the discussion by announcing there was homemade apple crumble or fresh fruit for dessert, and asked if anyone wanted tea or coffee.

They all chose coffee and Alex volunteered to make it. While he set up the coffee machine and spooned ground beans into the filter, he went over in his mind everything Simon had told him about seeing Sylvia.

"The first time was in a place I didn't recognise," he'd said. "The next time there was a little girl with her. In fact she saw me before Sylvia did. The third time Sylvia was in the garden at home. I'd run outside to get away from the fire, and there she was. I tried to get to her, but no matter how fast I ran, I couldn't reach her." At that point he'd started to cry, and said, "I wasn't dreaming, Alex, I know I wasn't."

Alex had tried to comfort him, but in a flash Simon had pulled away, dashed the tears from his face, and yelled, really yelled at Alex, "But how come, Mr Bloody Bigshot TV Medium, I can see her and you can't!"

Alex hadn't been given a chance to reply. Indeed, he didn't have an answer because he wondered the same thing, but Simon had stomped off, swearing that Alex was nothing but a bloody charlatan.

Anna came in to fetch the desserts and said Simon wanted tea with his apple crumble. When it was made, she put a large slice of crumble into a bowl, poured cream over it, and put it, along with a spoon and Simon's mug of tea, on a tray. Alex stepped forward to open the kitchen door for her, and as he did so, Simon came barrelling in, knocking the tray from Anna's hands. The crockery smashed on the hard tiles of the kitchen floor, and hot tea splashed over Anna's hand and up the wall.

Everyone came running from the dining room and for a long moment there was a stunned silence, until Simon looked from face to face and burst into tears.

This galvanised everyone, and while Felix steered Anna to the sink to run her burned hand under the cold tap and Alex began to pick up the pieces of mug and plate, Beth took charge of Simon.

"I'll take Pops upstairs and see if he'll go to bed," she said. "I think a rest would be a good idea."

Chapter 27
Simon

Woken by daylight seeping around the heavy curtains Simon presumed it must be time to get up and make Sylvia her mug of morning tea.

Tea. What was it about tea that nagged at his mind? There were fragmented pictures in his brain of a tray flying through the air, he could hear smashing crockery and a shriek of someone in pain, but he couldn't pull it all together to understand what it was about.

He put out his hand expecting to touch Sylvia's arm or the curve of her hip, but when he felt nothing but cool sheets he opened his eyes and stared in confusion at the ceiling. It wasn't the ceiling he expected to see.

His ceiling had swirls in the plaster and a pendant light with a beige fringed shade in the centre. This one was smooth with a light that had three bare, candle-shaped bulbs in brass, upward-curving arms.

Had he overslept? Pushing himself up so he could see the clock, he was further nonplussed to find there was no clock where it should be and no mahogany tallboy the alarm clock should be sitting on. The walls were painted a pale peachy colour, not papered with the blue and cream patterned wallpaper, chosen by Sylvia and put up by himself one rainy Sunday.

Confused, he pushed back the duvet and sat up, not recognising its cover either. He swung his legs over the side of the bed and searched with his feet for his slippers, relieved to see that he was wearing familiar pyjamas and his leather slippers were where they should be. He slid his feet into them, but when he stood the momentary comfort he'd felt slipped away and he felt tears of fear and alarm prickle behind his eyes.

He did not know this room.

Why wasn't he in his own home?

And where was Sylvia?

Looking around he realised that he might have been here before, in fact he was becoming more certain of it by the minute, but not being able to recall the rest of the house beyond this room made his heart pound, his head hurt.

Thoughts whirled through his befogged brain as he tried to recall getting into bed last night. He could see his clothes, all neatly folded, on a white rocking chair next to a low, white chest of drawers, but could not remember taking them off and placing them there. On top of the chest he could see his wristwatch, mobile phone and his wallet. He could not remember putting them there either. He noticed that there were shiny patches of skin on his hands. Reaching up to his face, he felt the stubble of a beard that must be several days' growth.

"Sylvia?"

Had he said that out loud? Now he was no longer in a bedroom, no longer in a room at all, but in a garden which he knew, yet didn't know. He turned a half circle and found himself facing a high wrought iron gate set in an archway in a stone wall.

So familiar, yet not.

Like a dream. Yet not a dream.

He walked resolutely forward, calling out for Sylvia. He couldn't have said why he knew she was there, he just did. His heart knew, his soul knew, that his beloved was near.

"Simon! I'm over here!"

There she was, behind the gate, waiting for him! He closed the distance between them and reached out his hand to take hers. They connected and the world stood still as they gazed at each other, not speaking because they didn't need to. Her happiness spread through him, and his into her until it felt as if the gate simply melted away leaving nothing between them. They were melded as one, enclosed in their own bubble where no harm could touch them.

Safe. Warm.

Together.

"Simon! *No!*"

At Sylvia's cry the world tilted, tipping him off balance. Sylvia reached out to hold on to him, pleading with him not to leave her again. But he was being pulled backwards now, unable to stop himself from tumbling over and over in the dark until her dear voice was lost to him, replaced by a loud and insistent buzzing in his ears.

With a heavy thud he fell to his hands and knees onto the carpeted floor, then pitched forward so that he was lying flat on his face.

Winded, confused, he rolled over onto his back and lay where he fell, his fingers digging into the short pile of the carpet. Carpet, not grass. That smooth ceiling above his head again, the light fixture coming in and out of focus. Wherever he had been, the place where his Sylvia waited for him, he was not there now.

He hauled himself up and walked slowly to the closed door, trying to orient himself. On a hook on the back of the door hung his faded blue towelling robe and he quickly pulled it on, tying the belt tightly round his waist, welcoming the familiarity of its feel and its smell. He put his ear to the door, listening hard for any sounds coming from the house, but he could hear nothing, no voices, no signs of people moving about.

Carefully, he eased the door open and peered out onto a landing. It was thickly carpeted in a different colour to the bedroom. In front of him a white balustrade guarded the staircase. He was in the end bedroom, there was a bathroom to his right and two other doors to his left. At last, he could hear other people downstairs, people talking. He went carefully downward, following the voices and the chinking sounds of cutlery on china plates until he was in the kitchen.

The conversation suddenly stopped and two heads swivelled to look at him.

"Dad! You're up! You've slept a long time and nearly missed breakfast. What would you like to eat? Eggs and bacon? Cereal? Toast?"

The woman who had spoken was looking at him expectantly, but her expression changed when he didn't—couldn't—answer her. Who was she?

"Dad?" She came towards him, and he stepped back smartly, his hands out as if warding off her approach. "Dad, what's wrong? Did you have a bad night again?"

Simon stared at the upturned face, the hazel eyes framed with rimless glasses looking at him with such concern. He studied the other person, a man with a shock of silvered hair. Who were these people?

And then he knew. He knew everything. It was as if someone had removed the top of his skull and momentarily removed all his memories from his brain, just scooped every single one of them out, and then poured them back in again and closed his skull with a sharp click.

His knees began to buckle but he caught himself and staggered backwards a couple of steps. Felix, for that's who the silver-haired man was, rushed forward and sat him down. Simon stared around the kitchen and almost laughed with the sheer delight of knowing where he was and who these two people were.

His daughter, Anna, and his son-in-law Felix. Yesterday, he remembered, there had been a lunch, a large gathering around the dining table. He remembered that Beth and her husband Alex had been there, and Paul, his oh-so-successful, entrepreneurial grandson. Paul should get married, he thought. No man should be without a loving wife, a wife like his Sylvia was to him and Anna was to Felix. Beth had let the side down a bit by leaving her husband, but she had been so sad after losing the baby. At least the separation hadn't been for long and they were together again now. Yes, he remembered everything and it felt so good. But wait, was someone else at the lunch? In his mind's eye he swiftly pictured the dining room and the people seated around the table. No, he was pretty certain he's remembered everyone.

He asked for scrambled eggs on toast and watched Anna happily bustle about making it for him. He was a lucky, lucky man, with his family surrounding him with such love and his beloved Sylvia waiting for him not far away. Did they know that she was close and he visited her?

A plate of food was placed in front of him and he picked up a knife and fork. Felix passed him the bottle of ketchup. He ate the eggs with relish and added sugar to the mug of tea placed before him by Anna.

At that moment Paul and a woman arrived, calling out a hello as they entered the kitchen. Had he seen the woman before? Simon wondered.

Paul said, "Just thought we'd call in on our way back to London. Thanks for lunch yesterday." Then he looked at Simon and his face softened with love. "Hi, Pops. Good to see you tucking into breakfast."

Anna then said to the woman with Paul, "Was Lily okay, Adele? Did you get her plan for the new shop sorted out?"

"Oh yes. Isn't it fantastic that she's confident enough to open another shop?" The woman held out her hand to Simon. "How are you today?" she asked.

Simon searched frantically in his mind for the identity of this woman, wondering why she was with Paul, why she seemed so comfortable here. He so badly wanted Sylvia. There were so many people in this room, but where was Sylvia? Where *was* she?

It was his last coherent thought as fear and anger overwhelmed him.

Chapter 28
Kallie

Smoothing out the disposable paper cover on the therapy couch, Kallie gave a swift glance around, and told herself she was ready for another busy Thursday in the DPU. There was a light tap on the door. Hmm, were they starting half an hour early today? She called out to the person to come right on in, and Trish popped her head round the door.

"You're wanted in the office, Kallie."

"Pam's office?"

"No, the main one. They're asking if you could pop up there now. It sounded urgent. Let me know when you're back and I'll bring the first guest in."

As Trish's head withdrew, Kallie wondered what on earth anyone in the main office would want with her. Had she done something wrong? She didn't think so, but couldn't help feeling a little nervous as she made her way to the oldest part of the sprawling building where the administrative team worked on the first floor. As she went in, she realised Trish hadn't said who she should ask for, and at least six people were sitting at desks working.

"Hi, I'm Kallie Harper. I was asked to come up here?"

"Oh yes, Kallie. It's Sasha who wants to see you, go straight in."

Sasha was Head of Personnel, making Kallie even more worried that this had something to do with her employment there. The door was open, but Sasha was scribbling on a notepad so Kallie knocked to let her know she was there.

"Ah, Kallie. Thanks for coming so quickly, I'm aware you're always busy in the DPU, so I won't keep you long. Have a seat."

Really curious now, Kallie took the chair on the other side of the desk.

Sasha opened a file and selected a typed letter from it. "Kallie, I have been having dealings with your mother's solicitor, under strict instructions not to inform you until a certain event had taken place. It has been a mighty uncomfortable time for me, I want you to know that, for I have not understood the need for such secrecy. However, my hands were tied by legal requirements drawn up by your mother's solicitor and agreed by our own legal advisors. I understand that you and she are virtually estranged, is that right?"

Taken aback by the directness of Sasha's question, Kallie replied, "I wouldn't say estranged. We don't see each other but we do talk on the phone. Not regularly, if I'm honest, but we try very hard to stay in touch." She gave a rueful smile. "I'm afraid we're not very good at it."

"Hmm. Well, Kallie, there's no easy way to say this, so I'll just come straight out with it. Your mother has been diagnosed with vascular dementia, and the event of which I speak is about to take place. She is coming here, as a full-time resident in the dementia care wing."

Kallie could say nothing, only stare. It was too much unbelievable information to absorb in one go. Celia hadn't said a word about her illness and now she was coming here? And she'd planned it all through a solicitor? How the hell had she managed it? If Kallie wasn't sitting down she'd fall down. She felt hysteria gathering somewhere under her ribs and had to fight hard to stop it rising and coming out in a cry of rage from her throat. Why had Celia gone about it this way instead of picking up the damned phone and telling her? Kallie would have helped her. She would have!

"Are you all right, Kallie? Shall I get you some water?"

"No! Um… no, thank you. I just need a minute."

"I understand the shock you must be feeling. If you ever need to talk to someone, you know you can go to any of the counsellors here, don't you?"

Kallie nodded, filing that information away for she might well be in need of counselling after this. Despite hearing what Celia had, a condition she knew nothing about but was in the right place to find out, Kallie felt embarrassed, even betrayed. How must it look to Sasha and anyone else here who knew about this?

After a struggle she found her voice. "When is she coming in?"

"Monday next week. Her room is almost ready and she should arrive about mid-afternoon. Kallie, you're very pale, would you like me to ring Pam and ask her to reschedule anyone booked in to see you today? It would be quite understandable if you'd rather go home."

Tempting though it was to walk out of this office, out of the building, into her car and just keep driving until she ran out of road or fuel, Kallie said she would be fine to continue. In fact she would rather continue, for the guests coming in for their therapies would help to keep everything in perspective.

After Sasha had assured her that her mother had made all the necessary financial arrangements and Kallie needn't worry about a thing as far as Celia's residency at Rainstones House was concerned, Kallie left her and scurried back to the hospice wing and the sanctuary of the DPU, wishing that Kevin was working today. He always cheered her up, and she was beginning to suspect, to hope, that he felt about her the way she was beginning to feel about him. She was meeting him for drinks tomorrow evening, so that was something to look forward to.

She let Trish know she was back and went to the treatment room to wait for her first guest. She would put all her worries about her mother to the back of her mind for the next few hours so she could concentrate on making people coping so stoically with their life-limiting illnesses feel just a little bit better.

Chapter 29
Alex

Alex rubbed the tiredness from his eyes and massaged his temples with small circular movements. He was exhausted by the filming schedule of the new Eselmont show, but everyone involved was in good cheer because two channels were negotiating over the rights to broadcast it. On top of that and his other commitments, he was worried about how poor Simon, a full-time resident now in Rainstones House, was sinking further and further into dementia. It felt like he was being pulled in too many directions, and he wondered which part of him would give first.

Today he had a rare Sunday off. He and Beth were about to go to Rainstones House, but first Alex needed to see his dad and have a little time with Amber to help recharge his batteries.

While Beth was busy elsewhere in the house he went into the living room and settled into his father's wine-red, deep-buttoned leather chair. Leaning his head back and placing his palms on the smooth, worn curve of the arms, he opened his mind and called.

His father was immediately there, with Amber playing on the floor at his feet.

"Hi, Dad. How's my little girl?"

"Amber's just bonny, as you can see."

They chatted for a while, Alex asking and being told that his father had not been able to communicate with Sylvia. By the time Beth called that she was ready to go out, about half an hour later, Alex was ready to go. He held Beth close as he told her that their little girl was absolutely fine, and by the time they were on their way to the care home, he felt able to cope with anything.

The smell of roast beef and cabbage assailed Alex as soon as he and Beth entered the dementia care wing. No need to ask what the residents had had for lunch then. He signed in the visitors' book for them both and trailed Beth into the lounge. It was decorated and furnished in a 1950s style to help the residents feel more comfortable.

As they got closer, he heard an angry, raised voice and recognised with a sinking heart that it was Simon, a sure sign that this was one of his bad days. When Simon came into view Alex could see that he had a face like thunder. Spraying spittle he was shouting at poor Anna, who looked very small in front of his towering rage as she tried to keep clear of his flailing arms.

"I do not want to spend another minute in this bloody awful place! Where is Sylvia? Tell her to get here right now, I want to go home!"

Rainstones House was as far from an awful place as you could possibly get, but there were times that Simon did not seem to know where he was.

Placing him in a care home had been an agonising decision for Anna, Beth and Paul, but one they'd had to take and they'd been so pleased to secure a place for him here.

His descent into the mean grip of dementia had been astonishingly rapid once he'd been fully diagnosed, almost as if the diagnosis itself had caused the acceleration. All too soon after he'd arrived to stay with Anna and Felix because he was no longer capable of living alone, Anna had tearfully admitted that she couldn't cope because his behaviour had worsened to the point he was unpredictable and a danger to himself.

They had all watched in dismay as Simon's memory lapses and mood swings became steadily more severe and frightening. More than once, Anna had discovered that he was missing from the house, and on one of those occasions she'd found him outside fumbling with a set of keys, trying to get into her car. Thank goodness he'd been trying to open the door with the wrong key and hadn't thought to use the remote because it made the blood run cold to think what might have happened had he managed to get into the car and drive off.

In between the episodes of manic behaviour, his periods of complete docility were a welcome respite, though still heartbreaking because it was as if he was there only in body, his mind having gone a-wandering who knew where. He didn't wash or shave unless he was told to. Sometimes he spent the whole day shuffling about in his pyjamas and slippers.

The final straw for Anna had been the morning he had walked into the kitchen stark naked, just as she was serving coffee and biscuits to some friends, and he'd become aggressive when she'd ordered him to go and put some clothes on.

The temper tantrums had been the worst thing, though, because they were so uncharacteristic against his normally placid nature, and his volcanic eruptions were truly frightening. And here he was, throwing another almighty strop at the one person who always seemed to be his main point of attack, Anna.

Beth started to rush forward to support Anna when it looked as if Simon might strike her but Alex gently held her back as Erin, one of the senior nurses, went to Simon and said something which calmed him down. He smiled sweetly at her and allowed her to guide him back to his chair.

Erin followed him, grabbing from the bookshelves his life story scrapbook that Anna had put together and gesturing to Anna to come and sit with them. Alex saw how Simon's body relaxed as Erin opened the book and pointed to some photographs, asking questions about them, and he admired the nurse even more as she continued to hold Simon's attention for a few minutes more while another ruckus was starting in the far side of the room. When she handed the scrapbook to Anna and went to deal with the next crisis after taking the time to say some reassuring words to her, Alex and Beth went over to join them.

Anna was visibly shaken and a little tearful, but Simon's eyes were closed, his head resting against the high-backed armchair. At last he looked totally relaxed, the face that had been so fearful, so confused, so angry, was slowly slackening to blankness.

After a few minutes, when it seemed likely that Simon would remain quiet and docile as he usually was following a fit of temper, Anna said she needed to go for a walk and get a breath of fresh air.

"Do you mind if I go with Mum?" Beth said to Alex. "We won't be long."

He said he was quite happy to sit with Simon for as long as they wanted, and the two women left. Mulling over the scene he'd just witnessed, Alex wondered how the staff dealt with these outbursts on a daily basis, not to mention the repetitive questions and behaviours. Respite was often short, with the whole thing starting up again, over and over, day in day out. Having mere admiration for the care staff was not nearly enough.

Erin was still attending to the wild-haired woman who'd started shouting abuse while she'd been dealing with Simon. The woman had almost tripped over a walking stick, Alex had no idea if it was her own or someone else's, and Erin was trying to soothe her with her soft voice.

Suddenly, the woman stopped shouting and set off round the perimeter of the room, not seeming focused on anything in particular yet walking at a cracking pace. Alex watched her, bemused that though she was moving with apparent purpose her face was as expressionless as Simon's.

A young woman in jeans and a pale blue sweater picked up the abandoned walking stick and placed it where it wouldn't be a danger to anyone, then she waited, watching helplessly as Erin called a young nurse to help and they gently steered the fast-pacing woman out of the lounge. Compelled to speak to her, Alex checked Simon to make sure he was still in his own world, then he went over to introduce himself.

"Hello. That was distressing for you, is there anything I can do? My name's Alex, and that's my wife's grandfather over there."

She gave him a tired smile. "I'm Kallie. That's my mother. I heard your wife's grandfather shouting before my mum started up. Awful, isn't it, seeing them this way? I didn't even know my mother knew so many swear words!"

Alex suggested that they sit down, placing himself so he had a clear view of Simon in case he came out of his trance-like state.

"Has she been here long?"

Kallie sighed and told Alex a little of how Celia had come to be resident there. "She lived in Cambridge, but when she was diagnosed she made arrangements to come here so she could be near me. The nurses tell me that this purposeful walking is quite common. They don't know why it happens. There are others here just like her, and would you believe they can walk themselves to exhaustion? Apparently, they get fed and given fluids even as they're on the move if needed, because they are so driven and trying to stop or restrain them only makes things worse."

"So they've taken her to the safe room?"

"Oh, you know about that? Yes, it's nice that this is such an enlightened care home. The organised entertainments, the sensory rooms and communal lounges like this one, I think they're wonderful. I just love all the 1950s-style furniture and everything, don't you? And to have a safe room where they can walk in safety, even go outside from there if the weather's good and they're determined to go out, it's so helpful. Honestly, though, it's weird watching them. They move as if they know where they're going, yet they go round and round in circles and never communicate at all. But who knows what goes on in their heads? Is your wife's grandfather like that?"

Alex heard the question but was distracted before answering because a man and woman had appeared from thin air behind her. Opening his psychic senses he asked if they had a message for her, but either they deliberately ignored him or he hadn't managed to reach them for they didn't acknowledge him in any way.

Thinking quickly to cover his brief distraction, for Kallie was looking at him curiously, he said, "I'm so sorry, I was thinking about what you just said. No, I don't think Simon does that walking thing; I'd no idea it happened to anyone until you told me. In fact, I'd very little knowledge of dementia at all until Simon was diagnosed. There's such a range of symptoms and outcomes, and everyone's different, it seems. Simon used to go wandering about when he lived with my in-laws but I don't know if he does that here. Most of the time he just seems to disappear inside himself, only coming back now and again to rant about something. We're just glad we have a wonderful place like this practically on our doorstep."

"Yes, it's an amazing place. The staff are so compassionate and caring. I've been to a few of the entertainments and the other week they had a couple of pet therapy dogs come in and the patients were allowed to stroke them. It amazed me how much those dogs lifted the atmosphere as soon as they came in and provoked such positive responses." She paused and sighed. "I was only familiar with the hospice side of this place until my mother came in to the dementia wing as a resident. My grandfather died in the hospice, and I work there as a holistic therapist one day a week. A friend of mine, a Day Patient Unit volunteer, her father's been here for years and years. Trish told me about it but I never dreamed I'd be visiting anyone in here."

"Trish? Trish Gartner?"

"Yes, that's right. You know her, obviously. Her father's completely bed-bound and totally unresponsive, isn't that awful?"

At that moment Anna and Beth came back from their walk in the garden, and Alex made the introductions.

"Your mum is a patient here?" asked Beth with sympathy. "Gosh, she must be young."

Kallie smiled. "She's not far off seventy. She was nearly forty when she had me. But dementia can strike at any age, even in children, so I understand. Mum's in great health physically, so she could be here for a long time."

Beth asked where Kallie's mother was now and she explained again about the safe room.

"I won't see her again today, because she'll walk herself to exhaustion and they'll put her straight to bed. She was only here a matter of weeks before her memory became severely affected and it wasn't long before she didn't recognise me any more." Kallie looked rueful. "Sorry, you don't want to hear all that when you're probably going through the same thing. It was nice to meet you, though I'm sure we all wish it was under better circumstances."

Kallie gathered up her coat and bag and left the lounge, giving Alex, Beth and Anna a small smile and a wave of her fingers. Alex followed her with his eyes.

"I know that look," said Beth. "Does she have someone with her?"

"Two people," he replied. "Her grandparents, I think. I could sense them when she and I were talking, but either they weren't aware of me or just didn't want to communicate. I think they're just watching out for her."

"Maybe Kallie's mum is their daughter and that's why they're here, watching over both of them?" Beth squeezed his hand. "Why don't you go outside for a bit, Alex?"

He set off to find his favourite bench, the one hidden from the lounge windows but with a good view of the striking water sculpture.

Once past the area that had been laid out as a giant checkerboard, Alex was pleased to find there was no-one else around. He sat down and contemplated what he'd just witnessed inside, allowing the gentle, musical sound of running water and the little tinkling bells to soothe him. He decided he didn't know nearly enough about dementia in general and Simon's condition in particular, and needed to do some research. If only he had the time! He shouldn't even be here now, but he'd come for Beth's sake and he was glad that he had.

"Would you mind if I sit here?" a friendly voice asked, bringing him out of his reverie. "It's my favourite place as it can't be seen from the house and I can get a precious few minutes uninterrupted."

Alex looked up at the slender figure in front of him, delighted to see that it was Erin, and invited her to join him.

She sat down beside him, her knees audibly clicking. "Sorry about that." She laughed. "My knees have always clicked and the years of bending and lifting takes a terrible toll on the joints, even when you've been trained to do it right. Shame Simon had to go into one of his strops just as you and Beth were walking in. Is Anna okay?"

"She's fine and you were marvellous, as always. It amazes me how you stay so calm. Would you like to be alone? I'd say you deserve some peace and quiet after what you've just had to deal with, but I suppose it's all part and parcel of the working day for you, isn't it?"

He made to rise but Erin placed her hand on his arm and gently but firmly prevented him from leaving.

"Actually, Alex Kelburn, I've been stalking you!" She laughed, making her face look years younger. "I've seen every episode of your TV show, I've read your book, and whenever you've come to the hospice to give one of your inspirational talks I've been sure to be there. Everything about you is absolutely fascinating to me and since your wife's grandfather came in I've been waiting for an opportunity just to talk to you! Can I ask you a question?"

She bit her bottom lip and a slow blush rose from her neck upwards as she waited for his response. He assumed she was going to ask if he could give her a message from a late member of her family or a friend, so he nodded, more than willing to help someone who worked as hard and as compassionately as she did.

Everyone noticed how kind, how gentle she always was with the residents, and the dementia lounge seemed a much duller place when she wasn't on shift. She asked her question but it wasn't at all what he expected.

"Where do they go, the patients who no longer seem to be aware of themselves or their surroundings? I mean, take Simon. One moment he's angry and shouting, the next it's as if he's simply left his body behind and gone somewhere else. Some of the patients are like that all the time, never having lucid moments at all, and I've always wondered... where do they go?"

Alex smiled at the question, glad that it was one he could answer. It might even help her.

She laughed, a little nervously, and flapped her hand at him. "Oh, it's probably a stupid question. They're not dead, are they, so how would you know?"

"It's not stupid at all, Erin. The best way I can describe it is that they're still here physically but their souls have crossed over, or partly crossed over. Simon says that he sees his late wife, he says also that they are very much together when he's over there, but he's always dragged back again even though he doesn't want to come back. I've come across quite a few cases like this."

"So... what you're telling me is, they've crossed over in all but body? Heavens, I should have guessed! I've always suspected they go *somewhere* but I never thought... oh, you've no idea how many people I've tried to talk to and just been dismissed as being fanciful or mad! Is it the same place, though? I mean to same place we go when we die, or are they stuck somewhere waiting for their physical selves to die?"

"Yes, that's it exactly. Not stuck, though. It's more a waiting place, a lovely place, where they stay until their bodies die and then they can go on."

She grinned at that thought. "You know, I overheard you talking to Kallie Harper. Her mother is another case in point, though she exhibits markedly different behaviour to Simon. Mostly, she's what we call non-verbal and non-engaging, but with occasional outbursts of swearing, which Kallie tells me she never did before. Then she has to move and keep moving. When they're like that they behave like clockwork toys that've been wound up and set going until they wind down again, yet mentally they seem to be somewhere else. We call it sundowning because they usually start late afternoon or early evening. If we try and stop them, as we used to do before care protocols changed, they can become really agitated, sometimes aggressive and they and care staff have actually been injured."

"Have you been hurt?"

"Only once, a cracking right hook to my jaw! I was bruised for days, but you can't get angry about it. They don't know what they're doing." She sighed and shook her head. "It pains me to say it, but when I started out it was accepted practice to restrain them when they got agitated. We had this horrid thing called the Buxton chair, which had a built-in table to prevent them from standing up and wandering away by themselves. It took time to make us realise that restraint could sometimes be more dangerous and increased rather than reduced accidents, but by the time I moved here things were already changing and I'm so glad things are different now."

"This seems like a wonderful place," said Alex.

"Oh it is, one of the best! Care in specialist homes like this one is so much kinder, I think, because the patient is at the heart of everything we do. We sit with the family and take as full a picture of their relative as possible, and we suggest that they put a scrapbook together that we can hold here, just as we did with Anna and Simon's grandchildren."

"Yes, it's what you used to calm him down just now, isn't it?"

"Exactly. As all the staff have access to these vital little biographies that set out some history and likes and dislikes, we have an idea of the patients' family, their past and their social lives and so on, and we can use the information to engage with them, or for distraction if we need it. Simple things, like asking them if they want a cup of tea, or giving them some small task to do, it all helps to make life a little easier. Back then we constantly tried to keep them in the present; nowadays we go into their reality and use gentle, persuasive techniques to divert and encourage them in ways that won't stress them."

She paused again, then her hand flew to her mouth. "Oh my goodness, listen to me rabbiting on! You've good ears on you, Alex Kelburn, and you've allowed me to monopolise you when you should be back inside with your family. In fact, we both need to get back before they send out a search party!"

Alex assured her that he'd enjoyed chatting to her and learning about her work. He would be delighted to talk to her again, he told her, for all the time she could spare.

They walked back together, separating when Erin was pulled away on some errand as soon as she was spotted by another member of staff. Alex headed back to Beth, Anna and Simon, and met Trish Gartner on her way out.

She smiled at him and he heard once again a low voice whispering, "*pat-a-cake*," as he did every time he encountered her at the engineering works, sounding like a soft breeze rustling late autumn leaves. All this time he hadn't been sure whether it was male or female, but now he was certain it was a male voice, and that ruled out Trish's great-aunt.

"Hello, Alex. I've been wondering if we'd ever bump into each other here. How's your wife's grandfather?" Trish asked.

"Oh, no change. How about your dad, how's he doing?"

"I can't believe he's still here. I don't want to sound callous, and I think you'll understand because of what you do,

229

but I really wish he wouldn't hang on like this. He's a hundred years old and he's been bedbound and totally unaware of his surroundings for years. How on earth does the heart go on beating when the brain is so damaged with this dreadful disease?"

"Do you believe in life after death, Trish?"

Trish gave a little laugh as she considered. "I think there are three kinds of people when it comes to that particular question, Alex. Those who, like you, believe one hundred per cent; those who say that death is the end of everything and so it's oblivion; and people like me who'd like to believe we continue in some form after we die yet can't quite be convinced of it."

Wanting to seize the opportunity to offer Trish some proof, Alex flexed his psychic senses, certain someone was trying to communicate with her through him. But the connection was still too weak and he could get nothing more so he had no choice but to leave it.

In bed that night, with Beth already fast asleep beside him, Alex lay on his back, hands behind his head, wide awake because his mind was so busy running over and over what he'd witnessed at Rainstones House and the conversations he'd had that day with Erin, Trish and Kallie. Each one of them had given him a lot to think about.

Why had the couple with Kallie, who were most likely her grandparents, not tried to communicate with him? Why, too, did the person saying *pat-a-cake* when he was with Trish not answer him when he acknowledged that he could hear him? And, the most puzzling of all, why hadn't he had any contact from Sylvia?

Chapter 30
Kallie

By five o'clock Kallie had tidied up the treatment room so it was clean and ready to use by the next day's therapists. She changed out of her tunic and trousers into shirt and jeans then, grabbing her bag and jacket, raced to the canteen for coffee and a chat with Trish before they went to the dementia wing. How fast time was passing, she thought. Thursdays were still her special days, and although she hadn't been at Rainstones all that long, it felt as if she'd been there for years.

Trish was already seated at a table by the window, two large slices of cake in front of her.

"I got chocolate and this one is coconut. Do you have a particular preference or shall we have half of each?"

"Half of each sounds good. I'll get the drinks, what'll you have?"

When they were settled they chatted about the guests they'd seen that day.

Trish said, "The new guest turned out to be a real live wire and comedian who had everyone in stitches. It's the joyful and positive days like today that keep me coming back week after week. How about you, you had a busy day, didn't you?"

"Yes, I did, practically back to back appointments. My nose is so full of aromatherapy oils this coffee smells like perfume!" She took a sip and pulled a face. "Tastes like it, too! I was thinking how nervous I was on my first day, but this has really become the highlight of my week. I just feel so bad that my mother has to be in the dementia wing, but... well, life takes some strange turns, doesn't it?"

She took a mouthful of the coconut cake as Trish agreed with her that life was, indeed, strange, then said, "Trish, can

I ask you something? That tall, good looking man, Alex? He introduced himself to me, and he said he knows you. Are you good friends with him, by any chance?"

Trish laughed. "I hope you don't have designs on him, Kallie Harper, because he's very much married and it would break Kevin's heart to learn your affections lie elsewhere. We're not personal friends, I work for him."

Kallie raised her eyebrows and said, "I heard that he's a psychic medium on the telly, do you have something to do with that, then?"

"Oh no, not at all. Remember I told you I had a part-time job in a steel engineering works? Well, Alex is the owner. I don't see him there often, though, he's too busy with the TV show and all the other demands on him. That's why he doesn't come to visit his wife's grandfather all that often, either. I have to admit he scared me a little the first few times I met him, I always wondered if he was reading my mind or something, but he's a lovely guy and so friendly. So, come on, why are you asking me about him?"

Kallie expelled a breath and told Trish she wanted to tell her the whole story but it would take far too long if they were to get over and see their respective parents.

"Kallie, they don't even know we're there! It sounds as if this is important to you, so let's replenish our coffees and you tell me what's on your mind. I presume you consider me a friend or you wouldn't have told me all about your relationship with your mother and your grandparents. If it would help you to talk about whatever's bothering you, then I'm more than happy to listen."

Kallie took a deep breath and told Trish about the strange things that happened in her house. She'd the electrics checked out and everything was fine. Things had settled down for a little while, but then, about the time she learned that Celia was coming to Rainstones House, it had started up again. It didn't scare her, though, she just wondered as to the cause of it.

"After my grandparents died it was things like the TV changing channels or suddenly the volume going really loud, lights going on and off, items going missing only to turn up again when I'd searched absolutely everywhere."

She told Trish then about the time the perfume bottle had tipped off the dressing table and filled the room with her grandmother's scent.

"That happened shortly before Mum arrived to stay with me, and then it happened while Mum was in the room and she saw it slide off the dressing table! I used to joke out loud, telling Walter and Verity to pack it in. Mum said she heard voices and saw shadows. I haven't heard voices but I do see shadows sometimes."

"And you're not scared? I think I would be!"

"No. I feel I ought to be, but I'm really not. I can't say exactly why I think this, but I'm really beginning to suspect that it might be my grandparents and they may be trying to tell me something. If it isn't them, I think I need some help to find out what's going on. I thought of approaching Alex if he was a friend of yours, but if he's somebody famous he's not likely to have time for me, is he?"

"Wow, Kallie, I certainly wasn't expecting all that. It actually sounds quite exciting, though I'm not sure I'd like to spend a night at your place! Your cottage is next to a graveyard, isn't it?"

She dabbed up the last of the chocolate cake crumbs from the plate and licked them from her finger as she considered Kallie's problem. "I'm on the fence when it comes to life after death and all that stuff, but do you really think it could be your grandparents? Alex is very approachable, you know. You've spoken to him, haven't you? Well then, you know he's not at all the arrogant celebrity type that plays on his fame, and I think you should talk to him. If he can't help you directly then maybe he can give you some advice. It's worth a try."

"I suppose. But I don't know that I can just go up and ask him."

Trish laughed and told her she'd just have to, or she'd regret the missed opportunity. She checked the time and said they could still go to the dementia unit for a few minutes.

Feeling bloated, Kallie regretted that she'd eaten so much cake and Trish laughed, saying she felt the same. The cakes in the canteen were really portioned far too generously, but they were irresistible.

When they got to the dementia unit, Trish went to her father's room and Kallie looked for Celia, but there was no sign of her. Sitting in the far corner, as if she'd conjured him up merely by wishing it, was Alex Kelburn. He was sitting with his wife and it looked like Simon Savarese was having a quiet episode, because Alex and Beth were just talking quietly between themselves. Unable to figure out how to approach him, Kallie decided to let it go for now and go on home.

Trish appeared at her side. "Dad's fast asleep so there's no point in staying. Oh, look! I see Alex is over there. Aren't you going to speak to him?"

"Oh, I can't, Trish! Look, he's with his wife. I can't just march up to him, can I?"

"Well, I don't know how else you're going to do it, unless you want me to ask him for you? Ah, he's seen us. Come on, Kallie, don't run away."

Kallie's elbow was held firmly by Trish as Alex approached them. Heavens, he was handsome, in that slightly dishevelled way that she liked.

"Hello, Trish, Kallie. How are you both?"

They both replied at the same time, then Trish said that Kallie needed to ask him something. Horrified and embarrassed at being put on the spot Kallie glowered at her, but Alex gave a friendly smile and waited for her to speak, so she decided it was now or never. She managed to choke out that she was having a problem with her house and she thought it might be haunted.

"Is it frightening you, or do you think someone's just trying to get your attention?"

"Um, perhaps a bit of both? It's been happening on and off since my grandparents died. They both went within months of each other, my grandmother actually died in the cottage so… maybe it's them? I'm sorry to bother you with this, I'm sure you're far too busy." Cheeks flaming, she tried to back away to make her escape, but Trish tightened her grip on her arm.

"Not at all," said Alex.

Kallie watched in silent embarrassment as Alex seemed to be listening to something no-one else could hear.

"Your grandparents are with you, Kallie. They have indeed been trying to get your attention, and as we're speaking I'm getting a good idea of what's going on." He turned to Trish. "And someone is trying to get through to you, too, Trish, but it's too weak for me to work out who it is yet."

"Really?" Kallie and Trish squeaked together.

Alex grinned. "I usually close down my psychic senses when I'm out and about otherwise I get bombarded, but I'm certainly aware of loved ones being with both of you. It will be too difficult to have any kind of communication here, though. Actually, it would help me to come to your house, Kallie, so would you like me to do that? Trish could come along too, if that's okay with both of you?"

Kallie stuttered that she couldn't possibly impose on Alex in that way, but upon his and Trish's insistence she finally gave him her address and they arranged a date and time for him to be there.

He went back to his family, leaving Kallie and Trish looking open-mouthed at each other, astonished that they were going to get the personal services of a highly renowned psychic medium, whether or not they fully believed in what he did.

Chapter 31
Alex

"What's happening? Dad? Dad! Where are you going?"

Hearing Anna call out, Alex and Beth came rushing from the coffee machine, but Erin had already moved in sharply as Simon evaded Anna's grip. She called to another nurse to come and help.

"Take him out, Caroline. Let me talk to Mrs Savarese."

Caroline had to chase after Simon, as he was surprisingly fast on his feet, but when she caught up with him, she gently steered him safely out of the room without touching him.

"Is this the first time you've seen him go walkabout?" Erin asked. "Don't worry, Raina is taking him to the safe room where he can move unimpeded and without danger to himself." She placed her hand on Anna's trembling arm. "This happens, we don't know why. It's as if they are driven by some inner impulse and they simply *must* move. It's recognised these days that it helps to just let them move freely, as long as they are safe, and not try to restrain them."

Anna seemed to be struggling to find her voice, so Alex said, "I know this happens, didn't you tell me it was called sundowning? But how long has Simon been doing this? How long will it last?"

"To answer your first question, it started a couple of days ago. I can't say how long it will last I'm afraid, because there's no time limit. Sometimes they walk for ten or twenty minutes, sometimes it's for hours. Sometimes they'll come back and sit quietly, other times they need to be put to bed because they are exhausted. It's distressing to see, I know, but your dad is safe, I promise you."

Anna was fighting back tears at how fast this appalling thing was happening to her father and Beth, close to tears herself, wrapped her arms around her as she said, "He doesn't even know us any more. Should we stay and wait to see if he comes back?"

Erin smiled kindly and shook her head. "I would suggest you go home. If you like I can make sure someone calls you later so you know he's okay and resting, but I do assure you that he'll be fine. All of us are used to these situations, so your dad will be well taken care of no matter how long he feels compelled to walk."

"I hate this bloody disease so much," whispered Anna, her face crumpling.

"I know, believe me, I know how upsetting this is. Perhaps you should all have a cup of tea before you leave, steady yourself before driving home."

Alex took over then, steering Anna and Beth to a table and returning to the vending machines where he'd been just when the ruckus started.

Trish, who'd been in the room too, came over. Alex knew she visited her father at every possible chance because he was very ill now and she was desperate for it to be over. The whole family wanted it to be over, for the poor man deserved the release his death would bring after all these years. At least, Alex thought, a good thing was that as far as they could tell he had never been in any pain.

Alex introduced Trish to Anna and Beth.

"I'm sorry," she said, "But I couldn't help overhearing what just happened. I'm about to go to the cafeteria before going home, it's more comfortable and the drinks machine is much better than this one, would you like to come with me? I could do with the company."

Beth replied, "I think that's a great idea. Thank you."

"You all go on ahead," said Alex. "I'd like to talk to Erin. I'll come and find you shortly and we'll go home."

As the women walked away, Alex sought out Erin.

237

"Is Simon okay?"

"I'm sure he is, Alex. We'll look after him until he's all walked out and then we'll put him to bed."

"Erin, you'll probably say no, but would it be possible for me to see him in the safe room? I needn't go in and I won't stay long, but I think I might understand more if I can be close to him. And if I understand, we'll all benefit from the knowledge."

The nurse looked at Alex for a long beat, her head on one side as she thought considered his request. At last she nodded.

"I wouldn't grant this to anyone else, but you're special, and I believe you when you say it might be helpful to us all. Okay, Alex. Follow me."

Chapter 32
Simon

As if from a long way away, Simon was conscious of a babble of voices and of being touched by unseen hands, but it felt like he'd been anaesthetised and all his senses were numb. He wanted to speak, but he couldn't get his throat and tongue to form the words. Nothing made sense to him except the sudden, overwhelming urge to move, just to walk and walk and walk until exhaustion took him back into a deep sleep and the beautiful dreams that were not dreams he treasured.

Oh, it felt so good to be on the move! To feel the oxygen filling his lungs and the blood pumping round his body, to feel his muscles flex, the tendons stretch and contract. He was vaguely aware that he was going round in circles in an empty room, the carpet and walls different shades of green, the ceiling summer blue, so it almost felt like he was outside.

He sensed, too, that he was not alone, that there was a tall, dark haired man standing by the door, arms crossed, like a sentinel. He knew him, but the name wouldn't come. What did it matter, though? It didn't matter at all. He didn't want anyone or anything to encroach on this glorious feeling of freedom, because he knew in his soul that if he could just go fast enough he'd go to where he really wanted to be.

Yes! The ground beneath his feet changed from grey carpet to green, sweet grass. The walls and ceiling receded and he was running beneath real blue skies, the colours of everything so intense he wanted to laugh out loud at the sheer beauty of it.

Now he could slow down, now he could stroll at leisure and smell the perfumes wafting in the air, hear the birdsong, feel the warmth of that strange purple-hued sun on his skin.

He'd been here many times before and knew where to go.

Eventually he saw the high wall in the distance, the length of it running side to side as far as the eye could see and beyond. When he'd come across it the first time he'd thought it was an impenetrable barrier, but then he had seen the gate. And behind the gate had been Sylvia, but it had been padlocked and neither of them could get it open. He'd kept coming and at last the chain had fallen away and they had simply looked at each other in wonderment before falling into each other's arms.

But each time was too short, each time he'd been pulled away before he was ready to leave and he'd felt that his heart would break to be torn from her so soon. Lately, the times they had together seemed longer and they would sit together and talk, yet it was never long enough and all too soon he was tugged back to this place of carpet, walls and ceilings.

There she was! She was seated on the grass, waiting for him as always, her back against the great stone wall, her face raised to the sun.

"Sylvia!" His voice echoed as he broke into a run, her name rebounding off the sun-warmed stones of the wall.

Her face beamed with a wide, joyful smile, and she rose to meet him. She wore a necklace of small white flowers with pink centres, and seeing how fresh, how lovely she looked, Simon ran even faster.

Within moments he had closed the gap and clasped her outstretched hands. She looked so young and he *felt* so young. For eons, they stared at each other, communicating with hearts, minds and souls. Oh, how he loved this woman, his true soulmate. Sylvia.

Without speaking and without letting go of hands, they sank down to the ground, cushioned by the warm, green grass. This is where he wanted to be, where he *needed* to be, and he knew Sylvia felt the same. She waited for him here, she'd told him, she would always wait for him. The barrier behind them would never keep them apart again, for she would not go back through the gate until the time came when he could pass through it with her.

He leaned forward until their lips met in a long, loving kiss. He told her how much he loved her and that he hoped never to leave her again.

"I made a daisy chain for you," she said, holding it out to him.

Laughing, he bowed his head to receive it, but before she could place it round his neck he felt it. The tug, that irresistible force pulling him back, dragging him away from Sylvia.

No! No, no, no!

Her expression changed to one of confusion and then alarm. She threw the daisies down and reached out for him but he was already too far away to touch her. He managed only to scream her name and to promise he would be back, and then, once more, his eyes were looking at carpet and walls and ceiling.

The sentinel was still there in the doorway, and he came running to catch him as Simon stumbled and pitched forward with an anguished cry.

Chapter 33
Alex

"So what happened with Pops in the safe room?"

Alex leaned back in his chair as he searched for the words to explain to Beth what he had experienced with Simon at Rainstones House.

"When he was in the hospital after the fire, he told me that he'd seen Sylvia. Naturally, I assumed that Sylvia was appearing to him in much the same way as I see Dad and Amber. In other words, she was going to him and he was able to see her."

"But you've never seen her, have you?"

Alex shook his head. "No. And I've wondered about that. I would have expected her to come through quite soon after she died, but so far, nothing. So, my expectation was that if she came to Simon while he was in the safe room, I would see her too."

As he talked, Alex felt like he was back in that room, standing in the doorway, watching Simon walk round and round, getting faster and seeming to have purpose, yet his face was completely expressionless.

Alex had flexed his senses, opening them wide, sending them towards Simon like radar, thinking that if Sylvia appeared in that room, he would be able to see her.

"What took me by surprise," he said now to Beth, "is that Simon, the *essence* of Simon, if you understand me, left the room! I was connected with him, albeit tenuously, so what I think happens is that he goes to Sylvia, not the other way round!"

Beth frowned, trying to comprehend. After a long pause, she said, "So, am I understanding this right... you're telling me that Pops crossed over? I know you've been there, but you were unconscious after the accident and you call it a near-death experience, but Pops is very much alive. He was even walking round that room. So how is that possible?"

Alex had been surprised himself when he'd realised what was happening. He knew that people with severe dementia, those who no longer knew who they were, had crossed over in spirit while their physical selves still lived. It was agony for their families having to watch their dementia steal their loved ones from them, but the person was unaware of the here and now. They were, in fact, happy on the Other Side.

He explained this to Beth, and while she tried to absorb it, said, "In Simon's case it seems he can help himself cross over by what the care home calls sundowning. He was talking to himself as he walked, and I heard him saying that the whole room was disappearing and he was outside. He talked also of some kind of barrier, a place where Sylvia waited for him, and then… oh, Beth! The look on his face as he called her name!"

He leaned forward and wiped the tears from Beth's face with his thumbs. "It was beautiful to witness, Beth. The sad part is that they can't stay together because Simon's body isn't yet ready to let go."

"So," Beth whispered, "they can be together but only for a short while? Until he's dies and then they'll be together forever?"

"Yes, that's about it. I hadn't realised, though, that they came and went. I've always believed that the spirits of those who were completely unaware of this side of life were over there completely, biding their time somewhere on the Other Side waiting for their bodies to die so they could cross over completely. Simon has taught me this isn't the case. He can cross over for short periods of time, but his physical self drags him back. It's sad, I know, for you to think of losing Pops after losing Sylvia and Amber, but he will be happy to go, Beth. Believe me. He will." He gathered her into his arms and let her cry.

She was and would forever mourn the loss of their daughter. She missed her grandmother every minute of the day, too. How could she cope with the loss of Pops too? But Pops was already leaving them, for his mind was fast disappearing, being stolen piece by piece by dementia.

Chapter 34
Kallie

Kallie waited with Trish, feeling ridiculously nervous. "Maybe he's not going to come?"

"He's only five minutes late, Kallie. Did you catch him on the local news the other night about the little girl whose remains were found on a building site?" When Kallie shook her head she continued, "Apparently the press got hold of the story and his involvement in it, and he agreed to give an interview ahead of the programme being shown. The presenter was trying to goad him about his work, but he was so calm, so articulate throughout. I see him in a whole new light now; you must see it if you can."

They both heard a car draw up, then a door slamming, followed by footsteps coming up the path. There was a sharp rap on the door.

"He's here," said Trish. "Now calm down and let him in."

Alex had to duck slightly as he came through the low door, apologising for being late. Kallie dismissed his apologies, saying she was grateful that he'd agreed to come at all. She went to make coffee, listening from the kitchen as Trish talked to him about the latest goings-on at his factory. It seemed an odd combination, Kallie thought, ownership of an engineering works and being a psychic medium, but then again, what kind of job *would* go alongside being a psychic medium?

She carried the drinks through and sat next to Trish, not having a clue what would come next. She'd meant to try and watch an episode or two of his TV shows on her laptop but had put it off and put if off until it was too late, and she hadn't known about the programme Trish had just mentioned. Now here he was, Alex Kelburn, in her living room, about to give her and Trish a personal reading.

Alex began, "Trish, I said someone is trying to make contact with you. Unfortunately, it's a really weak connection, but I'm pretty sure it's a man. What I hear is pat-a-cake, does that mean anything to you?"

Trish gave an incredulous laugh. "It's what my dad called me! Everyone else calls me Trish, but to Dad I was always his Pat-a-Cake. I was his youngest, you see, and I think he spent more time with me as I was growing up than he did with any of my half-siblings."

Alex frowned. "Okay. I think it *is* your dad that I hear, but he's still alive, isn't he?"

Trish nodded. "Yes, but he's not at all well. He's definitely fading and we're taking it day by day."

"Okay, that makes sense to me actually. I first heard the voice when you started working at the factory and no matter how hard I've tried I just can't get anything else. Let me work with Kallie now and we'll see if anything else comes up for you."

Kallie had to remind herself to breathe as Alex turned his attention to her.

"Kallie, you said you thought this house might be haunted. Tell me what's been happening here that led you to want to talk to me about it."

Still feeling nervous, and wondering just how much he was going to charge for this meeting, Kallie went through the timeline of events. As she explained about the electrics misbehaving and items going missing and reappearing, and the two times her grandmother's perfume bottle fell to the floor, suddenly it all sounded so ridiculous, so trivial. But Alex was listening intently, his focus entirely on her. Eventually her tale was told, and she tailed off not knowing what else to say.

After a silence she realised that Alex was no longer looking at her, but at a point just over her right shoulder.

"Verity," he said. "And Walter. They're here, Kallie."

Trish muttered, "Bloody hell," and when Kallie glanced at her she wasn't sure if her friend was excited, amused or scared.

"As you've told me so much, Kallie, I'm asking for something evidential that they can tell me, something I couldn't know. The most trivial details are usually the ones that provide the most compelling evidence. Ah! Walter is telling me that before he died he sent you out to make a pot of tea. He hopes you weren't too upset, but he really wanted to be alone with Verity when he took his last breath. It's a promise they'd made to each other. Verity says she told you that Walter was always with her in the months leading up to her own death, and he really was. They'd both known that Verity was ill but they had decided not to tell you."

Kallie swallowed back the tears that threatened. Was it really possible that her grandparents were talking to Alex, as if they were in the room?

After a short pause Alex spoke again. "Your grandparents raised you. You and your mother have never been able to get on, but they say you were wrong about her and they wish you could have seen that. Um, wait, Verity is showing me something."

Alex closed his eyes and Kallie could only stare stupidly at him while she waited for whatever was coming next.

"She's showing me boxes of wine glasses." He hesitated, eyes still closed. "You were clearing up and felt angry with your mother because she hadn't been helping you. When she said something about you washing the glasses, it escalated into an argument." He opened his eyes. "Verity was watching you both and it made her very sad because your mother left so quickly after that."

He went on, telling her snippets of things that had happened in a way that left her in no doubt that Verity and Walter were giving him the information. "You didn't mention the mysterious phone calls? Your gran is telling me that they found they were able to make the phone ring but realised they couldn't speak through it and it was worrying you."

Kallie was crying openly now, and so was Trish, who rummaged in her bag for tissues for both of them to mop their tears and blow their noses. But Alex wasn't finished.

"They were watching over Celia too, and knew about her diagnosis and what she was planning."

Alex appeared to be listening intently to something... or someone. Could he really hear Verity and Walter speaking? Kallie could hardly believe it, but he knew so much, had told her so many personal things, how else could he know?

Alex's attention came back to the room, and he said, "I think that's it for now, Kallie," he said. "They're withdrawing their energy from me for now, but please be reassured they're still close to you."

Silence settled in the room for a while, as Kallie took it all in. As she calmed herself down she began to feel a warmth flowing through her body. Wow, she thought, her grandparents were here, in this very room, and they were watching over her all the time! In the space of under an hour Alex had lightened her grief and shifted her perspective about life, death and in-between, and it was wonderful.

Trish asked Alex if he had anything further for her.

He shook his head. "I'm sorry, not right now. But the connection is getting stronger, I can feel it. It could be a grandparent of yours who knew about your dad's nickname for you, and it's their way of telling you they're close by because your dad's time is coming? I promise I'll work on it and I'll let you know as soon as I can."

When she found her voice to offer him another drink, which he declined, she then blushed furiously as she asked him what she owed him.

"Owe me?" He blinked in incomprehension, then laughed, throwing his head back. "Oh, I see! Your grandparents are highly amused at your discomfort, Kallie. I don't want any money from you, it's been my pleasure. I shall be on my way now, ladies, and maybe I'll see you both at Rainstones House soon."

When he'd gone, Kallie made more coffee for her and Trish and they talked about how amazing Alex was and dissected what they both thought was one of the most fascinating couple of hours they'd ever spent.

"What do you make of it, Kallie? He seemed to be giving you a lot of information that he couldn't have known."

Kallie nodded. "I know. It was astonishing! I had hoped it was Walter and Verity and now I know it is I feel just great." She looked all around the room and spoke up to the ceiling, "Thank you! Feel free to visit any time, I love you both so much!"

Trish laughed. "He didn't have anything for me, though."

Kallie asked about the pat-a-cake and Trish explained again how it had been her father's nickname for her for as long as she could remember.

"But he's not dead, so it can't be him. Maybe Alex is right and someone is around because Dad's going to die soon. Don't be shocked, but I'm hoping it will be soon. Dad's been in that care home for so long, and seems to be totally unaware of his surroundings. He needs to be released."

"I'm not shocked, Trish. I understand how you feel, I really do."

Trish considered for a moment and said, "Imagine being able to communicate with the dead. What must that be like? Would you like to be able to do it?"

"Yes, I think I would," she replied after a moment's thought. "At least, I wouldn't want to do it for strangers like Alex does, but I'd like to be able to see and talk to my grandparents at any time without having to have a go-between to do it for me."

Trish chuckled and nudged Kallie, saying, "But isn't it great when the go-between is someone as gorgeous as Alex Kelburn?"

Chapter 35
Kallie

The familiar scrawled writing had Kallie taking the proffered envelope with some trepidation.

"Where did this come from, Erin? It's my mother's writing so she must have done this ages ago."

"It was given to Sasha for safekeeping when Celia arrived here and she handed it to me yesterday to pass on to you when you came in. There was another letter with it explaining how she wanted things to be handled and why. I hope you don't mind but I have seen that accompanying letter as it was addressed to the staff of the dementia unit who had direct dealings with your mother, and Sasha particularly thought it might help me to read it before I gave this sealed envelope to you. Apparently, your mother understood her prognosis and wanted you to have this if, or when, she became unable to recognise you."

She gave a gentle smile and patted Kallie's hand. "I'm sorry that happened so quickly after she arrived. There's no knowing how fast any form of dementia will progress, and exactly which of the many symptoms each person will experience."

"Maybe it's just as well she's no longer aware because now she doesn't know what's happening to her, does she?"

Erin shook her head. "We don't know that she is truly unaware, but we just can't be certain once they get to the non-communicative stage. From what Celia told me, though, when she first arrived here, she had it all worked out from the moment she even suspected something was wrong. She didn't know if you would visit her, and she said she would understand if you didn't and no-one was to judge you for it.

From what you've told me you two certainly had a difficult relationship."

Kallie sighed. "That we did."

She smoothed the fabric of her tunic with one hand, looking down at the thick envelope she held in her other hand. After a long pause, she switched her gaze back to Erin, who was regarding her fondly and with so much sympathy Kallie was in danger of bursting into tears.

"Do you know what's in it?"

Erin explained that the envelope had remained sealed by the solicitor's stamp as it was meant for Kallie's eyes only. "So no-one here knows what's in it, Kallie."

Kallie sighed. "I wish we could have had a better relationship."

"I know it was awkward when your mum arrived and you found visiting her such a strain, but you kept coming and I'm sure in my heart that she appreciated it. As I say, no-one but Celia knows what's in that envelope and as she's given every other detail a great deal of thought then I imagine this is important. I suggest you take it home, maybe pour yourself a glass of wine, and open it when you know you won't be disturbed. Maybe it will help you understand her a little, Kallie, or maybe it's nothing more than her funeral instructions." Erin placed her hand over Kallie's and gave it a light squeeze. "There's only one way to find out."

Kallie gave a short, mirthless laugh. "God. I can hardly take it in. All my life Celia has surprised me, and not usually in a good way, and now this. I hardly knew her really, and seeing her struggle with dementia has just about broken my heart, because the chance for us to make peace with each other has well and truly gone. Maybe, probably, neither of us would have taken that chance anyway, who knows? But it's so desperately sad to see such a brilliant mind wiped out. In a strange way, I do miss her."

"Of course you miss her. Parents and children may not always see eye to eye, I've had a few fall outs with my own kids," said Erin. "But the bond is always there. Just you keep on coming and sitting with her, because I do believe that at some level she knows you are there. Now then, I need to get home. It's been a long day and I need my cup of tea the way only my husband can make it. I hope whatever's in that envelope brings you some sense of peace."

Kallie smiled, glad that it had been Erin, the lovely, thoughtful senior nurse, who'd been entrusted to pass on the letter. The other nurses were truly wonderful too, but Erin was extra special in Kallie's eyes, and she knew Trish felt the same way. As soon as she was able, she did as Erin suggested, went home, locked the doors, poured a glass of wine, switched off her phone, and opened this last communication she was ever likely to get from her mother.

The envelope had been sealed with a thick circle of red wax and Kallie struggled to prise the flap open and keep the envelope intact. Celia had scrawled across the front in two lines: Strictly Private & Confidential. Only to be opened by Kathleen Harper.

Kathleen. That hated name. But did she hate it really? Hadn't she changed it to even further distance herself from her mother? She'd always blamed Celia for the deep flaws in their relationship, but now, too late, she was beginning to realise that once she'd reached adulthood and been able to reason things out, she had to take her share of the blame for the sometimes awful way they'd behaved in each other's company.

She heaved a sigh, trying to picture Celia writing this shortly after she'd received the dreadful diagnosis. She could imagine the scientist in her taking over, that deep need to research, to analyse, to *know* as much as there was to know.

How sad, though, how dreadful, that Celia had learned of it just weeks after she'd returned to Cambridge when her broken arm had sufficiently healed so she could look after herself. She had never told Kallie, choosing to keep her in the dark until just days before she'd moved into Rainstones House.

To say she had been stunned and confused at her mother's arrival in the dementia care wing was an understatement, but Kallie had gone to see her that same evening. For the first few weeks Celia had been okay, there'd been very few signs that there was anything wrong with her, just some absent-mindedness and the constant hand-wringing that Kallie had never seen before. But the respite had been short and with the benefit of hindsight, Kallie had realised too late that her mother's strange and erratic behaviour while she was staying at the cottage with her was very likely to have been due to the onset of the disease.

The flap came open at last, with just a little tear at the edge where the wax seal was so firmly stuck. She extracted several thick sheets of writing paper, pale cream like the envelope, each page covered both sides in her mother's tight, untidy handwriting. Kallie reached for her glass of wine and settled back to read.

Chapter 36
Alex

Lying wide awake in the early hours, Alex yet again mulled over the events of the past few days and weeks. Flora and Rachel and their sad story; Sylvia's death and Simon having to go to Rainstones House; the reading he had done for Kallie and Trish. It had been disappointing that he hadn't been able to connect with whoever was calling out 'pat-a-cake' when he was near to Trish, but he was sure that would come.

So much had happened. He'd thought he'd known all he needed to know about life, death and the in-between, but he'd learned something new from all these things.

He'd discovered through watching Simon in the safe room that Simon could leave his physical body and visit Sylvia on the Other Side, and it seemed Celia was doing the same. He thought of what Verity and Walter had told him, *"Celia is here with us sometimes. She likes to watch over Kallie, as we do, but she doesn't, or can't, stay long. Her spirit is out of her body and her body calls her back because it's not ready to let go."*

They hadn't wanted him to tell Kallie this and of course he hadn't even so much as hinted it to her. They also mentioned a letter that Kallie's mother had written. Alex wondered if Kallie had received it and if it had helped. Kallie hadn't said much, but Alex had been able to tell there was a deep sadness for her in connection with Celia.

Now his thoughts wandered to Rachel. She hadn't yet been arrested and charged, but Alex felt it was just a matter of time and he was so sad that he was unable to help her when that happened. At least he'd been able to tell her what had happened to her daughter, he had brought her and Flora together for that brief time, and that was surely worth a great deal.

A glance at the alarm clock showed him it was ten past five, and though he had a busy day ahead of him he knew he wouldn't get back to sleep, so he decided to go down to the office and work through a few more of the fan letters Marcia had sent him

Rising quietly so as not to disturb Beth, he fumbled his way downstairs in the dark until he reached his study. Snapping on the light he sat at his desk and pulled the latest batch of correspondence towards him. He'd hardly started reading the first one, from someone telling him their four-year-old son seemed to remember a previous incarnation, when a psychic vibration disturbed the air.

Alex closed his eyes and allowed his mind to flex and open. Immediately he recognised who had come to visit.

"Hi, Alex."

As the little girl spoke into his mind, he became aware of other presences. One, though faint as if she was some distance away, was Grace, but the other one he couldn't identify. He hoped it was a relative of Flora's, someone who had come to look after her over there, now she had fulfilled her wish to communicate with her mother.

"Do you have someone with you, Flora?"

The little girl giggled. *"Yes I do! But she's finding it hard to talk to you. I think she's a little scared."*

This was delivered in a whisper, so Alex whispered back, *"Tell her there's nothing to be scared of, I don't bite! Is it a relation of yours, Flora?"*

"No. Not really and truly. But I've kind of adopted her as my granny, as I don't have one."

Alex gave this some thought. Rachel had told him that her parents had thrown her out and cut all contact when she'd got pregnant in her early teens. He'd been shocked beyond belief, that people could abandon their only child, especially in an age where pregnancy out of wedlock was no longer considered shameful. Why, he'd thought, couldn't they at least have placed her somewhere away from home until she'd had the baby? The baby, Flora, could have been adopted by a warm and loving family, and then maybe she wouldn't have lived the life forced upon her, and died the way she had so terribly young.

Ah well. No point in going over all that.

"I know what you're thinking," said Flora, shocking Alex back into the present. *"But Grace has explained things to me, and it could never have happened in any other way. I love my mum, I don't blame her for any of it."*

Alex smiled and said he was very pleased to hear it.

"Now then, young lady, so are you going to introduce me to your new granny? Shall we see if we can show her how to communicate?"

Laughing, Flora skipped from Alex's view and then reappeared, pulling along someone by the hand.

His jaw dropped as the figure appeared in front of him and his senses connected with hers.

"Sylvia! Oh thank goodness! I've waited so long for you to come through."

She looked beautiful, Alex thought, younger and, well, luminescent is the only word he could think of to describe her.

He could feel her trying to communicate, but he was unable to understand her. *"Flora, sweetheart, can you help Sylvia speak to me?"*

He watched as Flora skipped over to Sylvia and took her hand. Sounding very grown up, she said, "When I was standing by my grave Alex told me to speak to him with my mind. You just need to think the words and he hears them. It's a nice feeling."

Sylvia smiled down at the little girl and stroked her hair. She looked back at Alex and he could see her face tighten with concentration. At last, at long last, he felt their connection being made.

"Are you alright, Sylvia? I don't need to tell you how concerned everyone has been when I had to keep on telling them I hadn't been able to make contact with you."

"I'm sorry, Alex. I can't explain it except to say my whole focus has been Simon. I feel so stupid for not telling you all about my suspicions, it would have saved a lot of pain if I had. But he comes here, did you know that?"

Alex nodded. "Yes. It took me a while to realise that it was that way round, not you visiting him. He's okay, Sylvia, he's being well looked after at Rainstones."

"I know, but... it's so hard to watch him there, how he is. And every time he comes here it seems as if we have just a couple of moments before he's pulled back again. It's so cruel."

Alex said he understood, and that the only thing he could say was that things had to take their natural course. "He'll be over soon enough, Sylvia, you just have to be patient."

Flora came back into Alex's psychic vision, skipping around Sylvia, singing The Skye Boat Song.

Alex laughed, "So you've learned the whole song? You sing it much better that I do!"

Flora giggled and said to Sylvia, "Alex can't sing at all. HE sounds like a frog!"

"Charming," laughed Alex.

The little girl stopped her skipping and slipped her hand into Sylvia's. "Someone's coming," she whispered.

They all waited, and Alex called out as soon as the figures were near enough. "Hey, Dad! You've brought Amber, too, that's great. Come and meet Sylvia and Flora."

To Flora he said, "You have a granny, Flora, I think now you also have a little sister. How's that?"

As they clustered together, making introductions, Flora took Amber's little hand and told her she wanted to show her how to make daisy chains.

A new sensation hit Alex's senses, and he braced himself for the power that was Grace to enter the scene. She stayed a little way behind his father, Sylvia and the two little girls, spreading her arms as if to embrace the new family grouping in front of her. Her extraordinary eyes bored into Alex and she bowed her head. When she looked up again her face was lit with one of her rare and beautiful smiles.

Chapter 37
Alex

By mid-afternoon Alex had made good headway through the pile of letters Marcia had forwarded to him. Beth was at work, the house was silent, and he'd been so deep in concentration that when his phone rang his hand jerked, scoring a jagged black line across the page he was writing notes on. Seeing it was Paul's office he answered with a cheery hello.

"Good afternoon, Alex, it's Marcia. Some exciting news for you, I've just had a call from a gentleman claiming to know something about Flora's death."

"What!" His mind raced, and although he didn't believe it could be, he asked, "Not the man Flora says was at the house?"

"No. But he says he can tell you about him. He'd like to talk to you."

Stunned, Alex asked, "Is he genuine, do you think? Did he give you any information at all that makes you think he might be for real?"

Marcia's warm voice answered, "Actually, yes. His name is Gethyn Ewans and he told me he works at a hostel for the homeless in Manchester. He gave me the phone number, but I checked for myself that this place exists, and I rang them and asked if they had a man by that name on their staff. They put me through and I spoke to him again briefly. The police have the story and now he's keen meet you."

Alex couldn't deny the frisson of excitement that ran through him. Could it be that this man had answers that would prove Flora's and Rachel's accounts of what happened in that derelict house? He pulled his diary towards him to check how soon he'd be able to get to Manchester.

As if knowing what he was doing, Marcia said, "You don't have to go Manchester to see him, Alex. Gethyn has family in Salisbury and suggests you meet him at a café there on Saturday. I'll give you his number."

***

Alex was the first to arrive in the charming back street coffee bar that Gethyn had suggested. It was busy, but he spotted a trio of women vacating a corner table that was away from the door and the counter. He'd just shrugged off his jacket and draped it over the back of his chair when a man came in and he knew instantly that it was Gethyn Ewans. He was stocky, quite short, wearing his long reddish-blond hair in a ponytail. Alex guessed him to be in his late twenties, but when he came closer, he amended that to late thirties.

They shook hands and introduced themselves, then waited quietly until their coffee was brought over.

"Okay," said Alex, "You have me intrigued."

Gethyn wrapped his hands round his coffee cup and looked at Alex for a long moment, his blue eyes enlarged by the thick lenses of his round, gold-rimmed glasses. "Thank you for agreeing to meet me. I had already planned to come and visit my parents this weekend, so it's worked out for both of us. It's quite a story. I didn't know about the case and your involvement in it until I did a bit of research, and then I, kind of, got a firm nudge that I needed to talk to you."

Alex, not at all surprised by the soft Welsh accent, was however taken aback by what his words implied. His senses prickled and he said, "Are you...?"

Gethyn nodded his head. "Psychic? Yes, I am. Runs in the family, actually. My sister and a cousin both do platform work and private readings. It's not for me, though. Standing in front of crowds of people like you would be beyond me." He smiled, his gentle eyes crinkling at the corners. "I never ignore the nudges, though, and the gift certainly comes in handy with my hostel work."

Alex leaned forward, excited now. "So your own senses led you to believe what the man told you? What have the police said? No." He held his hands up. "Don't tell me about the police yet, just tell me the whole story as you heard it."

Gethyn began by describing the hostel, how they took in homeless people from the streets of Manchester and tried to help them.

"I was on night shift two weeks ago when this chap came in, Colin Collier. Ex-soldier. He was in a bad way, both psychologically and physically. Very sick. We fed him, let him take a long, hot shower, gave him clean clothes, and he agreed to stay the night. Many of them don't. Something keeps them on the streets, no matter how hard we try to get them to stay with us, to accept whatever help we can give them to get them back on track."

He paused, took a couple of sips of his coffee. Alex remained silent, giving Gethyn time to get the story out in his own time.

"When I did my final round that night before turning in—we have rooms for the night shift staff—I saw that the bunk allocated to Colin was empty. I went looking for him, worried that he'd upped and left. I knew he was in urgent need of medical care, and I really didn't want him to leave. He was in the backyard, lying on one of the benches we have out there for outdoor meals. It was a clear night, new moon. He said he liked to look at the stars.

"He had the kind of lung-rattling cough that I know from experience doesn't bode well, and I told him I'd arrange for him to see a doctor in the morning. He said it was too late for that, and he was ready to go anyway.

"He hadn't made eye contact once, not with me or anyone else, but he looked at me then, and I felt my senses ignite. It's a feeling you know well, I imagine?"

Alex nodded, already feeling he knew where this was going. He asked Gethyn to wait while he fetched two more coffees, then Gethyn started speaking again.

"Colin said he wanted to tell me something, a secret he'd held for a very long time but which he now needed to get off his chest. He explained that he'd been in the forces and was discharged for medical reasons. He suffered badly from PTSD, as so many of them do, but he had a supportive wife and a job on the building sites. It was all going well, but then his mental issues got worse and worse. Nightmares, flashbacks, that kind of thing. As happens so often, he couldn't get the care he needed, his marriage ended and he lost his job." He pushed the empty cup away from him and pulled the fresh one towards him, once again cupping his hands around it.

Alex murmured, "I can see how the tragedy unfolded. He lost everything, didn't he? So, just how did his world collide with Flora's?"

Gethyn sighed. "He'd been working on that particular building site but got laid off because of his increasingly erratic behaviour. He'd been living in shared accommodation following the marriage break-up, but losing his job meant he could no longer pay the rent and he ended up on the streets. When the weather took a turn for the worse he had the idea of breaking into one of the condemned houses for shelter."

Alex interjected, "And of all the houses there were to choose from, he picked that one."

"Yes. He said the boards had been removed from the kitchen window so he climbed in that way. He had no idea, of course, that the little girl was upstairs. He stowed his gear in one of the downstairs rooms then went out to scout around, see if he could find anything he could sell. When he came back, he opened the door and this figure just rushed at him, screaming. He didn't remember shoving her, but if he did it was a reflex action. She fell, knocking her head on the corner of the hearth."

"So it was an accident," said Alex. "It happened just as Flora told me."

"He insists he didn't mean to harm her. He didn't even know it was a child until he got a close look at her, and by that time she was dead."

Alex blew out his breath and ran his hands through his hair. "Wow. Did he tell you how he buried her, Gethyn? I mean, the ground would have been soft from all the rain, but she was buried very deep."

"He panicked at first, just thought of running and leaving her there. But there were rats, and he couldn't bear the thought of her being eaten by rats. It didn't occur to him that she wasn't there alone. He assumed she was a runaway. He knew the security code to get into the site office, he took a key to one of the diggers and…"

"Wow again," exclaimed Alex. "If he hadn't been able to use the digger maybe he would have left Flora there, and then Rachel would have found her. Too late, of course, but at least she wouldn't have had to go all these years not knowing where Flora was. Many would say it was a perfect storm of coincidences, except you and I both know there's no such thing."

Gethyn remained silent for a while, staring off into the distance. "You know, Colin still had the key to that digger. He showed it to me. He was distraught, sobbing as he told me about wrapping Flora in his sleeping bag and burying her. I asked him if he'd be willing to go to the police."

"You said they have the story, so I presume you called them, or took him to the station?"

Gethyn gave a wry smile and shook his head. "I wanted to contact them as soon as he'd finished his story, but he asked me to help him record his story first. Everyone was asleep, so we sat in the kitchen and he repeated it all while I filmed it on my mobile. His coughing got worse and worse, blood was coming up, so I called the attending doctor. Colin was admitted to hospital straight away and then I called the police."

Alex said, "So he validated everything Flora told me, and now the police know that Rachel didn't have anything to do with it."

Gethyn narrowed his eyes and looked keenly at him. "But she did have something to do with it, didn't she? Making Flora live that life. It was child neglect, at the very least. And had she lived, she'd be, what? Twenty, twenty-one? Would she have been able to escape the spiral that Rachel was on, or would she have ended up on the streets or in a hostel too?"

"Yes," replied Alex sadly. "You're right. And Rachel knows it. She'll still be punished by the authorities in some way, I'm sure. And to tell you the truth, Gethyn, she wants to be punished. So where is Colin now?"

Gethyn didn't speak for quite a while, and Alex knew the answer even before Gethyn gave it.

"Well, the police interviewed him at the hospital as soon as they'd seen the video confession. I think he held on just long enough to make his peace and then he let go. He died in the early hours the following morning."

Alex thanked Gethyn for taking the trouble to contact him and tell him this whole, tragic tale and they chatted about other matters for a little while before going their separate ways.

Driving home, he could only wonder at the twists and turns of fate that led Flora, Rachel and Colin to that condemned house.

Chapter 38
Kallie

Kallie gave up trying to sleep as soon as the dawn chorus started. Rising from her bed, she said good morning to Walter and Verity, wishing with all her heart that she could see them like Alex Kelburn did because it felt as if she'd never needed them as much as she did now. Alex's visit had clarified many things for her, but had her grandparents known about the letter? Well, if they hadn't, perhaps they'd both been reading it over her shoulder last night.

Had they cried as much as she had? She'd been so choked at times she had hardly been able to read some of the lines. All her life she'd seen her mother as this remote figure who hadn't wanted her and would have palmed her off to strangers if Verity and Walter hadn't stepped in and insisted they would raise her. She'd thought Celia unfeeling and unloving, argumentative and difficult. She'd hated her for not telling her who her father was. Well, now she'd never know, and it didn't matter. It really didn't.

Kallie had enjoyed a wonderful childhood, but instead of recognising that it was thanks to her mother, who had made sure of it by allowing her to be raised by two people who knew how to be the kind of parents Kallie needed, the two people who had always loved and understood her, Kallie had seen it as a desertion of maternal duty. But Celia had known her limitations, had known that she would not have made a good mother; it was simply the way she'd been made. She'd wanted the best for her daughter and had made sure she got it.

Never, not once in her life, had Kallie thought of Celia as a person with a history that had little or nothing to do with her. Never had she considered how her mother thought about things, how she felt. Everything was coloured by the fractious relationship they'd had, and Kallie had laid the blame for that squarely on the shoulders of her mother.

What kind of a daughter had she been not to see beyond the woman who cared nothing for appearances, the woman with a brilliant scientific mind who was revered in her field? Why had she never signed even a birthday or Christmas card for her?

Her mouth was so dry she could hardly swallow so she drank a large glass of fresh, cold water while the kettle boiled for tea. Trying to decide whether to go back to bed and drink the tea there, Kallie was instead drawn back to the couch, where the pages of Celia's letter still lay. How was she going to get through the morning at the salon knowing what she now knew?

All this time she'd been visiting Celia it had been nothing more than a duty and now she was desperate to see her, just desperate to talk to her. Celia might not hear her and would not be able to respond in any case, but Kallie needed to talk to her anyway. She needed to tell her mother how grateful she was, how sorry she was, how *desperate* she was that Celia should know that she loved her.

Tea, a cooked breakfast and a hot shower revived her, and having some of her favourite clients booked in meant she managed to enjoy her shift at the salon.

After a quick lunch back at the cottage, Kallie felt the return of her raw emotions as she walked into the lounge of Rainstones House. Her plan was to catch a quick word with Erin, sit with Celia for half an hour, then accompany her to the lounge for the afternoon's entertainment, a singalong with a quartet who sang songs from the 1930s and 1940s.

Kallie spotted Erin across the room and headed over. "Erin, can I talk to you for a moment please?"

The senior nurse turned with a warm smile. "Of course you can, Kallie. Have you heard from Trish about her dad?"

Kallie shook her head.

"He died this morning. Trish and her family are here sorting things out. They're all emotional, of course, but I know it's a relief for them. It's the longest I've ever known a patient be totally unresponsive."

"Thank you for telling me. I'll give Trish a call later. Look, Erin, I know you're busy and you've got lots to do getting ready for the afternoon entertainment, I just wondered..."

Erin glanced at the cream envelope Kallie held out to her, and Kallie could tell that she recognised it.

"Would you read it later, Erin, when you have time? Please? You look after her and apart from the very brief details she chose to share with anyone while she still could, you've no idea who she really was, just as I didn't. I honestly think she'd like you to read it, to know some important things about her life. And it would help me too to have another person, someone I trust, to share this with. If I'm asking too much, I'm sorry..." Kallie trailed off, embarrassed.

"Oh, Kallie, I'm touched, I really am. But are you sure?"

Kallie nodded and Erin took the envelope, promising that she would read it as soon as she could and return it. She briefly held Kallie in her arms, then gave her a little shake as she looked deep into her eyes.

"Go and talk to Celia, Kallie. Tell her you've read the letter. Talk to her and tell her how you feel."

Kallie let herself into her mother's room, so similar to the one where her grandfather had spent his last days in the hospice part of the building. The main difference was the absence of French doors to a patio, to prevent residents like Celia from going wandering by themselves.

Celia seemed to be sleeping, so Kallie sat in a chair beside the bed and waited for a while to see if she would wake. Eventually her eyes opened, but Celia merely stared upwards and did not acknowledge Kallie.

"I gave your letter to Erin, Mum," Kallie began. "I hope you don't mind, but somehow I thought you'd like her to

267

know more about you. She's a very special lady, don't you think?"

No response, not even a flicker or an eyelid or movement of a finger.

"Anyway, I wanted to talk to you, to tell you… to tell you how grateful I am you wrote it. It's… it's really helped me to understand you. To understand *us*."

She swallowed back tears. Her mother was never any good with emotional displays and Kallie, feeling that at some level Celia was aware of her and could hear her, was determined to say her piece without crying.

Somehow she had to give back to Celia what she had given her, an explanation of her own behaviour and a heart-felt declaration of sorrow and love. Not in writing, of course, that was no longer an option, but by spoken words. With a quick prayer to whoever may be listening, Kallie asked that all the words she needed would come.

Chapter 39
Alex

Alex, Beth and Anna were among the last of the invited relatives to arrive. When they'd learned of the singalong, Anna had asked that they all go along because Simon had an incredible memory for music and lyrics and she hoped that this would spark something in him.

Simon was quiet these days, with the sundowning happening every day at about the same time for the same length of time. Afterwards, he would go docilely to bed and sleep a straight ten hours, sometimes more. It still bothered Anna and Beth, but Alex understood now why he did it.

He led Anna and Beth to some seats and, spotting Kallie, said he wanted a quick word with her and he'd be back.

"Hi, Kallie." He looked closely at her, sensing that she was deeply emotional about something. She was pale, red-eyed, and she looked quite drained. "Are you okay?"

"I'm fine, thank you. Well, not really *fine*, but... Alex, did my grandparents tell you that Mum had written me a letter?"

Alex nodded. "Yes, and they asked me not to tell you because Celia had arranged under what circumstances you would receive it. I presume you've got it now? How is she?"

"Completely unaware of me, but I told her how much that letter meant to me. You know, I learned more about her from that letter than I did during my whole life, and it explained such a lot. I only wish she'd written it sooner. Years sooner, in fact. I've just spent the best part of an hour talking to her about everything, but there wasn't even a flicker to show that she'd heard me."

"Believe me, Kallie, she heard you and she knows how you feel."

Kallie blinked back tears. "I can't take it all in, not really. I'm so grateful to you, Alex, for giving your time to me. I don't understand it all, where Walter and Verity are and all that, and I can't for the life me imagine what it's like for you, but you've really helped me come to terms with all this. Oh, and did you know that Trish's dad died this morning?"

He nodded. "Yes. He came and told me himself, Kallie. He had a message for Trish which I will pass on to her as soon as I see her. Are you staying for the singalong?"

"Yes, though I'd hoped Mum would be able to come along."

Her eye was caught by a young man at the door, and Alex smiled inwardly at the way Kallie's face softened as she waved him over.

She made the introductions, "Kevin, this is Alex, who I've told you so much about. Alex, this is Kevin. He's a therapist here, too."

She didn't need to say any more, Alex thought anyone would easily sense what was developing between them, and he was pleased for them both.

At that moment, Erin announced the four singers as they came in and took their places in front of the audience. As Alex hurried back to his seat he was pleased to see so many residents, carers and family members there, ready to join in. Music was a wonderful therapy, and although he couldn't hold a note himself, he was sure it would be a very enjoyable couple of hours.

While the sounds of wartime songs sung by four young women immaculately dressed up in smart military uniforms, his eyes roamed from chair to chair, alighting on the patients and their relatives or carers one by one. He kept his psychic senses closed so he wouldn't be bombarded, thinking about how they existed on something like the rungs of a ladder. At the bottom, ground level were those who were like children, not knowing the year, the day or even the hour, but living cheerfully in the moment. A little higher up were people like

Celia and Simon, sometimes present in the here and now, other times residing on the Other Side, waiting for their physical selves to reach a natural conclusion and release them. At the top were those who had died and completely crossed over, people like Trish's dad.

His eyes continued to rove the room, and then he glimpsed Trish outside, crossing the garden towards the water sculpture. Whispering to Beth where he was going, he swiftly left the room.

By the time he caught up with her, Trish had seated herself on the same bench that he had sat on talking to Erin a week or so earlier. The air tinkled with the musical chimes of the little bells attached to the glistening quartz monolith. She looked up when she heard his footsteps on the gravel path.

"My condolences, Trish. Erin told me that your father passed this morning. If you'd rather be alone…?"

Trish smiled, a smile that reached her eyes. "Part of me feels I should be in deep grief, but really, it's a relief after so long."

"You don't have to explain anything to me. I was hoping I'd see you today because I've got something to tell you."

Trish raised her eyebrows at him as he sat down, turning his body slightly so he could look at her. Alex knew that if he'd said such a thing to her before he'd sat with her and Kallie in Kallie's cottage, she would have thought it ridiculous. But now he sensed her excitement, her willingness to hear what he had to say.

"My dad brought your dad to me this morning. Woke me up, in fact. Of course, I had no idea who it was, as I'd never seen him before, but Dad said this was the man I'd heard say pat-a-cake and he was your father. Other than his age, because you'd told me, I knew so little about him. I didn't even know his name!"

Trish tilted her head to look at him, a sparkle in her eye. "But you know it now?" It was almost a challenge.

"Howell Ashton. Once my dad made the link Howell was very clear and concise about the message he wanted conveyed to you. He said to tell you that although his spirit had been far away for a very long time, he had always been aware of how well he was being cared for here at Rainstones. He said he'd always been treated with tenderness and devotion, especially by Erin, who always went far above and beyond her duty."

"That she did. And does. Erin is a remarkable lady."

"Your dad was always aware of you, Trish, when you visited. He could hear your voice when you read to him and told him the latest news about the family, although it seemed a long, long way away."

He stopped then, allowing Trish time to digest all this.

The silence went on a while, and then Trish asked, "So where was he all that time, where is he now?"

"He was on the Other Side, a place of peace and wonder. I know because I've been there myself, and one day, if you want to hear it, I'll tell you the whole story about that. But I've learned from Kallie's grandparents, and my wife's grandmother and a little girl called Flora, that there's a place where people just sort of wait. They wait because they have unfinished business back here, or, in the case of things like dementia or coma, they wait for their bodies to naturally die so they can cross over completely. There is no pain there, Trish. They are happy, and I hope you can rejoice in the knowledge that your dad is truly free now."

Trish, having no words, reached for Alex's hand and squeezed it. He smiled and squeezed back.

"Shall we go inside?" he said. "I think the entertainment will be over soon, and then, if you feel like it, I'd like you to join my wife and mother-in-law, and perhaps Kallie too, for a drink?"

Trish nodded, and they both rose to return to the lounge.

As they walked, Trish said, "Alex, I saw you talking to Erin a little while ago. Does she know any of this? About you, I mean, and what you've just told me?"

"She does. And with your permission I'd like to give her a message from your dad too. He'd like to thank her, you see, because she always made him feel special."

"Of course you must tell her. Thank you, Alex. You too are very special."

Alex hugged her, thinking what an amazing time of it they'd all had, Trish and Kallie, Flora, his own family. He'd had no news yet of Rachel and wondered what was happening to her following Colin Collier's confession. But legal matters take a long time, he'd just have to be patient.

The quartet had begun to sing *We'll Meet Again*, inspiring many of the residents to sit up straighter, clap along, and join in the iconic song with smiles and shining eyes.

How appropriate, thought Alex, as he slipped into his seat next to Beth.

Chapter 40
Celia

My dearest Kathleen,

As I sit here writing these opening words, I wonder if I will be able to say all I need to say. I wonder, too, if you will read this, my last communication with you, or will the sight of my handwriting on the envelope make you want to tear it up unopened? We never could understand each other, so I can only hope that you will give yourself one last chance to get to know me as a person, and not just the mother you found so inadequate. I write in the full knowledge that by the time you receive this, I shall be dead or my disease too far gone for me to know. This letter may not give you all the answers I think you seek, but I hope it will help you.

So let me begin.

I think it hardly need to be said that I never had the least interest in fashion and make-up, like you and your grandmother, nor did I want to learn how to keep house, prepare meals and bake cakes. I preferred to sit by myself and read books. When Mum asked me what I'd like for a present for my sixteenth birthday I gave her a list of textbooks, suggesting she choose one or two. She said that what she'd had in mind was a new outfit or a trip to a stylist to have my hair cut, saying that it was as if I went out of my way to look plain. But she was wrong, because to say I went out of my way inferred a deliberation that simply wasn't there.

I was naturally gifted academically, and all I wanted to do was learn as much as I could. Domesticity was anathema to me, the acquisition of knowledge an absolute joy. My life's purpose, in fact. Any and all academic subjects fascinated me, especially the sciences, and I excelled at school.

At no time have I ever felt the need for friendships or romance. I confess that people and their emotions confuse me, and I know people found my direct and blunt manner disconcerting. I remained happily single as I studied for my degrees and my doctorate. It came as no surprise to anyone when I announced that I would be devoting my life to academia.

I gave my all to my work, considering myself very fortunate to research, lecture and teach in such a prestigious university. Never was I lonely. Who can be lonely surrounded by magnificent buildings, all of them steeped in history and filled with other academics and students who hung on your every word, not to mention a world-renowned library of books at one's disposal? I wished for nothing more, and that's the truth.

Of course, it's obvious that fate had other ideas, otherwise you would not exist and there would be no need for me to recount all of this, which is painful for me to do. I know you must have asked yourself a thousand times how I, a thirty-something with an aversion to relationships, came to have an affair. I often wondered that myself, actually, during the time the liaison lasted. However, as I couldn't explain it even to myself, I chose to simply enjoy it.

Our first encounter was in the refectory. I'd just come out of a lecture and I did not have much time before a tutorial with a very promising doctoral student, so had dashed from my office to get something to eat. When I reached the till I found that I had left my purse on my desk.

A man behind me in the queue offered to pay for me. I expected it to be a colleague from my own department, but my eyes met those of a stranger, the bluest and most piercing I had ever seen. I can only describe what I felt with a well-worn cliché: it was like being hit by a bolt of lightning. I said I would pay him back if he would tell me which department he worked in. He replied that my company over lunch would be payment enough, and led me over to a table. Even to this day, I still can't believe that I forgot I was supposed to be back in my study preparing for my student.

He was in his sixties, not particularly handsome, but he had a charisma that I had not encountered before. For the first time ever I was late for the tutorial, and I could hardly keep my mind on my work all afternoon.

I tried to focus, but I found myself constantly wondering if he was thinking of me, and that took me back to the angst and torment I'd witnessed at school as girls worried themselves into extreme silliness over whether so-and-so liked them or not. It was uncomfortable in the extreme, so I tried to put him out of my mind.

I never expected to hear from him again, but a few days later he sought me out, and in no time at all I found myself caught up in my first, my only, romantic affair. He told me straight away that he was married, but gave me the old line of 'my wife doesn't understand me' and I decided to believe it.

Of course our liaisons had to be conducted in secret and I had no problem with that. It was all so strange, so completely alien to me, I wanted simply to keep to myself that I was seeing a man who was attracted to me and didn't care what I looked like! He was fascinated by my intellect, as I was enthralled by his, and the physical side of things seemed a natural extension of that.

I was disappointed but not surprised when I found out he'd lied about his 'uncaring' wife and was, in fact, renowned for breaking hearts with his extra-marital activities, but by then I didn't care.

My work suffered, I became less attentive to my students and was apt to lose the thread or wander off-topic in my lectures. The changes in me did not go unnoticed and inevitably we were spotted together, and all too soon rumours about us started to fly.

I felt his withdrawal quite quickly after that. Everything was on his terms: when we met, how we met, where (usually my place) and how long for. The stimulating intellectual conversations dried up, and finally, as it should have done from the beginning, it dawned on me that I was being stupid.

But it went on for a few more months before I started to see what a selfish and shallow man he was beneath the veneer of intellectual sophistication. I realised that it was my emotional naivety that intrigued him, and my slavish adoration that kept him coming back for more. It became so stressful I ended it between us and threw myself back into my work. Weeks would go by, I would start to get back on an even keel, and then he would call and though I am ashamed to admit my weakness, I would allow him to come because he had awoken a physical need in me. We carried on this way for too long, with each quick, unsatisfactory visit leaving me heartsick, guilty, and used. But I was soon to learn through circulating rumours that he already had his eye on a new student.

And then I found out I was pregnant.

He became so cold towards me when I told him, even suggesting that he might not be the father. He shouted that he had his reputation to think about, a wife and family he wanted to keep, and he told me to get rid of the baby. If I didn't, he made it clear he would deny ever having anything to do with me, no matter what I said or did to prove otherwise. I don't know how he would have fought a DNA test, but that's a route I didn't need to take, because I knew the truth.

I thought of ending the pregnancy. How could I be a single mum at the age of thirty-nine, a full nineteen years older than Mum when she'd had me? But I couldn't go through with a termination, and I was sure I would be able to cope.

It soon proved otherwise. I was soon so out of my depth, so confused by the emotional turmoil within me, that I felt the only sensible action was to take an extended leave of absence from the university and return home to Mum and Dad.

All through my pregnancy it was hard not to resent the baby I was carrying (I do not say 'you' because, of course, I did not know you). My condition had forced me to take leave from the job I loved more than anything else in the world; I felt sick all day, not just in the mornings; I ballooned like a whale, not only my stomach but my ankles, feet and fingers too. I hated the indignities of the pre-natal examinations and was terrified of the birth and what would be expected of me once I had a baby to care for. I was even more terrified that I might not be able to return to teaching and research, for how could I do that and look after a child by myself? I was so confused, so disappointed in myself, that I considered adoption. Surely, I told myself, it would be the best thing, both for the baby and for myself, because I was not, most emphatically not, maternal in any way.

Oh, the horror on Mum's face when I told her what I planned to do. She insisted that I would love you once you were born, once I had actually gazed on your face and into your trusting eyes, but I didn't believe her. As my due date got nearer we went round and round in circles, me arguing for adoption, Mum and Dad telling me it would be the biggest mistake of my life.

But when you did finally come into the world and had been placed, clean and sweet-smelling in my arms, I did love you—I do love you, with all my heart—but I still did not think I could or should keep you.

My muddled thoughts were relentless and I thought my head would explode. I found it almost impossible to feed you and I wept and wailed about my shortcomings in that most basic motherly function until I was actually sick, alarming the nurses in the maternity ward. They assured me that bottle feeding you would be fine and I shouldn't feel guilty about it, and they called Mum in to try and calm me down.

She and Dad walked in together. Mum picked you up out of the cot and held you so naturally, so lovingly, I saw how she must have held me when I was a baby. They sat together by my bed, Mum cradling you, Dad holding out his hand so your fist could grasp his little finger.

He cleared his throat and, not quite looking at me, said, "We've thought it all through, love. You can go back to your job at the university. We will raise your daughter."

Mum was gazing down at you, then she looked up at me with tears in her eyes, and said, "She is our granddaughter. Our family. You can't just give her away. Please, Celia!"

I was so happy, so relieved I was at their decision. The thought of giving you to strangers was eating me up inside, but this generous offer literally made the sun shine that day. I knew what wonderful parents they would be to you, far better than I could ever be, and I would still be able to see you, to watch you grow up.

We went home the next day and Mum helped me immeasurably in the first few weeks. I was baffled by your needs, struggling to keep up with the constant feeding and dealing with the appalling nappies that had to be changed all too often. It didn't help that you were a screamer from the time you took your first breath! You were so hard to settle that it seemed to me that you already sensed my inadequacies and were determined to drain every ounce of strength and tolerance I had.

Only your grandparents could soothe you, so more and more they took over the care of you, making sure that by the time I was ready to leave and return to Cambridge you would not miss me.

I didn't give you a name until you were almost six weeks old. I suggested Mum and Dad decide what to call you, but they insisted that it was for me to name you.

"You are her mother," Mum said. "And she will be raised knowing that. You've had time with her now, so surely you have a name in mind?"

Until that moment I hadn't. You were 'the baby', but suddenly I knew what I wanted to call you: Kathleen, after Dame Kathleen Lonsdale, a heroine of mine. I know you don't care for the name and don't use it, but look her up and you'll see why I admired her so.

I visited at weekends, walking into the kitchen to find you standing on a little stool, helping Mum to make pastry for apple pies or sponge mix for cupcakes. All the things you two made together would have filled a bakery shop twice over! And you loved following her as she cleaned the house, clutching your own feather duster, copying her with your toy vacuum cleaner. You were the child they wished I had been.

You were always pleased to see me, but you seemed to instinctively know that I was not the type to get down on the floor and play at 'shop' or pretend tea parties, or want to help you delve into the dressing-up box that Verity had created for you, so you didn't ask me to join in your games. Your gran was your playmate, your confidante, the one you really loved, but I was fine with that because you and I got along well enough, considering the circumstances.

Well enough, that is, until you reached your teens and we started to clash over your future.

Of course I rather expected you to be like me, someone who loved books and school and learning. You proved to be very clever, so I didn't think it unreasonable to want and expect you to go to university and get a degree.

You had your own ideas though, and the eruption that occurred when I refused to allow you to leave school before you had even sat for A levels is forever seared on my memory. I'd had no idea until then that you possessed such a temper! How had it happened that I had one day left a giggly, amenable little girl who loved to make cakes and returned to find a sophisticated, stubborn young woman in her place? Who was this person with beads in her hair and artfully applied make-up on her lovely young face?

I'm sure I don't need to remind you of the day we had a complete meltdown of understanding that so irreparably damaged our relationship. You started by accusing me of neglecting my maternal duties, even though, surely, you'd realised by then that I could not have given you the blissfully happy childhood you'd had with your grandparents. You screamed that I had no right to tell you what to do, that I had forfeited any rights at all by choosing not to raise you, and although Mum tried to smooth the waters as she always did, you were having none of it.

And then you asked the question that finally broke us, the one question I would not answer. I can picture you now as if it were yesterday, a bundle of fury planted in front of me, hands bunched into fists, demanding to know who your father was so you could go and find him and tell him what a dreadful mother I was.

I will still not name him, but let me tell you this: he was a self-centred, narcissistic egoist who had no interest in learning anything about you. He may not even be alive by the time you read this letter, but if he is and you were to find him, he would only disappoint you. I say again, as I told you that day, Dad was all the father you'd ever need.

Our long estrangement following that row was deeply painful, and I was truly sorry to come crashing back into your life the way I did when I broke my arm.

I had hoped it would bring us closer together, especially as you were missing Mum and Dad so much, but I came to the conclusion long ago that our chemistry is of the volatile kind and not at all meant to mix. I did miss you, though, once I was home and was sad when I realised that you were happy to go back to the way things had been before.

That's why I did not contact you when I received the diagnosis of dementia. I had suspected it for some time, several years actually, but diagnosis can be tricky and it took a while to have it confirmed. I have researched it thoroughly and am fully cognisant of what is ahead of me. It is daunting, to say the least, but my pragmatic nature is guiding me through the things I need to do.

I write in the full awareness that the disease will progress from decision-making and day-to-day tasks becoming

281

difficult, as they are swiftly becoming, to the point when I will be incapable of independent living. My apartment and most of my possessions are in the process of being sold and the firm managing my finances have their instructions, so there will be no burden on you in any way.

I have made arrangements for admission to Rainstones House when my doctor deems it necessary, because I want to be near you at my life's end. I know full well what is ahead of me, whether it be slow or whether it be quick, and so I know that eventually I will not be myself and I will no longer recognise you. It is not the exit from life I had ever contemplated, but I doubt anyone does, do they?

I am a scientist and have never believed that there is anything such as a soul or a spirit, as I know you believe, but now I am facing death I have read many books about dying and am giving it due consideration. If our thoughts are energy and energy cannot be destroyed, maybe the thinking part of ourselves does continue to exist when we die? It's a comforting prospect.

If you do not visit me, I hope that somewhere in my diseased brain I will remember that on Thursdays you'll be working in the hospice wing so we'll be in the same building. It is admirable that you use your skills to ease the lives of those who are dying, and I am sorry I did not recognise this in you earlier. I am proud of you and maybe I will even try one of your therapies when I am there, if you allow it.

I want to thank you, my daughter. Thank you for not turning away from me when I broke my arm, though I would not have blamed you if you had. I am under no illusion that you found my presence in the cottage for those many weeks nothing but daunting, but in my defence, I was already exhibiting the early symptoms of dementia.

At the very least I can see two good things coming out of my illness. The first is that it has made me want to explain myself to you, in the hope that you will finally see that what I did when you were a baby was done out of love and an honest evaluation of my own maternal shortcomings. I am sorry you resented me for it, but I think you know in your heart that you were raised by the perfect couple, Verity and Walter. The second, and more important thing, is that I have the chance to tell you what a wonderful young woman you turned out to be.

With love
Your mother xxx

Introducing Alex Kelburn

Alex Kelburn doesn't just believe in the afterlife, he *knows* it to be real. A charismatic psychic medium, he works hard to bring comfort to the bereaved… until his own world is brought crashing down by an unimaginable tragedy. Devastated, he must choose between shutting down the precious gift he was born with, or carry on and risk losing the woman he loves.

Can he see beyond his own grief and pain to go on helping those who so dearly need him?

'Flight of the Kingfisher
ISBN 9780956795410
The Moon Tiger
2020

ABOUT THE AUTHOR

J Merrill Forrest's deep interest in the supernatural is a major theme in her writing. For more than thirty years Jane has researched her subject, visiting psychics, mediums, Spiritualist churches and séances, always keeping an open and questioning mind, always searching for evidence. At age forty she followed her long-held dream of going to university and gained BA(Hons) in English at Royal Holloway, University of London, and returned to academia ten years later to gain her MA in Creative Writing at Bath Spa University.

Find out more at www.jmerrillforrest.com

Printed in Great Britain
by Amazon

26265055R00169